LOVE, LIES, AND CRYPTIDS

M.L. NOLAN

M.L.
Nolan

M.L. NOLAN

Content Warnings

This book includes strong language, explicit sexual situations involving a character on the ace spectrum, references to the loss of a parent, and microaggressions against BIPOC, women, and LGBTQ+ people.

For Jess, Jess, and Jay. Thank you for being my
first readers and biggest cheerleaders.

Contents

CHAPTER ONE

THIS MAY HAVE BEEN A MISTAKE

Of course on his first day of a real, grown-up office job, Jasper would be late.

It wasn't his fault, really. He'd left exactly at the time he was supposed to according to his app. He was at the platform a whole five minutes before the train was supposed to arrive. But then five minutes passed. Then ten. And the sign under the awning marking the arrival of the train just added another five on top of that.

A Discord notification flashed across the screen from MixerKing13—a welcome distraction.

You regretting it yet?

Jasper raised an eyebrow, even though there wasn't anyone to see it. He spent enough time alone in his house, formerly his mom's house, that he was used to having fully emotive conversations even as he was just typing.

Regretting what?

Getting a job

I haven't even gotten there yet. MAX delayed due to "police activity." You'd think they'd be able to wait to harass homeless people until after rush hour.

We're saying unhoused now

Jasper cringed.

Sorry

You're good. I'm still in my pj's eating cereal suckaaaah

Srsly, why are you like this?

You luv it. Really tho, hope it goes well. Don't forget about me when you've got your media empire

I'm literally sending you a new episode to edit next weekend. I'm not going anywhere.

So you say

Jasper rolled his eyes, but then he noticed the time at the top of the screen and muffled a squeak. The woman in the Columbia rain jacket jumped, looking down at her ankles and high-stepping like a dressage horse as if expecting a mouse. Jasper chose to think the two actions had no connection to one another, but moved down the platform away from her all the same.

His sweater was already pilling with droplets of the noncommittal Portland rain; his red curls were undoubtedly floppy and plastered to his forehead.

Some first impression I'm about to make, he thought as the overcrowded MAX train finally (finally!) pulled to a stop in front of him.

Nico Juárez sat back from the computer desk, took off their black-rimmed glasses, and rubbed their eyes. It wasn't that it was too early—they had always been an early riser. It was just that staring at this presentation for the last three hours (and all weekend, but don't tell their boss) was tough on their thirty-year-old eyes.

They, along with Unified Theory Press's marketing manager, Evan Brooks, were due to present a new possible acquisition that morning at 10 a.m. to the publisher, Janet Kelly. The plan was to pitch the second in a series of books by canine mystic Hannah Hodge for acquisition.

("Canine mystic" meant she had a lot of mystical theories about dogs. Nico had tried to make her change it, but she considered herself too well-established already; they thought it made her sound like she was some kind of fortune-telling dog, but what did they know?)

This particular book included a lot of information about the legend of El Chupacabra. Ms. Hodge seemed to think Nico would be able to help supply information about it, though as a lifetime resident of the Pacific Northwest, they weren't exactly an expert in desert folklore simply because they had a Hispanic last name. They were, however, good with research and, when it came right down to it, not good at arguing with people who called themselves *mystics*.

The bell on the front door rang as the hinges of the old Victorian-turned-office's front door creaked. Nico checked the clock in the corner of their screen—8:30. About the time when the rest of the members of the press started arriving.

"Morning, Nico!" Clara Hewitt, UTP's publicity manager, called as she hung up her cherry-red rain slicker on the antique brass coat hanger. She threaded her fingers through her fine blonde hair and shook the roots in a futile attempt for more volume. "Do anything fun this weekend?"

"Finished up this presentation, mostly," Nico said, putting their glasses back on their face.

"Ugh," Clara groaned. "You didn't need to waste a weekend here. Janet's never turned down one of your proposals."

"Yes, well, some of us take pride in our work, Clara."

"Hey—I take *lots* of pride in my work, and you know it! You're lucky I need to go make coffee or I'd give you a lot more shit for that." The rubber heels of Clara's boots thudded on the wood floor as she walked back to the kitchenette. "Cute earrings by the way!" she called back over her shoulder.

Nico's hands flew to their ears, as if they'd forgotten about the enamel paw print studs they'd worn this morning. They were small, about as flamboyant as Nico was willing to get. They were new to the whole *accessories* thing and still very self-conscious about it, but the studs seemed apt for the occasion.

The door opened again, and they could hear Evan say, "Damn, dude, you smell like the whole dispensary."

He and house designer (and part-time pot dealer, despite the fact that cannabis was fully legal) Jack Stuart walked by Nico's office and straight to their desks. Nico's nose wrinkled a bit at the fact that Evan didn't check in with them right away, and at Jack's weedy scent, but they figured he'd get a cup of coffee and catch up with Clara, his work wife, first. He always seemed to be much more relaxed about pitches than they were.

Office and accounts manager Meera Chowdhury called out a bright hello as she came in right on their heels.

But Janet hadn't arrived yet, which was odd. She would normally have been there by now. In fact, she would normally have arrived at a similar time to Nico. Then again, she had been a lot laxer with her arrivals and departures lately. It was fine. Nico was sure she would show up before their meeting at 10:00.

Then they turned back to their computer and saw the bold subject line of an unread email in their inbox. It was from her. For some reason, they were struck with a deep sense of foreboding. With some trepidation, they clicked.

```
Nico,
Forgive the late notice. I had
thought I'd be dropping by this
morning to speak with you, but there
were some last-minute adjustments
to my schedule. There have been some
changes in the works at UTP for a
while now, which Brent will clarify
for you. Also, I've sent you some

additional editorial support.
J
```

Brent? As in Janet's son Brent? Nico was fairly certain he had been living in Los Angeles and pursuing some type of entertainment career. Well, "career" may have been generous. He seemed to be more focused on simply inserting himself at events with C-list celebrities and siphoning company money for various self-improvement workshops. Nico would say "cults," but it would be a bit hypocritical of them, their working at a paranormal publishing company and all.

"Hellooooo?" A nasal voice cut through Nico's confusion. "Where's my UTP family? Come out, come out, wherever you are!"

Nico cringed. They hated the use of the word *family* in a workplace scenario, never mind how much time they spent in the office. All the same, they wheeled their desk chair into the doorway. A man with close-cropped brown hair and a fully weather-inappropriate open-necked tunic with prayer beads on display stood in the center of the living-room-turned-bullpen, clutching a key fob and a green smoothie. Meera, Clara, and Jack peered over the tops of their computer monitors, all wearing puzzled expressions.

"Wow, that's a lot of linen." Nico jumped at the surprise of Evan's voice in their ear. "What's he doing here? Where's Janet?"

"I don't know," Nico hissed, still not having processed the confusing email they'd just scanned. "We have the Hodge pitch today, so hopefully she'll arrive soon."

"Hm. Do we?" Evan said. Nico scowled up at him. Confident, conventionally attractive, and effortlessly successful,

Evan should have been a total nightmare coworker. But somehow, he managed to be kind and dependable, and the two of them had an amicable working relationship.

"Hey, hey, enough chatter," Brent said, looking straight at the two of them. "Now, I don't know if she's let any of you know yet, but my mother will be OOO until further notice. I'm told that's 'out of office' in your lingo." He chuckled, and Nico bristled.

"Where's she gone?" Clara said as her painted-on eyebrows drew closer together.

"Well, that's her business. Respectfully," Brent said, not very respectfully at all. "I'm supposed to tell Nico that he'll be receiving some additional help with the editing and...I don't know, bookmaking side of things, I guess?"

A very unpleasant cold rush surged through Nico at the misgendering, but they weren't sure whether they should have expected any better.

"They," Evan corrected.

"What?"

"*They'll* be receiving additional help," Clara said. "Nico uses they/them."

It really was kind of the two of them, but it didn't lessen the sting or the weight of the additional attention on Nico. It was especially uncomfortable as Brent fixed a gaze on them like he'd stepped in some kind of mysterious slimy substance.

"Oh," he said. "Moving on...yeah. Go ahead and do whatever you were planning to do today, but tomorrow it'd be super if you'd all meet me in the conference room at 10:30 a.m. to get me caught up on all your goings-on."

Tomorrow? What could he possibly have had to do to cause that sort of waiting period, when clearly there was a huge disruption taking place?

"Clara and I have an author call tomorrow," Evan said flatly.

"Oooo...any way you can reschedule that?"

"Well, it's already been—"

At that moment, they were interrupted by the sound of something skittering in the front hallway and a strangled masculine voice saying, "Wait! No! Get back over here!"

—ell—

Jasper took the longest steps he possibly could as he strode toward the repurposed home that housed Unified Theory Press. It was a few minutes before 9 a.m. He'd hoped to arrive at 8:30, but he couldn't control the whims of mass transit, unfortunately.

Right as he mounted the stairs, he heard heavy breathing behind him. Normally he would ignore something creepy in favor of getting away as soon as possible, but in this case he turned to see what was following him. Standing behind him was a dog—a mutt of some kind, with wiry hair and a dopey grin.

"Hey, little guy," Jasper said, half crouching. "Where's your person?"

He felt a surge of anxiety. What was he supposed to do? Be late for work while he found the dog's owner? Maybe he could pop inside the door and let someone know there was a lost dog out there. This was Portland; undoubtedly they'd understand the importance.

In his urgency, Jasper opened the door without really thinking through his plan. Of course, the dog rocketed between his legs and into the room, claws scratching against the wood floor.

"Wait! No! Get back over here!" Jasper said, hurrying after it.

The office seemed to be all gathered in a central room, so everyone saw him scrambling after the mutt. He registered a cup of coffee go flying, heard a yelp and a man saying, "Oh fuck, sorry, Nico." A plump woman who looked like Mod-Cloth had thrown up on her leapt to her feet and scurried after Jasper and the dog until the two of them had corralled it between a heavy wooden desk and a tufted sofa.

Another woman, the only one Jasper recognized, called out an amused "Good morning, Jasper!" Then she turned away from the two of them, and Jasper's eyes followed to where a short, delicate-boned person stood, arms out as they looked down at the mess of brown liquid spilled all over the front of their white button-up shirt. They shot him a stormy look, and *oh* they were quite pretty, weren't they?

"That's your new assistant over there, Nico. Jasper, come here and let Clara take care of the dog," she said.

Jasper's stomach dropped. First impressions, indeed.

The woman in the faux-vintage dress handled finding the dog's owner as Meera marched Jasper into the front office and started clearing off a table stacked with old files.

"What are you doing? I've got those all organized!" Jasper's new boss was saying as she collected the mountains of papers. Jasper couldn't help but notice how resonant their voice was in spite of how small they were.

"Oh, don't be silly, Nico," Meera said. She had a bright, pleasant trill to her voice, and as unwelcome as Nico was making him feel, her mood was definitely making up for it as far as Jasper was concerned. "You haven't touched any of this in months. Trust me, I know. My desk is right there."

"I don't know why I wasn't consulted about hiring an assistant," Nico muttered, and Jasper tried not to take it personally. Tough not to, though.

"Because Janet knew you would try to stop her, and you really do need one." Meera had fully cleared the desk, and she pulled out the extra chair so Jasper could sit in it. "There you go, Jasper. Sorry you're stuck with them. They're in a bit of a grumpy mood today, but they're a good person once you get to know them."

Jasper waited for her to move out of the way before approaching the desk. He was very aware of his size, and how people tended to be nervous if he seemed to hover over them.

Then Meera was gone, and he was left with his new boss, who was currently staring at him with intense, searching brown eyes.

"So are you some kind of cryptid enthusiast, then?" Nico said.

In spite of himself, Jasper giggled nervously. Very professional. "Um, no? I mean, they're fun, but I kind of just needed a job."

Nico didn't drop their gaze, and Jasper felt his stomach flipping as he realized with horror that he really liked the feel of it. *Jasper, why are you such a freak?*

"So you're not a Bigfoot hunter or some nonsense like that?"

Jasper giggled again. *Goddammit, stop.* "No, no, I was a lit major, so I'm afraid the only monster I know anything about is Frankenstein." Or at least it said he was a lit major on his very creative résumé, which, hopefully, nobody would ever bother to check.

There was the sound of a sharp intake of breath. "Surely you mean Frankenstein's *monster*, right?"

Oh shit, that was a rookie mistake. "Yes! Yes, Frankenstein's monster. Totally what I meant." He laughed again, but he felt that impossible-to-control burn in his cheeks.

Nico sat back in their chair, and Jasper took in the way their elegant fingers curled in their lap. His eyes jerked back up to their face just as quickly when they said, "I'm afraid I've had some things that require my attention come up today and nobody told me you were coming, so I won't be able to train you on much. You'll have to ask Meera for an employee handbook or something. I have things to do."

"Um. Oh. Okay," Jasper stuttered. "I'll just...okay."

His unsettlingly attractive boss turned back toward their computer monitor, and Jasper tried not to audibly sigh with relief.

Maybe MixerKing was right. Maybe this was a mistake.

Chapter Two

No Hard Feelings

The conference room chair, of course, was distractingly uncomfortable, arms squeezing against Jasper's sides. However, it was just one more uncomfortable part of what was sure to be an extremely uncomfortable meeting.

The conference table itself was an old-fashioned dinner table made of heavy varnished wood; it was the kind made for families with seven or more children. Limited light from the cloudy late morning filtered through a wall full of casement windows. On the wall, a large photo of a hairy white man in a very Pacific Northwest plaid flannel shirt looked down at them. Jasper made a note to ask someone who it was later.

From what he'd heard around the office after Brent had left the day before, there'd been a major upset moments before Jasper had arrived for his first day. Now, everyone was tasked with bringing their new boss up to speed. There was a part of Jasper that was grateful for this meeting, as he was desperate to know what was going on in every way possible. On the other hand, looking at all the faces at the table, particularly Nico's, this didn't seem to be a time to celebrate.

"Well, team, hit me. What are we looking at?" Brent rubbed his palms together like a low-rent stage magician.

Everyone looked at each other, and Jasper would have slumped in his seat if he weren't clamped in place by it.

"I'll go, then," Evan finally said with false cheer, turning and raising an eyebrow in Nico's direction. Jasper leaned back to allow the look to pass between them. "Maybe we could start with the latest book acquisition—the new Hannah Hodge. It'll be our second book with her, and Nico and I have prepared a report with her last book's sales figures and our proposed table of contents."

He passed a paper-clipped stack to Jasper, who started to slide it toward Brent.

Brent sat back and put his hands in the air as if to absolve himself. "Oh, don't give me that. I won't read it."

Jasper swore he could feel the temperature in the room drop a degree. The temperature radiating from Nico might have dropped two.

"Okay…," Evan said. His smile was slipping already and changing into something more tentative. "I can read off some of it if you prefer?"

"Hm," Brent murmured, leaning back in his chair. Despite the fact that his slender frame did actually fit in it, his legs were spread out with enough gusto to make it seem too small.

"What do you mean, 'hm'?" Nico nearly snarled, and a condescending smile pulled at Brent's mouth.

"Now, Nicky, it's nothing to freak out about," Brent said. Nico bristled, and Jasper heard a sharp intake of breath from Clara's direction across the table.

"Don't call me *Nicky*," Nico said with an expression like they'd bitten into an unripe piece of fruit.

Brushing past this, Brent said, "I was only wondering if books are, like, the thing anymore."

"Could you, um..." Evan interrupted himself to clear his throat. "Could you elaborate?"

"Well, I'm just wondering if people *really read* anymore, or if we should be branching out into other forms of media," Brent said.

Clara sat up and adjusted her cat's-eye glasses. "Actually, there's tons of research that says readership among the twenty-five-to-forty age group is higher than—"

"Ooo, I wasn't finished, Sarah," Brent said with an obviously fake wince, continuing before she could object. "Anyway, I'd say we should hit the brakes on any book acqs for now. Also, if you're thinking about striking any deals, you should definitely talk to me about it before you talk to the author. I am in charge, after all," Brent said.

"That's not normally how we do things," Nico said with an audible choke in their voice. Jasper glanced at their hands, which were going white gripping the arms of their chair.

"Well, it's how things work now. I'd like us all to be a little more open-minded. We need some new blood...shake things up. Get out of our comfort zones, right, Jasper?" To his deep dismay, Brent threw an exaggerated wink Jasper's way. Nico turned and fixed an icy glare on him.

Dammit.

They'd always heard that when some people have painful experiences, their minds dissociate. However, Nico had never been fortunate enough to experience that disconnection. Instead, when bad things happened, time seemed to slow down so they could experience every excruciating moment more powerfully.

"Do you have any new media acquisitions in mind yet, then?" Evan said, apparently refusing to accept what Brent had just said as the last word. "Because if not, this book would be a great tentpole revenue stream to hold us over until we find one."

Brent seemed to consider it. It rankled Nico, though, the way he stared at the ceiling and bit his lip as if he were trying to decide which protein bowl to order. The gall of this man to pretend to deliberate over something so important to all of them, as if he knew better.

"Now when you say tentpole..."

"It means it'll be a healthy midlist title that should help float us if our bigger gambles don't pay off," Clara said. Again, Brent looked at her as if he was surprised she was speaking at all. It didn't surprise Nico that he would be a male chauvinist, but the lack of surprise didn't calm their anger.

Another sound that was supposed to seem thoughtful, and then Brent said, "I don't think this 'midlist' thing is thinking big enough. Every book we do should be a best-seller."

"Do you even know the first thing about publishing? Or how any type of business works at all?" Nico blurted, and they felt the horrified energy of their assistant's eyes fixed on them. So be it. Better that he knew Nico's tendency to lose their filter at the first sign of trouble.

There was a sickly silence as everyone stared at Nico, or at Brent, or from one to the other. Nico felt their cheeks burning. Why couldn't they just learn to shut up?

"How about this?" Evan said. "Maybe we can talk about our acquisitions strategy later and move on to other things?"

As much as Evan was trying to help, this also was an offensive solution. Acquisitions was Nico's job. If they didn't have that, what did they have?

"Let's just parking-lot this whole conversation," Brent said. He drummed his fingers on the table a couple of times, then, without another word, left the staff sitting dazed at the conference table.

Seconds later, Nico stood and made for the front door. They were half-afraid they'd throw up in the rose bushes outside, but the nippy midmorning air blew away some of the nausea, to their enormous relief. Their relief was short-lived, however, as they heard the door open behind them and Jasper following them out onto the steps.

"Um...sorry, mmm—um...Nico?"

"What?" Nico snapped. They assumed Jasper had been about to call them "Mr. Juárez" and caught himself at the last minute. There was no proof, and it wasn't terribly charitable of them to think, but all the limited charity they'd had for the day had already been wrung out of them.

"I just…" Jasper lowered his voice. "I just want you to know I'm not, like, in cahoots with that guy or anything. I know there's a lot going on, but I'm on your side."

Nico couldn't help the disgusted confusion on their face. It was such a presumptuous thing to say. Nico didn't appreciate being seen like that.

"On my side? How would you know whose side you're on? You've been here all of five minutes. Now, I need to clear my head. By myself."

Without a glance behind them, they turned on their heel and made their way up the sidewalk.

— ele —

If there weren't so much hurt involved, it would be funny how catastrophic the past two days had been. Sure, Nico came off as an asshole, but considering how they'd just been treated, it was understandable that they wouldn't be at their best.

Still, it hurt.

Maybe Jasper should just start looking for another job, or double down on promoting his Patreon and look into his options for private health insurance.

But no. This wasn't over. Jasper refused to let it be over. Private health insurance was hella expensive. Plus, he couldn't accept the idea of someone disliking him as much as Nico seemed to (especially someone so cute, if he was honest with himself).

He'd show them that he meant what he said.

Meera's face greeted Jasper as he came back inside, tail between his legs. Her big eyes swept the room, and she beckoned him to her desk.

"I'm sorry, Jasper. It's not normally like that here," she stage-whispered.

Jasper broke into the nervous giggle that had clung to him since childhood. His mother had hated it, but he was never able to stop. It seemed to charm Meera, though, and her face broke into an affectionate smile.

"I'd apologize for Nico's behavior as well, but it's their job to do that," she said with a touch of sass. "Some of it is obviously..." she jerked her head in the direction of the stairs leading to Brent's office, "but they're probably also cranky because they have low blood sugar."

Jasper laughed again. Then he had a thought. "Actually, I meant to ask—is there a coffee shop nearby? Maybe a place with pastries?"

Meera's eyes lit up. "Yes actually..."

⁓ ✐ ⁓

Nico knew they had been needlessly mean to Jasper. His expressive blue eyes really did look sympathetic, but that hadn't stopped Nico from taking their frustration out on him. Nico couldn't possibly be welcoming, or judicious, or any of the things a good leader should be under pressure.

It had been nearly five years since they started working at Unified Theory Press. They'd gone straight through college to graduate school, then had a flurry of unpaid internships before finally landing the editorial assistant job. For the first three years at UTP, they worked right under Janet, faithfully putting in more hours than was legal. They proved themself enough that they were made a senior editor when the original publisher retired and Janet replaced him. In a town without many publishing jobs available, having a senior position before thirty was an anomaly.

Nico had spent the last ten to twelve years completely engrossed in getting to this point. How were they supposed to know their accomplishment was so fragile? How could they predict that one LA trust fund brat could come in and demolish their security like a bully kicking over a sandcastle? They also felt betrayed by Janet, to whom they'd been fully devoted for years. It was silly—of course a private business owner would have every right to put whoever they wanted in charge, and Brent was her son, after all. What right did Nico have to be upset? What kind of unresolved mommy issues were they projecting onto their boss right now?

It was downright embarrassing.

They crossed the street, narrowly missing a cyclist, who shouted a passive aggressive, "*Excuse me*," over their shoulder. At last they stopped in front of a converted craftsman house, trotting up the black painted steps. Their feet had led them to Blossom & Crow, a gothic-themed book store where UTP had many an author event. It also happened to belong to Nico's lifelong best friend, Andie Silvana.

Nico strode through the door, which was already propped open by a cast iron corvid statue. A quick look around the shop proved it was empty of customers, or that whoever was in there was tucked into a corner in the back of the shop.

At the counter, a slight-bodied goth with long, black hair bent over an open paperback. They glanced up at Nico and grinned, looking as casually delighted as if they'd won $20 in the lottery.

"Well, hey there stranger." They shut the book—some gothic romance dreck. Nico knew Andie had better taste than that, but they were clearly indulging themself.

"Why are you talking like a cowboy?" Nico sneered.

"I'm not. If I were talking like a cowboy I would have called you 'padnuh.' 'Stranger' is more film noir. Now what's got you all riled up, padnuh?"

Of course they could tell something was wrong. Andie was nothing if not perceptive, and Nico had always plainly worn all their emotions on their face.

Nico leaned their elbows on the counter and hung their head. The story emerged in what felt like a single run-on sentence—how they came into work yesterday and Janet had disappeared, leaving an entitled fool in her wake; how they had been saddled with a new assistant they didn't know how to handle. All the while, Andie stared at them with folded arms, tapping fingernails coated with chipped black polish.

"Sorry if I sound like a dick, but getting an assistant sounds like a non-problem," they said, cocking their head and shifting their weight to the other foot.

"But I've already gone and yelled at him, and he's very...I don't know...," Nico flailed a hand as if they could catch the elusive word in midair, "gentle. I don't know how to deal with soft people. You know this."

"Sure," Andie said curtly, as if they were any better.

"And I've never had to manage anybody before. I haven't had to deal with that whole hierarchical thing," they continued.

"That's not true, you know how all that shit works. Everyone under capitalism does," Andie said.

Except for people like you who get to be their own boss, Nico thought ruefully. But they couldn't say that. It would just be mean for no reason. Again. Plus Andie would undoubtedly put them in their place, and that was always terrifying.

Instead they said, "Yeah, but I don't know how to be on top!"

Andie's eyes went wide, and Nico immediately realized how that sounded. They hid their face as Andie shook with laughter.

"Jesus, Nico, you sure do have a way with words."

Nico groaned. "You're disgusting."

"Thank you. It's gotten me far in life," Andie said. "And now that you've got that out of your system, take a deep breath, and stop being an ass. The dumbass boss thing sucks, but you should totally enjoy getting an assistant. Just try to be nice. I know you've got it in you." They reached across the counter and gave Nico a slap on the upper arm.

"*Ow*," Nico winced. Andie had a tendency to give handshakes and hugs that were just a little bit too aggressive.

"Sorry friend." They shrugged then nodded toward the velvet sofa on the far wall. "Want to hide out here for a while?"

Nico checked their watch (yes, they still owned a watch, like a professional should). They sighed.

"I should go, actually. Besides, I think even I would break that ancient thing over there if I sat on it."

Andie rolled their eyes. "Alright, well, hugs."

Mumbling a goodbye, Nico went back outside, where the sun was starting to burn a hole through the cloud cover.

—ell—

Jasper's confidence had thoroughly bloomed as he walked through the double doors to his and Nico's shared office, carrying a tray of two drinks and two pastries. He had, of course, dropped off Meera's order first—a caramel latte and biscotti.

Nico started babbling before they turned toward him. "Jasper, I need to apologi—oh!"

"A little bird told me you liked a good cappuccino," Jasper said brightly. The surprised look on Nico's face almost completely made up for their lashing out earlier. "Do you want a plain or a chocolate croissant to go with that?"

"Oh, um...ch-chocolate sounds delightful," they stammered, and uh-oh, that was much too enticing. Jasper pushed back against a surge of gloating triumph (that soaring feeling *was* triumph, wasn't it?). He set the drink and the paper bag containing the croissant on their desk. Nico moved their hand as if to pick it up, then set it back in their lap.

"I want to apologize for how I acted earlier," they said. They were focused on Jasper's white Converse sneakers. It was surprisingly demure, and Jasper felt another pleasant flutter in his chest. "It was very unprofessional of me. None of this is your fault."

Jasper smiled. "No hard feelings," he said. "Hope you like your croissant."

"Oh, um, yes. I'm sure I will," they said.

Their eyes finally found Jasper's, and he couldn't help but see in them unexpected vulnerability. He realized suddenly that they were probably a lot younger than they'd seemed at first. He thought that he'd gotten the upper hand, if only for a few minutes, but instead he was hopelessly disarmed.

This was going to be much more complicated than it needed to be.

CHAPTER THREE

NOBODY'S GETTING FIRED

Jasper had meant to get up early this morning and do some recording, but that was a lie apparently. Putting on semiprofessional clothes, getting stuffed like a sardine into a train to and from the office, only getting a half hour for lunch, walking on eggshells around his supervisor—these were just a few of the things that made this job way more taxing than he'd expected.

He'd been used to overworking himself when he'd been juggling his own business and taking care of his mom. It was exhausting looking out for a mother who didn't really like him much while also trying to run an audio-based business on the down-low. Either he'd gotten away with it, or she'd just never said anything, but he was pretty sure he would have gotten an earful if she had heard him.

There was something about moving through the world and being around other people that demanded a completely different type of energy. Jasper wasn't even an introvert, not really, but when he came home every night that week, all he wanted to do was stare at his laptop. That did not involve setting up his microphone and pop filter to record the script he had written.

Come to think of it, the script wasn't even all that good. He made a note to revise it again before he sat down to work.

It was okay, it really was. Today was Friday, and it wasn't like he had a vigorous social life to take up his time. He'd have plenty of opportunity to record this weekend and get MixerKing the audio by Monday.

When he arrived at work, he tried not to make too much noise getting settled at his desk. Nico seemed deeply absorbed in whatever Word doc they were looking at, and the last thing Jasper wanted to do was break their flow and make them dislike him even more than they already seemed to. He might take up a lot of space, but spending years with someone who was very sensitive to sound had trained him to be silent as a spirit. He probably would have made a great cat burglar.

"Editor-folks! Got a minute?" Evan's voice broke the silence and Nico's chair squeaked with the way they jumped.

"Dammit, Evan," Nico said, and Jasper bit his tongue trying not to laugh. "Look, could you come back a bit later? I'm trying to refine this—"

"Tell me that's not the Hodge proposal still," Evan interrupted. "Nico, he's not going to read it."

"Yes, but he's also probably going to get bored and then Janet..." They trailed off.

Evan shook his head. "As much as I want that too, we can't expect it. We need a different strategy, and I think I've got one."

Jasper looked from Nico to Evan, a little knot of interest balled up in his stomach. Then Evan gave him an ingratiating smile, the kind a charming person gives you before they ask for something disappointing.

"Jasper, do you mind giving us a minute?"

"Yes, please, Jasper," Nico said without an ounce of the same care.

With an involuntary wrinkle of his nose, Jasper stood. "Fine," he said, failing to avoid being passive-aggressive about it. "Maybe there's coffee."

"Oh, there's definitely coffee. Good coffee, too." Evan gave him a personable pat on the back as Jasper headed to the kitchenette and tried not to pout.

—⁓⁓—

The way Evan came in, as if he had some subversive plan to retake control of Unified Theory, was foreboding, but Nico decided to indulge him. They fully turned toward him and folded their hands primly in their lap. It was the sort of posture they used to avoid for being too schoolmarmish, but now that they weren't concerning themself with all that masculinity business so much, they hadn't been suppressing it.

"Well, as you might remember, the twentieth anniversary of *The Unified Theory* is next year." Evan raised an eyebrow and waited for Nico to pick up on the implication. They had been waiting for Janet to discuss that very thing with them, but if they waited much longer, it would end up being a twenty-first anniversary edition, or they'd have to wait until the twenty-fifth.

"I suppose we should get that started. We're late on it already," Nico said.

"It shouldn't be too difficult to put together since it's basically already written," Evan said. "To be a new edition, it needs to have what...fifteen percent more content?"

"Something like that," Nico said. It was actually twenty, but Evan always gave them this disappointed look whenever they'd correct him on something he deemed too minor. "What are you suggesting?"

"Well, I say we present this to Brent as something that is guaranteed to make us a lot of money. It's the reason the business is still running." Evan paused dramatically, as if his point weren't completely obvious. "And in return—"

"We leverage the Hodge book. Got it." Nico supposed that sort of subterfuge would have to be the new normal if they were going to get anything done with Brent around. They weren't sure that they liked it. They had never been good at lying or hiding their feelings.

"Hey, don't look so glum, Nico." Evan relaxed back into Jasper's chair, and suddenly it looked very much like *Jasper's* chair—a place where someone else shouldn't be sitting. "So, how's that new assistant working out for you? Kind of adorable, isn't he?"

Nico sputtered before they could put a sentence together. "I certainly haven't been having such infantilizing thoughts about him, and I don't think that kind of talk is appropriate for a supervisor/employee relationship."

Evan put his hands up in exaggerated innocence. "Sorry, I meant it fully platonically, I swear. Like, he seems like a sweet guy." He stood, then gave Nico a very unflattering wink.

"Well, if you're finished being extremely presumptuous, I would like to reassert my boundaries," Nico said witheringly.

Evan stretched his hands over his head, the next words coming out half as a yawn. "Assert away. I'm just saying that we've known each other a long time, and you can use whatever kind of help you can get."

Nico couldn't possibly say what that meant, but before they could protest, they were interrupted by a loud clanging.

"Oh shit," Evan muttered. "He found the bell."

There was an old-fashioned handbell sitting on the corner of Meera's desk, accessible to anyone in the office. Anyone was allowed to ring it when there was a particularly interesting announcement to be made. Usually, that just meant Janet or sometimes Nico announcing the acquisition of a new book. Meera had also rung it herself once when she'd announced that she was getting married to her husband, Joe. However, Brent now held the bell in his hand, and Nico dreaded what might come next.

The kitchen was small, but Jasper supposed it could have been worse. This having once been a house, one side seemed to have been torn out to make space for a table where people (or more accurately, two people—four max—at a time) could set their things or eat lunch.

Currently Clara was pouring heavy whipping cream into a mug of steaming coffee. The mug sported a large fluffy cat with stripes curled around the name of a local bookstore. Meera was fixing a cup of hot black tea, a light hint of bergamot competing with the smell of steeped beans. If Jasper's body didn't require at least forty ounces of heavily caffeinated coffee per day, the smell alone would be enough to make him rush for a tea bag of his own.

"I just don't get it," Meera was saying. She and Clara had clearly been midconversation when Jasper had appeared. "It seems so salacious, listening to something that makes you all tingly like that. Or at least that's how my cousin Ruchi described it. I was like, please, dear, I do not want to hear about something so personal from my little cousin."

The pleasant lilt in her voice made the subject matter not chill Jasper's blood quite so much. But it still felt like someone had dropped an ice cube down the back of his shirt, and not in the fun way.

"I actually think it's not that big a deal," Clara said. "I know some people just do it to relax, like listening to music except it's just speaking or sounds that are repetitive or soft or something like that."

"Maybe." Meera looked skeptical. She turned from the counter, giving Jasper a bright smile. "Jasper, have you ever heard of ASMR?"

There was nothing sly in Meera's expectant glance. She couldn't possibly know. But on the other hand, Jasper even opening his mouth right now could reveal that something was up. It was okay, he'd been hiding his work from his mother for years—he could handle some near-strangers at work.

Oh no, the pause had gone on too long.

"Are you not one of those *very online* people, Jasper?" Clara said. Her tone was nonchalant, but Jasper suspected he was being felt out. In the past, that tone had come from people looking for a way to get under his skin, but he convinced himself she was seeing whether or not they could be friends. How was that for emotional growth?

"Oh—oh yeah, I've heard about it—" he rushed. He hoped he sounded very innocent. "Just... coffee, you know?"

Clara laughed politely and stepped out of the way of the carafe.

"I'd say I'm online a normal amount. And by normal I mean probably way too much," he joked as he poured coffee into his mug. It had a light fruity smell, and he glanced at the bag of coffee, branded with the name of a roaster he would always pass walking from MAX to work. He wondered who among them was the coffee nerd. Nico? Jasper was *very* interested in what Nico might actually like.

Clara laughed a little more genuinely this time. "So then you've got to know."

"About ASMR? People whispering into microphones?" Jasper took great care not to turn around and to keep his voice light and breezy. "Yeah, sure I do. And, yeah, Meera, I wouldn't worry about your cousin. Most people just use it to relax or fall asleep or as background noise. It doesn't have to be sexual."

"Doesn't *have* to be!" Meera said it like a gotcha. "So sometimes it is."

"Oh yeah, it definitely sometimes is."

Clara cocked her head and gave Jasper an unsettling squint as if she were scanning a street for the address of a place she'd never been.

Before Jasper had to think of another evasion, he was literally saved by the sound of a bell coming from the front. The wash of relief receded when he saw the dark way that Meera and Clara looked at one another.

"What's that?"

"He found the bell," Clara said in a hushed voice. "Come on, y'all. Let's hear it."

Gripping the handle of his mug, Jasper followed Meera and Clara toward whatever doom awaited them.

"Up and at 'em, UTP peeps!" Brent crowed.

Nico couldn't suppress a cringe. It was far too early in the morning for that (although any time of day was too early for Brent's energy as far as Nico was concerned).

"I just wanted to plant a little seed here, and I think it's something you'll all be hyped about!"

Of course he would use a dangling preposition. *Typical.*

"Who here likes podcasts?" Brent's eyes swept the room. Meera and Clara both raised nervous hands. Nico felt like there were bugs crawling up their arms, but they kept them both firmly in place.

"I've been doing some research about how we can make this company more profitable, and I think we've got what we need for a pivot to audio! We'll be talking more about this on Monday, but I wanted to give it the weekend just to marinate. I'm heading out to the coast right now, but I'm looking forward to hearing your ideas Monday!"

Nico's stomach dropped, and they felt their jaw do the same.

"You're leaving now?" Evan said. His words sounded like they were coming from the surface of the pool into which Nico had just been shoved. "You just got here."

"Yup! Just wanted to come and check in with all of you first and give you the good news. Can't wait to talk about it more on Monday!" He waved his hand, key fob dangling from his fingers. "Keep being excellent!"

Then he was gone, leaving the office in total silence. Nico's eyes flicked over to where Jasper stood, gripping a cup of coffee. Idly, they thought that the man didn't look nearly as upset as he should. But why would he? He didn't seem to know the first thing about what a publishing company would be.

He should have known that a book publishing company wasn't a podcast production company, though. That much should have been clear to anyone with two brain cells to rub together.

"So like…" Jack broke the silence. "Are we all getting fired or what?"

"No," Evan said quickly. "Nobody's getting fired."

"You don't know that," Nico said sourly.

"Well, until I see evidence to the contrary, I'm just going to assume our jobs are okay. We'll just need to… pivot, I guess." The dwindling cheer in Evan's voice was still more cheer than anyone should have had right now.

Also Nico *loathed* buzzwords, especially ones like "pivot."

"Well, I guess we've got to continue our conversation, don't we, Nico?" Evan said.

"Maybe we should do it over drinks," Clara said.

Jasper turned toward her like she'd just suggested they partake in an impromptu naked bike ride. It actually reflected Nico's thoughts perfectly this time.

"*After work*, obviously." Clara rolled her eyes. "It's definitely a happy hour Friday if there ever was one."

Nico released a rattling breath. And just what were they supposed to do for the next seven hours, knowing that their job here was getting more obsolete by the second? They glanced up at Jasper, who was looking at them with wide, concerned eyes, and felt like something was trying to claw its way out of them from the inside. It was anyone's guess whether or not they should let it.

CHAPTER FOUR

MORE. HOPELESS. ROMANTICS.

*Y**ou're still getting the stuff to me Monday, right?*

Jasper gulped and put the phone back in his pocket. Seeing as he was sitting at an outdoor table at a brewery near Unified Theory, the sun just starting to duck behind the West Hills as he waited for the rest of the team, he was starting to worry about his deadline. But why should he? This was just tacking a few extra hours onto his time out in the world. That still gave him the full weekend to work.

Across the table, Jack ducked his head down and took a puff on a vape pen. The two of them had walked over together, and the thought *friend?* had briefly flitted through Jasper's mind. However, as the skunky vapor cloud wafted toward him, Jasper thought that friendship would involve more compromise than he was willing to make.

Jack held out the pen to him.

"Oh, nah, I'm good. Thanks, man," Jasper said. Talking like that was an unusual code switch, but it had just sort of happened. He was sure once the others got here he'd be a little more himself.

Hopefully not too himself. The slipup earlier while talking to Meera and Clara had spooked him. He was still a little embarrassed about the way he'd made money for the past several years. He knew he shouldn't be—Portland was pretty liberal, and he considered himself sex-positive, but...well, you just never knew. That was a part of his life better kept separate.

"You smoke?" Jack said.

"Not really," Jasper said. "Makes me too sleepy."

"Oh, you should be using sativa instead," Jack said. "It's a lot better for walking around. Everybody thinks weed is all the same, but it's really not. Something out there for everybody."

"Eh, well, I just haven't really been interested."

It felt suspiciously like he was being evangelized. He wasn't sure what would be worse, this or if Jack was trying to convince him to come to church with him that Sunday. He'd definitely fallen for that one several times in his years in school, always feeling let down when he realized the person he thought wanted to be his friend was just trying to collect one more soul for the Lord.

"Or if you're just more into the body high, CBD oil can be pretty great..."

God, where were the others?

"Jack, stop trying to sell him weed," Clara shamelessly shouted across the patio, and Jasper felt the corners of his mouth lift—felt his entire mood lift, actually. "Meera sends her regrets. Joe is out of town and she's got to get back home to the dog."

Clara and Evan approached, Nico skulking behind them with their hands in the pockets of their linen pants. They'd dressed a lot like a classy middle-aged woman today, complete with what looked like an artist's smock and a steel pendant hanging over their chest. Somehow it was really working for them, but Jasper supposed they could wear anything and he'd be perfectly interested. Hell, they could wear nothing at all and—*nope*, nope, not going there.

A nudge against his arm made him aware of his blush. "What are you drinking?" Evan said, then jerked his head toward Nico, who was still standing. "This one's buying the first round for being shitty to you this week."

"Excuse me?" Nico said.

"Oh, that's not necessary...," Jasper protested.

"Whatever—it's fine," Nico said, turning their intense gaze on Jasper. If anything, Jasper felt like he should be buying Nico a drink. It seemed like they'd had a pretty awful week, and for Jasper, this was all so new he couldn't possibly be shaken in quite the same way.

"Um...IPA, I guess?"

Nico rolled their eyes, "Yeah, there are about fifteen of those."

"There are *three* of those," Clara said. "He'll have the hazy, and I will too. Thanks, Nico!"

"Same," Evan sang out at them.

"I'm good with water," Jack said, taking another puff of his pen.

A squint told Jasper that Nico had no intention of buying Jack a drink anyway. "Alright…," they muttered, walking inside.

"Sorry about them," Evan said. "They're pretty shaken up with Janet taking off like that."

"Sure, sure, I get it. It's okay." Jasper forced a smile, and Evan and Clara both looked at him skeptically.

"They just really don't like change," Clara added. "We'll keep them in line for you."

Soon, Nico returned, setting four opaque bright orange pints on the table. Jasper took a moment to be impressed that they could carry four at once so easily. Did they like coming to places like this a lot?

"Much obliged," Evan said to Nico. Then, horrifyingly, he gave Jasper a very direct look and slid away so the only place for Nico to sit was between the two of them. From his facial expression, it couldn't have been incidental.

Was he that obvious?

⁓ℓℓ ⁓

Unbidden, the thought arose in Nico's mind that sitting next to Jasper was preferable to sitting across the room from him. As anxious as they were about having to manage somebody, Jasper had a sort of considerate and attentive way about him that made them feel much more interested than they normally would.

Then again, who was to say that attention wasn't just due to their position of power over him? Could their ego be so big as to make such a mistake? Even thinking this way about a subordinate was not very professional, so they stomped hard on the thought.

All the same, they should be cordial. After all, they weren't in the office.

"So aside from the new nightmare boss—not *you*, Nico—how are you liking Unified Theory so far?" Evan asked Jasper. He was leaning forward with both elbows on the table, giving Jasper the directed attention that made people fall for his charm so often. If Jasper didn't have a bit of a stammer already, Nico might think he was taken by it.

"W-well, I don't know. I'm happy to be here, I guess." He gave a nervous (*cute*) little laugh, and Nico felt their brow furrow. They cleared their throat but said nothing.

"Do you have any questions for us? I'm in a very talky mood right now," Clara said, as if that were an unusual occurrence.

Jasper gripped his glass with both hands and looked down at the caked-on yellow paint of the tabletop. "Well, it's a little stupid, but, um...what does Unified Theory actually mean?"

"I'm surprised Janet didn't mention it," Nico said. They felt a little flash of shame that he hadn't felt comfortable enough to ask them. But then, they hadn't been particularly approachable, had they?

Jack's high-pitched giggle sounded across the table. "What *did* she mention, though?"

"He's got a point," Evan said with a smirk.

"*Aaaaanyway*," Clara said, calling attention back to herself, "I'm guessing you haven't heard of the unified theory of the paranormal." Opening his mouth, then closing it again, Jasper shook his head. "It's this theory that says everything paranormal comes from the same energy. Like aliens, Bigfoot..."

"Nessie," Evan added.

"Yes, Nessie."

"Mothman," Jack said.

"Mothman and his juicy ass!" Clara threw her hands in the air in excitement. Nico choked on their beer.

"Ghosts, fairies, *all of it*, are just all manifestations of the same thing," Clara said. She was beginning to do that thing where she started speaking with her hands, and Nico began to get concerned for the safety of her half-empty glass of beer, and their own dry-clean-only smock.

"Anyway, it's just a matter of the person looking at it."

"So that guides our acquisitions strategy." Nico was still looking at the table, but they saw Jasper's head swivel toward them in their peripheral vision. "Meaning that all of our books are about those sorts of appearances. Mostly it's cryptids. Mythical animals and whatnot."

They glanced at Evan, who was looking at them with something resembling surprise. This was why they didn't like speaking up—people looked at them, and they couldn't always tell what they were thinking when they did. It was unsettling.

"So do you guys, like, believe in that stuff?" Jasper asked.

"No," Nico said immediately.

"Oh yeah," Jack said at the same time. Evan shrugged and Clara wrinkled her face up, eyes rolling toward the sail-like awning above them as if she were trying to decide on the spot whether she believed or not. Nico knew she didn't. Why would she put on a show for Jasper?

"In any case," Nico interjected, "the founder believed it. The one who wrote *The Unified Theory* in the first place."

"Dick Glenn," Evan said with a very immature grin. Jack snickered, also very immaturely.

"*Richard Glenn* detailed all the different types of psychic phenomena in his book, and it made quite a lot of money. It's still our biggest revenue stream," Nico continued.

"Yeah, and then he fucked off to the middle of the woods to hunt Bigfoot." Clara finished the last of her drink. "Another round?"

～ele～

The sun had almost fully disappeared, a cloud layer was coming in, and Jasper was almost done with his third IPA. He'd already decided to wait until rush hour was over, not feeling like standing armpit to shoulder with a bunch of strangers while he was tipsy. Plus, it felt nice to be sitting next to Nico, and they were being very nice to him right now. He didn't really want to let go of that feeling of contentment and approval yet.

"So!" Evan slapped a palm on the table. His voice had climbed in volume, which wasn't that odd for someone who was a beer ahead of everyone. Clara had switched to water, so Jasper assumed he had a ride home if he needed it. "What do we think happened to Janet? I think she may have run off with a new boyfriend."

Nico scoffed. "What a terrible reason to abandon your responsibilities."

Jasper frowned, or at least he thought he was probably frowning. He couldn't quite feel his face like he usually could. When was the last time he'd had this much to drink?

"Uuuuh, if you're gonna do that, I think falling in love is the *best* reason, don't you, Jasper?" Evan's eyes were wild with mischief.

"Leave him alone, Evan," Clara said warningly.

In his heart, Jasper thanked her. However, his mouth rebelled. "It's okay. I actually don't think it'd be so bad." Nico shot him a surprised look, straight into his face, and Jasper tried not to glance away in embarrassment.

"Yes, Jasper!" Evan clapped his hands together with delight, as if he'd transformed into a teenage girl discovering her new friend's crush. Fuck, maybe he had. "More. Hopeless. Romantics." Evan clapped along with each word.

At least Jasper could feel his face well enough to know he was blushing.

It was another hour before Nico finally stood up, and Jasper slid out of the bench to let them out. He found himself grabbing both their empty glasses and making his excuses to head back home. It was certainly the alcohol that was making him feel brave enough to walk out with Nico.

"You headed to MAX?" Jasper said.

"Usually, yeah," Nico said, a slight slur making their words somersault adorably. "If we're doing that pitch for Unified

Theory next week, I've gotta go back to the office for a little first."

Every protective instinct surged in Jasper. "You're kidding, right? You've been drinking! And it's the weekend!"

"I do it all the time!" Nico said. Their voice rose to a defensive pitch Jasper hadn't heard from them yet. "Well, I mean, not the drinking part, but—"

"That doesn't make it better!" Jasper said. "Fine, if you're going back to the office, I'm coming with you, and then we're going to MAX together."

As he said it, Jasper felt his guts plunge like that free-falling moment at the top of a roller coaster. Oh well, the words were out there now. He had to follow through. Plus, he hated the idea of Nico walking through the dark streets alone. Hopefully they wouldn't read too much into this.

Nico stopped in the middle of the sidewalk to scrutinize Jasper, who held his breath as if any movement would scare them off. Finally, they released a very beleaguered sigh and turned.

"Okay, fine," they said. "Come on, then."

CHAPTER FIVE

BETTER THAN GETTING MUGGED

It didn't take Jasper long after the two of them had reached the old, dark house to start doubting himself. As Nico walked around flipping switches, the quality of the light was alien. It felt weird to be here at night, as if the antique furniture and office supplies spent their time gossiping while the place was empty.

The office echoed with Nico's footsteps, and Jasper was gripped with the need to do something other than stand and wait by the office. Nico had a key, but he didn't. It was weird that they'd lock the room, given that if someone got into the building to rob them, all they'd have to do was break the glass. On the other hand, Nico seemed like the sort of person to just do it as a formality, or out of misguided paranoia.

"I'm going to make some tea, or, er, something." It annoyed him how sloppy his words had become. "Do you like tea?"

"What?" Nico shouted from upstairs. They'd been taking an unexpectedly long time to come back after climbing up there to search through...well, Jasper wasn't sure what. "Oh. Yesss...should...probably."

Jasper waited in vain for the end of that sentence. It never came. He let his shoulder bag thunk to the floor.

After checking that the front door was locked, Jasper ducked under the bottom of the wooden steps into the kitchenette and started to boil water in the electric kettle. There were tins from a local tea company, and Jasper felt a touch of relief at the familiar dark-gray-and-black insignia. Among the different tins was a chamomile blend that had been his mother's favorite, and he felt a very unwelcome knot in his throat.

He cleared it and shouted, hoping Nico could hear him. "What kind do you want?"

"Meadow, please," they shouted back with unexpected breeziness. The light tone almost made up for the fact that now Jasper had to make his dead mom's favorite tea for his boss. Was that a bad omen? Jasper drop-kicked the thought from his mind and took down the tin of Meadow, as well as some Lord Bergamot for himself.

The light in the kitchen had taken on a blue tint, like he was in a transgressive indie film from the early aughts. Who installed a stupid fluorescent light in this old Victorian house? Nobody liked them.

In his judgmental haze, he turned too fast and almost knocked over the kettle, smacking his wrist. Christ, he was a mess.

No, no. It was okay. He was just drunk. Normal people got drunk all the time and it was no big deal.

Yes, Jasper, normal people get drunk and party and have casual sex in their twenties, which you didn't do. Normal people don't get drunk in their thirties and then hang out alone with their bosses that they have a crush on and should definitely not have sex with.

Well, shit.

As if that wasn't bad enough, another very unpleasant thought struck him—that he had perhaps been too pushy when insisting he come with Nico to the office. Had they been too nervous to say no to him? They were so small, and Jasper did his best to make himself as nonthreatening as possible to small people, but maybe the beer had made him lose his usual discretion.

The kettle clicked off, and he poured the hot water over the metal tea balls steeping in their mugs, setting a five minute timer on his phone. As the timer on his phone counted down, a Discord alert lit up the screen.

You alive tho?

Oh god. MixerKing. There were light, uneven footsteps and creaking wood as Nico descended the stairs.

Yep. Finishing up at work

Why

It's Fri night bro.

Wenr to pick something with bosa

Dafuq?

Shit, apparently beer led to fat thumbs. There was a loud clanking of keys and the squeak of a door opening down the hall.

Sorry, the boss needed to pick something up at the office n m waiting to walk thm to the train

Fuuuh...this the hot one or the annoying one?

Hot one

Shit

LMAO enjoy ur night then ;-)

Better come up for air so you can get me the shit on Mon tho

It's not what you think

Yeah, ok

Jasper cringed and put his phone back in his pocket, waiting what seemed like an eternity until the timer finally sounded. He tapped the spent tea out of the strainers and into the compost bin, then picked up the mugs, praying that he wouldn't trip over his damn feet on the way. He needed to get it together. If he was late, MixerKing would know exactly why, and then there'd be no end of shit-talking.

When he reached the office, Nico wasn't at their desk. Instead they were sitting on the floor and...oh god. Jasper definitely struggled to keep from sloshing tea over the sides of the mugs.

Nico had taken their hair out of the high bun they usually wore, and it now fell in charcoal-black waves around their shoulders. It was thick and luminous as a raven's wing, and Jasper felt like some very ugly fish was flip-flopping inside his beer-soaked stomach.

Thankfully, they didn't look up from the book in their lap until they heard the thunk of both tea mugs being set on their desk. They reached out with both hands and made a pathetic, pleading sound. It was mortifyingly cute, and Jasper was certain he would be having a heart attack from anxiety before the evening was through.

"Okay, okay, take it easy, greedy Gus," Jasper heard himself saying, to his horror. As he lowered himself to the ground, Nico let out another puppyish sound of frustration, and Jasper couldn't suppress his giggle. "Oh my god, what is that noise you're making?"

"Shut up…," Nico whined, and Jasper laughed even louder. "Stop it. I'm your boss."

"Yeah, yeah, sorry. Why are you here again instead of going home?"

Some of the playfulness drained from Nico's face, and Jasper almost wished he hadn't asked. "We're going to try to get Brent to do an anniversary edition of this book, and I had to hunt the cop—I mean, hunt down compy. Goddammit. Copy. I'm a bit more inebriated than I thought I was."

"You still managed to say 'inebriated,' though, so how bad could it be?" Jasper said.

This time Nico actually smiled at him. It might have been the first time he'd seen it—no, it was definitely the first time. There was a light curl to their mouth, but what was really striking was the way their eyes lit up. They were a little red, a little unfocused from drinking, but they were bright and amused all the same. Jasper felt like throwing himself out the window; this was too much.

Then their face fell again. "You know, you didn't have to come. I shouldn't be taking up your Friday night. I'm sure you have other things to do."

"No, no, it's okay," Jasper said too quickly. "I mean—I hope I haven't made you feel uncomfortable. I can go now if you'd rather." That was it, this was too much. He put his hand on the ground to start to get to his feet, but before he could, a smaller hand rushed to cover it. Jasper froze.

"Wait!" Nico said. They looked startled with themself and pulled their hand away. "I mean, no, I'm not. Uncomfortable, I mean. It's nice not to have to be here alone. Sometimes it's creepy late at night, I'll give you that. I've been known to..." They bit their lip as they stopped short, then picked up their mug to take a sip of tea. It was much too hot, and they hissed in pain as they set it back down again.

"Been known to what?"

"I've..." They murmured something inaudible.

"What?" There was no way Jasper would drop this.

"Sleep on the couch over there when I work late. So I don't have to walk home in the dark."

"Nico, no!" Jasper said, voice hitting a much higher note than usual. "That's terrible!"

"Okay, well, it's better than getting mugged," they said. "Besides, up until now I rather enjoyed it."

At this, their head dipped back to the book. Jasper didn't press that issue any further; it was obvious they were very distressed about it, and he didn't want to poke at a raw nerve.

"Would you tell me about that book, maybe? Please?"

They clapped it shut and displayed the cover, a black-and-white illustration of mythical figures twisting around one another with a bold red title reading *The Unified Theory*. Smart of them not to put "paranormal" on the front cover, Jasper supposed. Gave them the opportunity to go mainstream, which they had. Come to think of it, Jasper remembered seeing this book in a rack at a grocery store when he was younger and wondering idly what it was about.

"Just what we said at happy hour," they said, a little of the familiar sharpness returning. "Every chapter is a different kind of beast or entity, and Glenn goes into a long explanation of the way these different beasts affect people's lives and act as metaphors and such." They turned it over in their hand. "Should I read some of it to you?"

There was that whirlpool in his stomach again. "If you want."

Nico took a sip of their tea, now cool enough to manage, then opened the book. "Oh, I'm not going to read the introduction," they muttered. Then they looked up as if caught sneaking a cigarette after swearing they'd quit. "Although, Jasper, you should read it at some point. Introductions are very important in nonfiction, actually. At least for editors."

"Noted," Jasper said with a smile. He leaned back against the desk leg. It was very uncomfortable, but he had no intention of going anywhere when his very adorable boss had offered to read to him.

The first chapter was about the fae, how they were found in countries all over the world, their tricky natures, and their light and darker sides. It wasn't groundbreaking, but Jasper knew from living in a city full of hippies his whole life how many people devoured this type of thing. He could hardly follow the words anyway, as his already-fuzzy concentration was completely focused on Nico's voice. It was smooth and precise as a well-played woodwind instrument, maybe an alto saxophone. Maybe Brent's idea about them getting into audio wouldn't be so bad for them after all.

After a while, Nico's sonorous voice developed a bit of a rasp, and they closed the book. "So, we've got followers of Glenn, but also specific groups who've decided to study each of the different creatures. A bit like Campbell if you want to give him that much credit." That last sentence was subtly sarcastic, and Jasper couldn't help but giggle. He was rewarded with another pleased grin from Nico, this time with a little teeth. "Yes, perhaps I'm not showing the proper respect."

"I couldn't care less," Jasper said. The stress he'd felt earlier was starting to ebb, he realized. Nico was much easier to be around right now than during the day. Maybe that was a little dangerous, but Jasper was having too nice a time to give a shit. "You don't have to be a true believer to do a good job with something." Jasper had intimate knowledge of that fact. Very intimate knowledge.

"Right?" Nico said with a little too much emphasis. "Anyway, you should definitely read this. I'm still shocked Janet didn't say anything about that. Especially if she was putting you in editorial."

"Sorry," Jasper said, hardly knowing why (yes, he did—he was a compulsive apologizer).

Nico shrugged. "Not your fault." Then they clapped the book shut. "Anyway. Maybe we should go?"

"Already?" Jasper said.

"I thought you said we shouldn't stay…?" Nico gave him a puzzled look.

"You're right. Just surprised you listened to your lowly assistant," Jasper said.

This time Nico laughed. They *laughed*. It was soft and breathy, and something he could see becoming an addiction.

With some effort, Jasper got to his feet. He felt bold enough to reach a hand down and help Nico up off the floor, and his face warmed a little at the softness of their hands. There was a single smooth callus on the inside of their middle finger, undoubtedly from holding a pen too tightly year after year.

As Jasper washed out their mugs, he heard Nico exclaim, "Dammit!"

Jasper finished what he was doing and clicked the lights off before hurrying to the front. "What's wro—oh. That's not good."

Despite how sunny it had been earlier that day, it was now *pouring* outside. Nico sat on the couch where they'd admitted to sleeping from time to time, looking desolate.

"Hey, don't worry. I can order us a Lyft." Jasper took the phone out of his pocket and grimaced as he opened the app. It was already after ten o'clock. "Looks like we can't get one until...Jesus, half an hour? Is something going on tonight?"

"I think I saw something about a protest downtown," Nico said through their hands, where their face was currently buried. "I just need a minute."

Jasper sat down next to them. "It's just a little rain..."

"It's not that," Nico said with a shuddering breath.

"Then what is it?"

Nico was suddenly remembering why they tried to avoid alcohol as often as possible. Their mood could turn on a dime, and after a week full of jolting change, this tiny inconvenience was like knocking over the first domino in a row. They were sinking into the horrible mood that they'd been staving off with busywork all week. Now that they were forced to sit down, everything was catching up to them.

"I'm just so tired," they finally answered. They wiped their hands down their face before sitting up to face Jasper, and they were able to read unmistakable concern on his face. Maybe it wasn't necessarily concern for their well-being. It could have been concern that he would have to take care of his pathetic half-drunk boss who was ruining his night. They didn't have the energy to decide which was correct.

"Let me just order that Lyft, okay?" Jasper said. "It might take a while to get here, so you can talk to me. That is, if you want to. We can just—you can just read or look at your phone or—"

"That's okay," Nico interrupted. "Go ahead and order it."

Jasper nodded and tapped at his phone. They took a few deep breaths, trying to balance on the swinging bridge of their emotions and not fall off in front of their assistant. He was being so sweet. He deserved better than to have to deal with Nico's meltdown. Plus how would he ever respect them again if they let themself fall into that space?

"So..." At the sound of his voice, Nico's head jerked up from where it was lying on the back of the sofa. "Why did you become an editor here? You know, if you don't believe any of this stuff."

To Nico's relief, it was a distracting question. "There aren't many book publishing jobs in Portland, much less editorial ones. I was just lucky. Besides, the subject matter is fairly harmless, and some people find great comfort in it, so I don't mind much." Aside from the cultural appropriation and the self-centeredness and the disturbing devotion of each philosophy's practitioners. "Also, I suppose we all want to feel like we matter. That we're adding value to the world."

Jasper was sitting with his head resting on his hand, body turned toward Nico and eyes fixed like magnets on their face. And dammit, those magnets were pulling the honesty out of them, no matter how hard they tried to clutch it against their chest.

"I just suppose this whole shake-up has made me doubt whether I have anything valuable to offer at all. If this business changes to something that I have no talent for...then I'm just one more worthless person again." They let out a bleating sound that was supposed to be a laugh but definitely didn't sound like one.

The couch shifted under them as Jasper inched closer, then stopped short. "Nico, you're not worthless. Even if you were to lose your job tomorrow, you wouldn't be worthless."

And it was this sincerity that finally pushed Nico over the edge. Suddenly their eyes were swimming with tears, and Jasper leaned forward to wrap an arm around their back. Before they could stop themself, both Nico's arms were tight around his middle and they were sobbing into his sweater.

"Hey, hey, hey," he said, voice soft in Nico's ear. "I know, I know, it's a lot, isn't it? But you're doing wonderfully. It's going to be okay."

He made a shushing noise, and the hand that was resting on the back of the couch moved to cradle Nico's head. At the sound, so close to their ear, the hairs on the back of Nico's neck prickled. His voice resonated through their chest as he spoke, and they shuddered.

"You're afraid right now, and that's so valid, but you're strong. You can do this."

Then he was...humming? It was almost subsonic, quieter than a whisper, but Nico could feel it everywhere. The goose bumps on their neck worked their way down their spine, and they relaxed under the warmth of his speech like it was a weighted blanket. Their eyes started to fall shut and they released a held breath. It wasn't until Jasper's hum was cut off by a sharp intake of breath that Nico realized their lips were grazing his throat.

They pulled back much more slowly than they should have, and their hazy eyes met Jasper's. His were also half-lidded, as if he'd managed to hypnotize himself as well. His gaze had barely dropped to their lips before Nico closed the inches between them.

One frozen moment, then Jasper's mouth yielded to them. He tightened his grip around their back and dug his fingers into their hair. Nico had never felt so held in their life. The give and take of their lips and tongues mesmerized them so that they felt like they'd fallen into a new, stretched-out timeline. The press of Jasper's body was warm, soft, and even more reassuring than his words had been.

It went on for too long, much longer than it would have had Nico been totally sober and in control of their mood. Their kissing was punctuated with quiet sounds, attempts to draw away from one another followed by dreamy looks that would pull them right back together again.

It was impossible to know how long they would have continued if Jasper's phone hadn't pinged with the notification that their car had arrived.

It wasn't until they were home that they realized they'd left the damn book on the couch.

CHAPTER SIX

THOUGHT CRIMES

"Typical," Nico muttered as the minute hand clicked to five minutes after nine and Brent hadn't arrived. Clara, Meera, Jack, and Evan also sat around the conference table, and Evan had insisted on leaving an open chair between himself and Nico "for your assistant." He'd even had the nerve to wink, as if he *knew*. But he couldn't have known. Nico reminded themself of that fact with unnecessary violence.

They didn't really want to think about why Jasper wasn't there; they assumed there would be a voice mail once they returned to their office with his voice saying he wouldn't be in today. Or maybe ever again.

Christ, what the *hell* had they been thinking, kissing him like that? It was so unlike them. They didn't just go around kissing people, basically ever. There had been some half-hearted attempts with Andie back when they were teenagers, and a couple of college romances that had gone nowhere. They'd been told they weren't confident enough by one woman, that they hadn't made another feel desirable enough. They'd even been told they were too *frigid* by the one and only man they'd gone out with, leading to one of the most unpleasant evenings of their life as they'd stubbornly tried to prove him wrong.

So why, why, *why* the hell had they kissed their assistant after their first week of work? In the office? After an evening of drinking? Clearly, they just weren't meant to have an assistant. Either they behaved rudely or they stomped over boundaries in the most inappropriate way possible.

It had been some very, very nice kissing, though (*shut up, Nico*).

The door swung open and everyone's heads snapped toward it in expectation. Jasper started at the weight of every eye on him.

"Sorry," he mumbled, his eyes scanning the table until they settled on his seat next to Nico. Maybe they weren't great at reading expressions, but that was clearly a look of embarrassment. Hopefully some of that was just from his tardiness, but that seemed like too much optimism today.

He pulled the chair back and sat down, setting down a fancy tablet and stylus that Nico had been reading about online. Nico might have distracted themself from their angst by asking about it had Jasper not chosen that moment to shoot them a bashful smile. Now there was no hope of their being able to talk about anything sensibly, because they were filled with frustrated confusion. Was that an "I'm pretending nothing happened, and this is okay" smile, or was it an "I think we're dating now" smile? Or something else entirely that Nico hadn't thought of?

Before they could recover their thoughts, Brent chose that moment to arrive. He strode to the conference table without an ounce of shame and plopped into the empty wooden chair. For a moment, his expression shifted to pained surprise at the hard landing. It served him right.

"Good morning," Evan ventured. Nico wondered whether there would ever be a point when he'd drop that faux-positive attitude, because they could see themself getting sick of it quickly.

Brent barely nodded in response before rubbing his hands together theatrically. "Okay! I'm excited to hear all the yummy ideas you had this weekend! Let's go—you!" He pointed at Jack.

Jack jolted out of his slumped position. "U-um...," he started, blinking red, woozy eyes.

"I was actually thinking," Clara jumped in to save him, "that we could give you a rundown on our in-progress projects and then maybe that could set the framework for the conversation."

"Sounds like setting constraints to me." Brent frowned.

"Constraints lead to good design, though, don't they, Jack?" Evan's head was turned away from Nico as he looked at Jack, but he was undoubtedly winking again.

Jack nodded his head vigorously. "Yeah, definitely."

Leaning on his forearms with a put-upon sigh, Brent focused on Evan. "Fine. Go ahead."

Evan nodded at Clara, and she said, "We were talking before you arrived and thought it would be helpful if we discussed what was happening immediately and then move backwards."

Brent laughed. "Well, I certainly don't like to hear that you were talking about me."

After a brief hesitation, Clara continued, stumbling a little over her words. "We've got Sparkle Sanders's unicorn book coming out a week from tomorrow, and I've spoken with Andie at Blossom & Crow and everything is on track for the launch event. And Evan's been working with her social media team to coordinate the art contest, which has been getting a *lot* of entries."

"Lots of fun artwork. Her team is taking care of all the printing costs, so we'll be able to display more than just the winning pieces," Evan said.

Fun seemed generous; to Nico, it was just a lot of aggressive colors. The fact that Andie, who had a goth aesthetic, was hosting an event celebrating someone named *Sparkle* seemed very ironic.

"Do we have merch?" Brent said.

"Merch?" Nico couldn't help but sneer.

Brent's eyes were suddenly on them, hostile in response to their tone. "Yeah, merch. Like, t-shirts, toys, those little"—he shook his pen in the air like it was a magic wand—"pom-pom things that look like tails."

Evan laughed and put a hand over his mouth, then cleared his throat. "This is a family event, Brent." Nico turned to squint at him. Why was that funny?

The palm of Clara's hand hit the table as if to call attention back to her. "We don't. It's not really something we do, normally."

"Well, that should change—so jot that down, Sarah."

"It's Clara," she said, somehow smiling despite the situation definitely not calling for it. "The event is only two weeks away, so it might be a little too late for this book, but maybe we can start scouting out some places for next time."

"Okay, who's going to do that? Jasper?" Brent said, clapping his hands.

Jasper sat up with a strong jerk, and Nico wondered if he'd actually been nodding off through all this ridiculousness. "Yeah! Yes. Sure. Can do."

"We also had something else we'd like to discuss with you," Evan said, and Nico's stomach seized as they realized what he was about to suggest.

"Not yet," they found themself whispering.

"Sorry, friend," Evan whispered back, then spoke up again. "You might already know this, but the *Unified Theory* book's twentieth anniversary is coming up next year, and since that's our biggest moneymaker by far, it would be smart to put out a new edition. Add fifteen—"

"Twenty," Nico muttered.

"*Twenty* percent new content, get a new, to-market cover, and get the next generation of readers interested in it all over again," Evan said. "And, as maybe a bit of a compromise, we could release the Hannah Hodge book afterward to piggy-back off that success."

The air in the room was thick with silence as Brent sat, tapping his pen on the table. Nico felt like they were going to throw up.

"We could release it as an audiobook as well," Clara added, and Brent's face lit up.

"That's promising. And of course that's going to be a slam dunk. Can't go wrong with *Unified Theory*, right?"

The atmosphere softened just a little, but Nico wasn't quite satisfied yet. "And the Hodge book?"

"I don't see how there's any innovation in that," Brent said, as if he were telling Nico they'd just lost the first round of a competition show.

"W-we can record something for that, too," Jasper jumped in out of nowhere, so suddenly that Nico nearly dove under the table. "Create some bonus materials that people can only access if they buy the book."

"Oooo, ambitious. I like this guy," Brent said with a smarmy grin. A surge of protectiveness welled up in Nico out of nowhere, and they felt themself turn their body fully toward Brent as if to shield Jasper from his gaze. "Are you volunteering to spearhead that?"

There was a pause, in which Nico didn't turn to see Jasper's expression. They were too busy glaring at Brent. They'd be damned if the man tried to scoop their assistant out from under them.

Oh, Nico, another poor choice of words.

"Right, well, great job today, champs. You've got the thumbs-up for both. Just don't talk about me behind my back anymore, 'kay?" Brent stood up, snapped his fingers, and pointed at each person at the table in turn. It felt unsettlingly like they were the subjects of target practice. Then he turned and bounced out of the room.

Clara's mouth was hanging open as if she had much more to say. In fact, Nico was certain she did. She shook her head and cleared her throat. "Well, go us, I guess?"

"Up top!" Evan leaned across the table, and Clara reached up to slap his hand. He turned to receive a high five from Jasper, then leaned across Jasper to Nico, who knew better by now than to try and avoid it.

It was a win, but it somehow didn't feel like one.

❧

It was a miracle that Jasper hadn't walked into a meeting in progress. He had barely rolled out of bed an hour before, missed his usual MAX train, and had to wait ten minutes for the next one. It had been a long weekend. On Saturday morning he woke up with a hangover-husky voice. He certainly couldn't record sounding like that, so he'd put it off. Then he'd continued putting it off until he was up until 2 a.m. finishing the recording session from hell.

These things were only ten to fifteen minutes long. Why was it so difficult this time?

Okay, okay, he knew why. But it wasn't fair.

As Jasper pushed his exhausted body up from his chair, he heard a cheerful voice from across the room. "Jasper, could you come over to my desk real quick? I have to ask you something," Meera said.

At first he felt a wash of fear, as if she could read his filthy thought crimes. *Relax, Jasper. She can't tell you were thinking about having dirty sex with your boss all weekend.*

Nico had already disappeared, as if they were purposefully trying to escape him. He tried to tell himself not to take it personally, but of course he did. Jasper had made a mistake—crossed a line that couldn't be uncrossed. He'd be surprised if he still had a job at the end of the week.

It would be a nice distraction to talk with Meera for a little while. When they reached her desk, she pulled open a drawer and brought out a key.

"Joe and I are going to Disneyland Friday through Tuesday. I don't know your situation, but our housesitter fell through, and I know you like dogs." She winked at him.

For the first time, he really looked at her desk and realized it looked like Mickey Mouse had thrown up all over it. There was a picture of her with who he assumed was her husband in front of the big Sleeping Beauty castle wearing mouse ears, a bobblehead of that blonde princess who sang that one really annoying song everyone was obsessed with a few years ago, and an elaborately decorated coffee mug shaped like a muscular man covered in tribal tattoos. That last one seemed a lot less innocent than she probably meant for it to be, but who was he to judge?

But in the middle of it all sat a photo of a Welsh corgi, grinning at the camera with its tongue lolling out to the side.

"Yeah! That sounds great! What's their name?"

"Lady," Meera beamed, because of course it was. "So what do you think? You can come over Thursday night to meet her, and then come over after work Friday? I'll leave lots of snacks. Oh! And money of course."

"You've got a deal." Jasper grinned. "Can't wait."

Meera grinned back with relief, thanking him with a prim hug around the shoulders.

It was a relief to have had such a wholesome interaction before going back to face Nico. It cleared a lot of the salacious energy from his mind. Hopefully there was more "cheerful dog sitter" in his step than "horny man who spent all weekend jerking off" now.

Before he could sit, Nico stopped him. "Could you close that door?" they said without turning from their desk. Once Jasper had shut the door, Nico finally turned.

"I owe you an apology," they said, eyes glued to the hands they'd folded in their lap. "What I did on Friday was very unprofessional—a violation, in fact. I would fully understand if you wanted to report my behavior to Meera, and I promise there'd be no retaliation. A-and, if you wanted me to resign..."

This was not at all what Jasper had expected. Wasn't *he* the one who kissed Nico? He wracked his brain, trying to remember. It had all been such a blur, and he'd assumed that he'd been the one to initiate it. But maybe it had just gotten mixed up as the fantasies he'd had this weekend had all overlapped.

Wait, wait, wait, Nico had kissed him, then! He tried not to let the excitement show on his face, which was much easier to do when Nico looked up at him with miserable eyes.

"Nico, it's okay." He wanted to say he liked it, but that was a dangerous idea. "You were in pain," he decided instead. "I didn't really mind."

Nico's brow wrinkled, and damn they were cute. Jasper felt like he was being dealt a series of shallow stabs to the heart.

"Yes, but that's no excuse," they said.

"Really, I'm not going to report you," Jasper said, feeling the excitement draining from him through the imaginary holes in his chest. "We can just...pretend it didn't happen."

Slowly, slowly, Nico's face softened. They nodded. "Right, if you're sure."

"I'm sure," Jasper said.

Nico smiled, looking relieved.

The good news was, they didn't say anything about it for the rest of the day. The bad news was, they also didn't say anything else to Jasper for the rest of the day.

CHAPTER SEVEN

TOO MANY BAD VIBES

The glass door swung open with a rattle and a clunk. There was even more rattling as Brent and his multiple sets of beads appeared in the doorway of Nico and Jasper's office. He looked like he'd just finished his keynote speech at an overpriced meditation retreat.

"Jasper buddy, could you join me in my office?" As usual, his voice was too loud for 9:30 a.m. Jasper wondered what kind of green juice made a person act like that. He didn't want to talk with Brent about the throat-clearing properties of different microgreens, though. That was much too personal.

Nico turned slightly from their computer, but only enough that they could catch Jasper's eye. They didn't seem to want to look at Brent, and who could blame them?

"Sure." Jasper pushed out of his chair. After all, Nico wasn't his only boss. They weren't even the boss with hiring and firing power over him, and frankly, Jasper had been a little miffed at them this past week.

Yeah, maybe they were pretending they hadn't kissed. That didn't mean they had to overcompensate by icing him out. There'd been so little talk this week; Nico had given him some instructions about where to find the company style guide and given him a few trade memos to edit (which they'd then proceeded to review themself and tear apart with red pen).

Then they had the nerve to be annoyed that he spent time doing research for Brent on that pointless merchandise project. What exactly did Nico expect, that he *not* do it?

Jasper pretended they weren't looking at him. He didn't really feel bad about it.

Yeah, right.

Brent walked away before Jasper was even out of his chair, and Jasper took long strides to catch up with him.

The office was about what Jasper had expected from a guy like Brent. He didn't know whether it had been the same way when it was Janet's—they'd met up at a café for his interview. Regardless, it looked like a hipster tchotchke catalog. There were dishes of opaque crystals, and a large glass ball on a plinth that had to be a fire hazard. A concrete Buddha watched over a trickling fountain in the corner.

Notably, the computer had been unplugged and set in the corner on the floor like it was waiting for the electronics firing squad. The only clue that Brent could even get emails at all was an iPad propped up against the side of the desk, its screen fully dark.

Jasper allowed himself a moment to wonder if Brent could actually read.

"Have a seat." Brent gestured to the far side of the desk, where there sat a large yoga ball. Anxiety zipped through Jasper's body. There was a nonzero chance he'd break that thing. At best, he'd be sitting so low his knees would be up to his ears.

"I um...let me get a chair from the hallway." He scurried out to grab one before Brent could argue.

When he got back, Brent had a judgmental wrinkle in the middle of his forehead, and his hands were clasped on the desk like a displeased vice principal of a high school. And it wasn't even in the sexy way.

"So how's Nico been? He seems like a pretty big downer," Brent said.

Anger flared in Jasper's belly. "*They've* been fine," he said, not wanting to give away anything else. Maybe he was annoyed with Nico right now, but he'd also take their side over Brent's any day.

Brent scrutinized him, and Jasper suddenly had a panicked thought that there might be hidden cameras in the office that had caught their activities last Friday night. But no...Brent wouldn't have waited an entire week to say something about a situation like that, would he? Also, he couldn't be that focused on tech with the way the computer was piled up in the corner.

"Well, if you're getting too many bad vibes, we can always move you upstairs by me," Brent said, his tone just a little too cheerful when presenting the idea.

"I, um...no, no, probably better not to," Jasper said before he could really think about it. Who knew what kind of fire he'd be jumping into by getting closer to Brent? It had to be a thousand times worse than working with Nico. At least he liked Nico (against his better judgment), even though Nico apparently didn't like him much. This guy, though, he'd probably have to go on weird wild-goose chases for kale-based baked goods or something.

Brent bounced a couple times on his own yoga ball, using the pretense of turning to look at his tablet, which still wasn't switched on. "And how's the merchandising research going? Find anywhere good for us?"

"Um, yup, going fine."

Without any follow-up, Brent soldiered on. "So what I really wanted to ask," he said, "is about your experience with audio."

It felt like someone had dropped an Alka-Seltzer into the glass of Coke that was his stomach right now. How the *fuck* did Brent know about that? He kept his face as still as possible, hoping that initial burst of fear didn't reveal him.

"Oh, I guess I have a little. Just you know, a little. Not a ton." Great work, Jasper. Really pro lying. An intrusive vision of Brent stealthily joining his Patreon and listening to his work flashed across his brain, and oh god, he was going to be sick.

Brent laughed. "Very modest of you. Janet told me that you had a few years of experience creating audio content under your belt." His eyes flicked down, Jasper realized, to under his belt, and he wondered if *that* was something he could report to Meera when she got back from Disney-land.

Then the memory of his interview with Janet returned to him. He realized that he had, indeed, told her he had some experience with audio. It was just that he'd only mentioned the audio drama he'd been scripting for the past several years. He'd conveniently left out the bit about how he'd never actually recorded or produced any of it yet. Instead, he'd linked her to one of MixerKing's other projects (and, yes, yes, he'd gotten Mixer's consent, and he'd been happy to do it).

"Uh—oh, oh, yes, that's true," he said with an embarrassing giggle. "But I don't see how that's—"

"Well, isn't it obvious? You can train up the others in how this sort of thing works."

Jasper was over the hump of worrying about his own secrets now, because this was a flat-out ridiculous idea. Why would this guy think it would be better to hire him than an actual professional?

"I mean, if you already have the knowledge, a little practice should get you up to speed. Besides, independent podcasters make it big all the time. We'll get started while I look into getting us a studio."

Money. He was doing this to save money—that was what was going on. Cheap bastard.

"'Kay..." was all Jasper could manage.

"Anyway, I was hoping you could schedule a little training sesh for the Monday meeting. What do you say?"

No. "Yeah, okay, sure," Jasper said. "Like...just a presentation of how to, like, talk into a mic or..." Goddammit, he was going to have to put *everything* on an external hard drive, and clear all of his browser history, and all his passwords, and...

"Whatever. You'll come up with something." Brent waved a hand, then pushed to his feet. "Now I've got to get to a meeting. Ciao!"

Ciao? When was the last time somebody said that, the '80s? Jasper sulked as he followed Brent and his jangling beads and key ring down the stairs. He vaguely watched the man walk out the front door before almost running into Nico, who was standing at the bottom of the stairs with their arms crossed.

"Mind telling me what that was all about?" they said. Clara, Evan, and Jack were all the way on the other side of the office, but that didn't mean their voice didn't carry over to them. Plus, all three of them were shamelessly looking in his and Nico's direction at the moment.

Jasper tried to keep his own words hushed. "Not really? I'm just supposed to give a presentation on audio stuff on Monday apparently."

Nico's eyebrows shot up. "Oh, so I suppose you're just going to ignore the project I gave you yesterday."

And that was about as much as Jasper could handle this week.

"Yeah, well, I don't know what you expect from me," he said, volume rising. "Which one of you signs my paychecks exactly?"

Nico looked at Jasper as if he had just knocked a stack of manuscripts off their desk. *Fuck.* That was too far.

"I-I'm going to take my break," Jasper said. Before he could make an even bigger fool of himself, he hurried out the front door.

CHAPTER EIGHT

HE PREFERS YOU

Nico watched Jasper disappear out the front door, their mouth hanging open in the aftermath. They had no time to react to his audacity, only to stand like an event speaker whose mic had been suddenly shut off.

A whistle behind them snapped them out of their shocked reverie.

"Think we should have a talk, friend," Evan said, pulling up to stand beside them, hip slightly cocked in a half-hearted attempt not to loom over Nico's small frame. Normally they'd appreciate the effort, but at the moment they were more focused on dreading what he had to say.

The sound of plastic wheels alerted Nico that Clara was also rising from her desk. Fortunately, Jack still had his soup-can headphones on and was zoned out, staring at his screen, probably on Reddit again.

Evan was already in Nico's office, and Nico had no choice but to follow him inside. Clara followed and shut the door behind her. When Evan gestured for her to sit down in Jasper's chair, she waved him off and stayed standing.

And if they weren't going to sit, Nico sure as hell wasn't going to.

"So, you seem to be having some issues with management," Evan said, false lightness in his voice.

"Oh, so you noticed," Nico responded dryly. "Is that what you came in here to say?"

"Nico, you don't need to be defensive, we're on your side," Clara said. She looked sidelong at Evan, as if trying to communicate with him telepathically. God, the two of them must have been talking about them outside of the office.

"What is this, then, an intervention? Are you going to cart me off to dickhead boss rehab?" they said, pushing back a chunk of damp hair that had fallen out of its elastic.

Another look passed between Clara and Evan, this one much more impatient. "Dude, we're not trying to—" Evan started.

"Dude?"

"Sorry, gender-neutral dude," Evan added quickly.

Dude wasn't gender-neutral; Nico didn't care what anyone said. However, something told them now wasn't the time to die on that hill. They were already holding a shovel and had dug half their grave here.

"You've just been very short with him all week, and he's been doing his best," Clara said. "He's not going to know what to do unless you teach him."

"He's not going to do anything I teach him if he's doing what *Brent* tells him to," Nico spat. "Besides, I did teach him things. I taught him how to review memos, I showed him where the style guide is, I'm having him review sub-missions, and—"

"Yeah, and you stayed after work every night redoing everything he did," Clara said. "And if I noticed, then he definitely noticed."

"Not every night!" Nico huffed. "He's spent most of that time doing useless research for Brent, and now apparent-ly he's going to spend the rest of the day working on some presentation for Monday morning. I mean, is he even my assistant? Because why should I waste my time giving him things to do if *he's* just going to take up all his time."

They took a deep breath, as if surfacing from choppy waters. The sympathetic look on Clara's face was halfway to infuriating. Sympathy and condescension were iden-tical twins as far as Nico was concerned.

Fortunately it was Evan who spoke, and his look was much less forgiving. "That is in no way Jasper's problem. Imagine how he feels being pulled back and forth like that."

"Plus he obviously prefers you, and you're kind of screwing that up," Clara said.

Evan turned to her as if she'd just let slip the spoiler of the latest popular prestige TV show. "You think so?" His voice was high and breathy, hungry for gossip.

Nico felt a pang of paranoia at the idea that perhaps the two of them had walked by the office last Friday night and somehow seen them through a window. But that was phys-ically impossible, wasn't it? For a second, they considered arguing, but they realized that then they'd probably just give themself away.

However, they realized this second part too late and sputtered nonsense words. Evan turned back to them, eyebrows higher than ever and hands to his face.

"Ooooh, is that what this is? Is this sexual tension?" he said through fingers covering his lips.

"Evan, stop it," Clara said.

It was absolutely not sexual tension, at least not on Nico's side. Not that they didn't find Jasper...appealing? He certainly had an attentive and comforting way about him, which made it all the more important that Nico *not* let down their guard around him. Obviously the last time that had happened had been disastrous.

"Sorry," Evan said, clearing his throat and dropping into a lower register. "That was unprofessional of me. The point is, you need to be more patient with him. And Clara's right. He likes you more than Brent, but if you keep being an asshole to him, you might pull off the miracle of being the most hateable person in the office to him. Is that what you want?"

Dread crept up Nico's spine. They knew they weren't the most tractable person on the planet, but the idea of Jasper liking them less than Brent (the absolute shithead) was intolerable. Unable to look their coworkers in their faces, they picked at their glossy black nail polish. It didn't help—it only made them feel like even more of a mess.

"No," they finally said as they forced themself to look back up at them. "I'll try harder."

"There ya go." Evan reached over as if to pat them on the shoulder, then thought better of it and pulled his hand back. Nico was thankful. They didn't feel much like being touched.

Just then, the bell jingled on the front door and the wooden floor creaked. Jasper appeared at the door to Nico's office, looking surprised at the sight of the three of them standing there. He bit his lip, eyes flying from face to face until they settled on Nico's. Nico wondered if they looked contrite, or intimidating, or if they had any control over the way they were perceived at all.

(Gods, every day was a new existential crisis lately.)

Jasper took a step into the room. His shoulders were rounded as if he were trying to shrink. "I just, um...I'm sorry for snapping at you, Nico. That was wrong of me, and I..." His gaze floated over to Evan and Clara.

"Sorry, we'll go," Clara said. She grabbed Evan by the bicep and dragged him out of their office.

"I-it's alright. It's come to my attention that I haven't been very fair to you lately anyway," Nico said. "I guess I've put you more on edge."

"Well, yeah, but still—" Jasper started.

"No," Nico said. "No, I'm the one who's supposed to be mature here. I mean, I appreciate your effort to be mature as well, but..." They sighed. "I'm just sorry, okay? I will try to do better."

Jasper nodded a couple of times, and his forehead un-scrunched. Hopefully that was a good sign. "It's alright." Jasper sat down in his desk chair. "Thanks for saying that."

Nico sat down as well. They were still a little nervous but feeling tentatively good about the situation. Before they could say anything else, though, Meera's phone rang. There was the sound of a chair pushing backward, and soon Evan's cheerful voice rang through the office as he answered the phone. That cheer quickly turned strained, which could only mean one thing.

"Yeah, just give me one second," Evan said. "Okay, you're on."

"Hey there, Unified fam." Brent's shout nearly blew out the phone's speaker. "I'm on the road, and I thought I'd update you on a couple things."

Why the hell had he not made whatever announcement he had to make before he left?

"I just talked to Uncle Ricky," Brent said.

Uncle Ricky? Surely he didn't mean Richard Glenn. Then again, perhaps he'd been more present in Janet's life during Brent's childhood, an idea that Nico was not excited to entertain.

"He's said that he's very excited to create a podcast with us for the twentieth-anniversary book."

Nico's stomach dropped. "I'm sorry, what?"

"Nico." Brent's own tone went flat at the sound of their voice. "That's right. We're going to record a podcast with him. I told him to expect a call from you to coordinate. I already let Jasper know that we'd be needing him to give us a tutorial on podcasting Monday."

Nico looked at Jasper, their anger surging all over again. Jasper looked plainly scared this time, and Nico glanced away so as not to make it worse.

"Okay...but we're still doing the book, right?" Evan said, hovering over the phone as if he were a hound waiting for a ground squirrel to pop out of it.

"Yeah, yeah, whatever, you can coordinate all of that with Uncle Ricky," Brent said. Nico could almost hear him waving his hand dismissively. "Anyway, gotta jet!"

The line went dead, and for a moment there was total silence.

"What the fuck," Clara finally said.

"I know, right?" Evan said.

"Nico, I swear I didn't know—"

"Yes, I believe you, Jasper." Nico held up their hand and swallowed their annoyance.

"Do any of us even have any real experience in audio anyway? That's an entirely different skill set from what we do. Not to mention different contacts. I mean, mostly...maybe there's some crossover." Clara's voice decrescendoed. Ever the pragmatist, she turned to her computer screen, very likely bringing up her contact database to see if she had anything relevant.

"I know a guy with a podcast," Jack said, headphones clasped around his neck like a choker. It was the perfect accessory to go with his early '90s flannel aesthetic.

"Yeah? What's it about?" Evan said. There was a challenging edge to his voice, even worse than the one he'd used on Nico earlier.

"Oh...it's like...just some guys fucking around and stuff," Jack said.

"Sounds hot," Evan said as he sat heavily in his desk chair.

Nico glanced at Jasper, who was staring down at his hands in his lap. Well, this was exactly the sort of situation where Nico was supposed to be a good boss, wasn't it? It was their job to make sure Jasper didn't feel too uncomfortable, or at least not any more uncomfortable than the rest of them. They weren't sure they could imagine how anyone could feel worse than them right now.

Their sigh had the intended effect of getting Jasper to look up at them.

"I suppose I'm the one who will have to speak with Richard Glenn. Not to change the subject"—although changing the subject was, in fact, the only thing they wanted to do right now—"but I was about to send you on an errand."

"Uh...okay."

The ghost of a smile tugged at the corner of Jasper's mouth. Nico almost mirrored it, but they just didn't have a smile in them at the moment. Not after all that. Instead, they turned around and picked up a big manila envelope off their desk.

"Could you go out to Clackamas and have Hannah Hodge sign this contract?"

Jasper frowned. "Oh! I took MAX today, but...is...?" He sounded like he was trying to recover words he'd spilled all over the floor. "Is it...what's the address? Maybe it's close by the orange line."

"I actually took my car to work today, but now that I have to deal with this *podcast* issue"—the word tasted sour in their mouth—"I don't really have the time. I'm sure I can trust you with it, yes?"

"Um..." Jasper clamped his slack mouth shut and suddenly took a very focused interest in polishing his glasses. Nico caught Evan looking over the top of his computer monitor, brows low over his eyes.

"My insurance should cover it in case you get in a fender bender. It isn't a big deal," Nico said, even though they weren't completely sure that was true. Very swiftly they were regretting this, but it was too late to take it back now, not without looking like they didn't trust Jasper with the job. God, now Clara was looking at them like they'd been possessed by sentient nanobots too.

"Sure, sure—yeah, okay," Jasper said. He gently took the envelope from Nico and gave them another weak smile as he pushed to his feet.

Well, why shouldn't Nico trust him? He was a careful person. He was friendlier than Nico and seemed like someone the authors would like. He could handle this.

"Address is on the envelope," Nico said. There was a rebellious little shake to their voice that they really resented. "It's the green Subaru."

As if that narrowed it down in this town.

"The green Subaru with the um...with the Bikini Kill sticker," they added.

Not much better, but it should be the only one on this block with one of those. Hopefully.

Jasper nodded, and now the smile was bigger—hopefully not because he was judging Nico's taste in music. Probably he was happy to have been entrusted with something. He nodded a couple of times, then turned to leave. Nico managed to contain their anxiety until he was out of sight.

CHAPTER NINE

CARBUNCLE

The whiplash Jasper felt from this morning had literally given him a headache, but that was fading. Things seemed to be looking up. He had a little bit of a high, even if that high was laced with anxiety. It didn't really hit him until he was pulling onto the 84 that he was driving his boss's car.

Oh god, and his crush's car, too—couldn't forget that!

It was a typical Subaru, old enough to have a CD player. When he turned the car on, he'd been blasted in the ears by some very yell-y band he didn't know. It was a little more high-energy than he'd have expected from Nico, but then he supposed he didn't know the real Nico all that well. Nico didn't come across as the type of person who wanted people to know them all that well.

One thing Jasper did know was that he'd have to readjust the seats and mirrors back to normal before he returned the thing. They were so tiny!

It surprised him how unkempt the interior was, but he couldn't say he wasn't charmed by it. It was just a little messy—he spotted at least two different cardigans draped over the seats, and there was a mug, an actual ceramic mug, sitting empty in the front seat cup holder. If he hadn't already thought everything about Nico was cute, this might have made him a little judgmental, but instead it was just endearing.

Christ.

It turned out the house wasn't exactly in Clackamas, but more outside the city on several acres of land. Half an hour after leaving Unified Theory, and after a few wrong turns that took a while to recover from, he pulled up to a metal gate in front of a long dirt driveway. The house he saw was the same as a lot of the older farmhouses out in this part of the county; however, the place itself wasn't much of a farm. He didn't see any crops, just a lot of overgrown grass, feral blackberry bushes, and scattered conifers.

There were also more than a dozen dogs, all crowding the gate as if Jasper were their favorite rock star. Some stood on their hind legs, balancing with their paws on the rails like they were ready to reach through to him. Others hopped around barking. Tails whipped manically.

How the hell was he supposed to get through this gate?

He stopped and pulled up so he wasn't blocking the road. Before he could call Nico to see what he should do, he realized there was no signal (because of course there wasn't). Jasper was proud of how little he'd been panicking lately, given the circumstances of his life. However, he was already operating on frayed nerves this morning.

As he considered getting back into the car and driving to a coffee shop to call Nico, there was a loud snapping sound from the other side of the fence. In one sweeping motion, every dog's head turned, and they started running away from the fence as if pulled by the gravity of a new planet.

The gate opened automatically, and Jasper, not believing his luck, pulled up toward the house.

A woman stood at the base of the rickety white steps. Hannah Hodge, Jasper presumed. She was dressed head to toe in camouflage, as if she were about to take the entire pack on a hunting trip. Her face was hard-lined, her build sturdy, as if she slept outside in one of the fenced-in kennels he'd spotted beside the house.

"You must be Jasper. Nico told me you were on your way," she said. Jasper winced when she immediately shouted, "Come!" right afterward. Her voice was husky in the way one would expect of someone who spent a lot of time bellowing commands at a crowd of animals.

Jasper could only manage a weak "That's me."

There was a stampeding rumble as the pack returned, a few of them trying to wrestle away a ratty duck toy from the cow dog running near the front. There was a contraption on Hannah's wrist that Jasper assumed was a weapon of some kind. He hoped that it hadn't been picked up just for his benefit.

The cow dog dropped the disgusting toy at Hannah's feet, and the rest of them swarmed around Jasper. He squeaked and jumped as he was goosed from behind, and he turned and saw a shockingly large black dog. It came all the way up to Jasper's hip.

"That's Gwyllgi," Hannah said as she attached the toy to the mechanism on her wrist. "Naturally you've heard of the Black Dogs of English folklore. That's what the Welsh called them. My little baby here doesn't have those red eyes, but his breath don't smell that great." She gave a baying laugh, as if scandalized by her own bad grammar.

She turned away to fix a squinting gaze on some faraway point, then shot the toy through the air and across the property. Most of the dogs took off after it, while a few couldn't be fooled so easily and continued to swarm around Jasper. A German shepherd reared up on its hind legs to balance its front paws on Jasper's belly. Jasper hunched over with an involuntary huff—just enough for the dog to lick his face.

It wasn't Gwyllgi, but its breath didn't smell that great either.

"Knock it off, Laika," Hannah said. "Just give her snout a nudge, would ya?"

Jasper felt like putting his hand near Laika's mouth might be a tactical error, so he chose instead to turn slightly away and follow Hannah toward the front door. At the last moment, he had to fight his way back to the Subaru to grab the manila folder with the contracts inside.

While the smell from the kennels outside had been a little ripe, the inside wasn't much better. It was pretty much what one would expect, as there were even more, smaller dogs inside. There weren't only several terriers and toys, but the walls and tabletops were covered in dog art from every era—from regal Renaissance dogs to sentimental tacky paintings of hunting hounds that looked like adaptations from a Sears family photo shoot.

"Do you like dogs?" Hannah said as she removed the device from her wrist.

"I-I, um, I guess so?" What was he supposed to say? No?

"Never met a dog I didn't want to put a collar on." Hannah barked with laughter. Jasper laughed sympathetically, even though she hadn't really told a joke—it was just a really weird way to say it. He might be good at hiding things in general, but he wasn't great at hiding his discomfort. Be that as it may, Hannah didn't seem to notice.

"Sit down, sit down," she said. Jasper sank into the only available chair (upholstered and coated in hair). "Do you know about my book? Nico said that you're their new assistant, so I'm guessing the answer is yes."

"Kind of?" Nico had not been very generous with information about the books, and Jasper had to admit it was a little insulting. But maybe if they trusted him with their car now…

"Give you three guesses what it's about." Hannah laughed loudly again and didn't notice, or didn't care, when Jasper flinched. "People throughout history have made so much of the cat. The sacred feline. The dog has largely taken a back seat when it comes to companion animals and mysticism. Would you like a drink?"

Jasper blinked at the abrupt change of subject. "A drink? Uh…" Normally he wouldn't touch anything that someone offered him in a house this filthy, but he had driven for half an hour already, and he certainly wasn't going to enjoy the dregs of whatever Nico had in that ceramic mug.

"We have…" She rummaged through the fridge, then hooted with amusement. "Ginger ale and… ginger ale."

"Ginger ale it is, then!" Jasper said with exaggerated politeness.

There was something a bit houndish in the slope of her nose. Jasper wondered if it was true that people grew to look like their pet dogs and, if so, which one of the pack she was best paired with.

Rude. That was a rude thought. Shush, Jasper.

When she emerged from the kitchen, she was holding a cup of ginger ale with no ice. It was full to the brim, and he hoped the glass was opaque by design, but that was probably too optimistic. Thirsty as he was, he couldn't get himself to bring the thing to his lips. Instead, he set it next to a dark stone Egyptian-style statue of a hound and opened the manila envelope.

"So, Ms. Hodge, do you have—"

"Have you heard of the Carbuncle?"

"The what?" He looked down to see a fluffy white toy poodle, its paws balanced on his knee. At least it probably had been white. It was currently a bit yellow.

"Well, yes, that's Carbuncle! But the Carbuncle is also a mythological Chilean creature. Some think it's a shellfish, but others still think it's a glowing white dog. That's why I gave him his name," she said with a self-satisfied grin. She sat in the chair opposite him, which was also covered in white (possibly Carbuncle's) hair.

"That's nice—oh! No, Carbuncle, that's important." Jasper said. He held the contracts over his head now, as Carbuncle had snapped at it. Dammit, he also realized he'd forgotten to bring a pen. "Do you happen to—"

The sentence went unfinished, as Hannah had launched into her plan to take color photos of each of her dogs and pair them with every chapter in the book. Jasper was fairly certain Nico hadn't written that into the contract, but he wasn't particularly interested in revising that and having to come back again. Not that he seemed to be able to get a word in enough to have her sign anyway.

"You haven't touched your ginger ale! Go on. Don't you like it?"

Jasper cleared his throat. "Oh, um, sorry, yeah," he said and took a sip as she resumed her storytelling. It smelled like dishwater, and he suppressed a gag.

She seemed intent on giving Jasper a crash course in the mythology of dogs, which wouldn't be such a bad thing in a different situation. It might even have been interesting to him if she weren't ignoring everything he tried to say and if he didn't have someone back at the office who he desperately wanted to please. As it was, his boundaries were being pushed, and so was his already thinned-out patience.

Eventually he gave up doing anything but smiling and nodding. God, he'd have to work on Brent's damn presentation over the weekend. Well, that and complete all the content that was supposed to go up on Patreon Sunday night (because obviously he couldn't just throw an audio file on there without context—ugh).

Ironically, the thing that finally stopped her monologue was Jasper's stomach growling.

"Got a pup in your belly there?" She laughed again, and Jasper clamped down on a surge of anger. To be fair, it might not have been a comment on his weight, but he wasn't feeling particularly charitable toward her right now. "I was about to heat up some chili."

Jasper swallowed bile and checked his phone. The first thing he noticed was that it was already almost 1 p.m. The second was that he had a message from an unknown number.

What's taking so long?

Is everything alright?

Did my car break down?

"Actually," he said, taking advantage of the slight gap in the conversation, "it would be great if you could sign these. Nico needs me back at the office."

"Oh, he can spare you for a few more hours," she said. She waved off the contracts he held out and walked over to open the fridge. "I still haven't introduced you to everyone."

Hours? Jasper schooled his face into a neutral expression and looked down at his phone, trying to figure out the right words to get Nico's help without making it seem like he'd been abducted by a serial killer. He settled on—

Apparently I have to meet all of the dogs before she'll sign.

He sighed and set the phone facedown on the table next to the half-drunk, milky-colored glass of ginger ale. Naturally, he picked it up again two minutes later, and there was already a response.

I'll be right there.

CHAPTER TEN

(NOT SO) STRAITLACED

They should never have let Jasper go by himself. Trying to show they were confident in him had backfired, and they couldn't help being slightly annoyed—not with Jasper, although they were a little bit at first. The annoyance was with themself. Jasper was an open and accommodating person, and Nico had sent him to a woman who was always ready to walk straight through a boundary. Nico had plenty of experience with her to know how she could be. They should have known better.

At least the universe took some mercy on them, and the Lyft driver was silent for most of the way. He was listening to some melodramatic string music that was likely a score for some video game. It was a signifier of questionable taste as far as Nico was concerned, but they were traveling on the company dime, so they knew they shouldn't be too upset.

It wasn't Nico's first time at Hannah Hodge's house, so they knew to wait until she'd called off the pack of dogs from the fence, knew to ignore her offer to sit down, and—most of all—remembered to bring a pen. She had tried to protest their taking Jasper away in the middle of "lunch," mysterious brown glop in a bowl, but Nico did their best impression of a steamroller to get him out.

If they had been there alone, it would have been impossible. In fact, the first time they'd been alone with her, they'd been stuck there all afternoon. They were also certain they'd mentally blocked whatever she had fed them for lunch. When they'd come back so late, it was one of the only times that they'd heard Janet raise her voice. Nico had already done enough of that for the week.

In Nico's Subaru, the Le Tigre CD played at a slightly more reasonable volume than they'd been playing it at this morning. They had to pull the seat all the way back up to reach the accelerator and brake pedal and huffed with weariness as they adjusted the mirrors.

"I'm sorry. I was going to fix that before I gave you the car back," Jasper said. His voice was quiet, his expression grave.

Dammit. The last thing they had wanted to do was make Jasper feel guilty. They'd already done quite enough of that, plus put him in a situation where he had to get pawed at by a Humane Society's worth of hounds.

"No, it's fine. I'm sure you were." Double dammit, that sounded disingenuous as well. They tried to pry themself away from self-reproach as they did a three-point turn and navigated back to the road.

After a few minutes, Jasper was still quiet, and Nico really didn't know what to say to break through the tension in the car. They wanted to apologize, but they weren't sure what they should say they were apologizing for. Maybe discussing something unrelated would help?

"Are you a Le Tigre fan?"

They caught Jasper's head turning from the corner of their eye. "Who?"

"You left my music on," they said, trying not to make it sound accusatory. They weren't sure they were successful, but there was no point in looking over at him. It wouldn't have revealed much, plus they needed to watch the road. Drivers were very inconsistent in this area of town—some slow and meandering while others in way too much of a hurry.

"Sorry, actually I'd never heard of them?" Jasper said, as if it were some kind of failing.

"Don't apologize," Nico said. "It's not for everyone."

"No, I mean—I like it. I just didn't expect..." This time, they chanced a look and saw that Jasper was biting his lip. "I didn't expect you to be into something like that."

"Why wouldn't I be?" Nico said.

"Well, you seem a little more straitlaced than that," Jasper said.

Nico held on to their next statement for a couple of seconds, wondering if it was inappropriate, given what they'd already been through. Then again, maybe it would break the tension caused by last week's drunken faux pas as well. It was probably too much to hope, but worth a try.

"Jasper, I thought it would be clear by now that there's nothing straight about me," Nico said, deadpan.

The words hung in the air for a terrible second.

Then Jasper bubbled over with laughter, putting a hand to his mouth and smothering an "Oh my god." Nico felt themself smile as the pressure in the atmosphere between them evaporated. They shot a look at Jasper from the corner of their eye and saw his head bowed, a little bit of red in his cheeks, and the raised corners of his mouth peeking out from behind his fist. Something inside their chest warmed at how pleased he looked.

They probably shouldn't be paying so much attention to his mouth, but here they were.

"We should get lunch," Nico said before they could stop themself, "since I so rudely interrupted yours and Hannah's meal."

"You're kidding me, right?" Jasper said. "You probably saved me from getting botulism."

"No doubt. But since I put you in that position in the first place"—Nico cleared their throat—"which I'm sorry for, by the way...so...yes. Maybe lunch as penance?" Nico held their breath.

"Sure," Jasper said. "Yeah, that would be nice. Thanks."

They settled on a ramen place a few blocks away from work. Maybe it was a missed opportunity to go somewhere deeper in Southeast, less hipstery, but in the end, Nico's practicality and the desire not to have to find parking twice won out.

And, of course, the desire to make this look as little like a date as possible.

While Nico planned to expense this to UTP as well, there was something about handing over their card to pay for both theirs and Jasper's lunch that made the hair on the back of their neck stand up. Refusing Jasper's offer to pay made them feel less self-conscious. Being contrary always seemed to do that, though it became clearer with every passing day that the habit wasn't serving them very well.

"Are you going to be alright taking care of Lady after such a harrowing canine experience?" Nico said after the two of them settled on one of the wooden tables outside. They were rather proud of themself for proving they did pay attention to what Jasper did with his life. It was the bare minimum, but all the same.

Jasper jumped a little at Nico's words, and the soft-boiled egg he had balanced on his chopsticks plopped back into the bowl. "Oh, yeah, she'll probably cancel out the trauma, honestly. Meera brought me home so I could meet her last night. She doesn't smell like shit. Oh! Sorry!" His eyes widened.

"For what?" Nico said.

"Oh, just, you know...cursing in front of my boss," he said with a breathy laugh.

Nico cocked their head. "Jasper, I don't give a fuck whether you curse or not."

For the second time today, Jasper's hand flew to his mouth to cover a grin. Nico wished he wouldn't hide it. They liked the way he smiled. It felt genuine, not like the smile someone used when they were trying to placate or charm them. They tried to keep their face expressionless in contrast, but it was a losing battle, and they both let themselves laugh until Nico noticed they were getting looks from the passersby.

The air felt sufficiently cleared to switch to a more serious topic.

"Jasper, I owe you an apology for the past couple of weeks," Nico said, laying their utensils across the top of their ramen bowl.

"You already apologized once today," Jasper said.

"Yes, yes, I know, but then I literally threw you to the dogs, so I feel like it should be restated." They realized that the way they'd said that might also have been considered too brusque. God, why were these things so difficult? "Granted, it's been a while for me, but I know starting a new job can't be easy. Unfortunately, I'm not known for my flexibility, and I allowed the fact that too many changes happened at once to color my treatment of you."

Maybe they were imagining it, but they felt that warmth was radiating toward them from the other side of the table, where Jasper was sitting. It was a strange sensation, but also very encouraging. They forced themself to look up and briefly met his gaze before focusing on the collar of his shirt.

"It's been brought to my attention that I could be doing a better job of training you, and maybe not being so untrusting of your skills. So, I'm sorry for that."

"Yeah, it was...well, I accept. Again," Jasper said. "I've got to do what Brent asks, you know? But I want to help you too—more, actually. That guy is..."

"Loud?"

"Clueless?"

Nico picked up their chopsticks again. "Fucking annoying."

"Nico!" Jasper laughed again and Nico beamed behind the lump of noodles they'd brought to their lips.

There were a few minutes of companionable silence, where they simply enjoyed their lunches. The clouds had parted, and tiny green buds and new branches shot a checkerboard of foliage across the patches of blue sky above them.

"So, what kind of editorial experience do you have?"

There were several coughs from across the table, and Jasper wiped his mouth with a napkin. "Sorry. Just, other than college, it was mostly digital QA type stuff. Honestly, I-I didn't think I'd get the job, but...if you want, I'll do extra reading after work and—"

"Jasper, relax," Nico said, feeling a little guilty (and a little frustrated) that they'd gotten him worked up again. "Where did you go to college?"

"OSU," he said.

"Did you? So did I. When were you there?"

"Uh—" Jasper suddenly became very interested in the tabletop, eyebrows drawing together. "Sorry, I feel really old. Like, 2005?"

Odd. Nico felt they would have remembered having Jasper in at least one of their classes. "Did you do English lit? I'm not sure how we would have missed each other."

Jasper bit his bottom lip, face still scrunched up. "I just did a minor in it, so maybe that's it."

"Could be," Nico said. Maybe it wasn't so strange. Their years in school had been lonely, lonelier than they should have been for a college student. It was their own fault. They'd never really been good with making friends, for obvious reasons.

It was a little frustrating—that someone with so much less experience than them could just land an editorial assistant position. This city was full of underemployed people with graduate degrees who would kill for this job.

But that wasn't Jasper's fault. Best not to dwell on the injustice. What was done was done, and Jasper seemed eager to learn and work hard. Perhaps Nico was acting with generosity right now, but they did plan to hold him accountable. It was against their nature not to.

They flipped their phone over and checked the time. It was almost three o'clock, and they had both almost finished their lunches. Some of the pleasant energy had gone away, and they were a little unsure of what they'd done to make that happen.

"Well, 2005 was a long time ago. I'd be happy to help you refresh your skills," they said, hoping that would help them recover the comfortable feeling of a few minutes ago.

It seemed to, judging from the way Jasper said, "Oh! That would be great! Thanks!"

Nico nodded, relieved. "I know you've got something else to work on today, so we can start Monday."

The walk back to work was quiet, but that was okay. Nico was pleased with themself and high on fresh air. They weren't quite sure what they were going to do to help Jasper, but they had a whole weekend to figure it out. The prospect almost helped them forget about the terrible phone call they'd put off in favor of rescuing him from Hodge.

Hopefully that wouldn't poison their good mood, but chances were very slim.

Chapter Eleven

A Little Vacation

That was the second roller coaster of a Friday in a row for Jasper, two bizarre crests of a tide of two unsettling workweeks. First there was the very uncomfortable meeting with his boss, then getting in a low-key fight with his other boss, then getting trapped by a pack of dogs and their human ringleader, and then...

Nico insisted on getting more endearing every day. It was like watching a slow-burn horror movie, except the horror was Jasper's growing, unrequited attraction. Because it *was* unrequited. The kissing had been a mistake, he kept telling himself. Nico didn't like him like that, no matter how kind they had been by the end of the day. They'd just been drunk and vulnerable, and Jasper had taken advantage of that and...*stopstopstop.*

He really needed to give up on these thoughts, rewind the unraveling spool of feelings that the last week had yanked out of him. The best he could hope for was that a weekend with a corgi might cool his feelings a little bit.

Plus Meera's house shouldn't have inspired anything but wholesome thoughts. Maybe there was an uncomfortable amount of cutesy paraphernalia for Jasper's taste—Mickey Mouse pillows on the couch and a giant Sleeping Beauty castle bedspread in the guest room—but at least it was immaculate. All the DVDs were lined up in alphabetical order, and he'd spent at least ten minutes before he found the kitchen trash can, it was so well concealed behind a pure-white cupboard door. Jasper wondered what kind of high-paying job her husband must have to be able to afford this kind of house and, apparently, a cleaner.

It felt like a little vacation to be somewhere other than work or his house, which still had the stink of loneliness and long-term illness no matter how much interior design magic he tried.

Also distracting him this weekend was the sobering task of going through MixerKing's notes on his latest recording.

> You sound fckin wrecked, and not like in a wanna-smash kinda way. I've marked where you might want to re-record, but if I were you I'd redo the whole thing.

There were a lot of time stamps on that list for him to check. Like, a lot. And there was no way he was going to re-record this *and* have it remastered by the time he was supposed to post it. He'd argue that the women who made up his core audience liked a bit of a rougher quality of voice, but then, MixerKing probably had a better idea of what women liked than he did, him being heterosexual and all. Or maybe not? That wasn't an argument he was interested in having.

The argument was simply that he wasn't redoing it. It'd have to be mediocre. Hopefully he wouldn't lose subscribers over it, but they were all pretty loyal. He could probably get away with one shitty week.

God, at some point he hoped he could move on from this. Part of his reason for working at Unified Theory was so he could start shifting his focus to passion projects like his audio drama. He had, no joke, almost two hundred pages of notes for a multiseason queer horror story that he thought was fucking dynamite. And, sure, maybe that sounded delusional, but he clearly had a good enough voice and worked hard enough and was a skilled enough writer that he'd supported himself and his mom pretty well for the past several years.

He was just starting to get very in his head about the whole thing when he felt two small points pressing against his shin. Peering over the top of his laptop, his eyes met Lady's wide brown ones over her open, panting mouth. She was one of those calico corgis, small with white, red, and dark brown fur.

It was hard to get upset about his *meh* vocal performance when this goofball was staring at him, pointy ears at attention. After yesterday's misadventures, she was doing some heavy lifting to repair his opinion on dogs. She was doing a bang-up job. Also, she really seemed impatient to get out of the house.

"You and me both, girl," he said as he pushed to his feet and retrieved the leash hanging on the wall hook by the front door. It was hilarious to watch her try and jump for it. The poor thing was so small she had absolutely no chance.

But Jasper knew plenty about wanting impossible things, didn't he?

There was no point in putting this off anymore. Nico took a big breath and reached for the phone. As they did, it started ringing, and they snatched their hand back with a yelp.

The display screen read *Richard Glenn Unif.*

Well, that was unsettling.

Before they could second-guess themself or succumb to the surge of anxiety inside them, they picked up the phone.

"Unified Theory, this is Nico," they said.

"Nick! Great to hear your voice again. It's been ages," Richard Glenn said. His voice rang with a good-old-boy timbre, like he was calling from the front seat of a rattly old pickup truck. Nico knew for a fact that, whatever he drove around up in the Washington woods, he always showed up to the UTP office in a BMW.

"Sounds like my nephew's got us a new project, doesn't it? Why don't you give me a little rundown?"

Immediately a swooping feeling seized Nico, like the way they used to feel when they'd jump off the top arc of a swing as a child. They honestly didn't know what they were supposed to be doing with this project; it was why they'd been putting off this call for so long. Well, that and they knew they'd be relentlessly misgendered, but that was a daily occurrence, even in Portland, no matter how they presented themself. Naturally it would happen with a self-centered, aging man who could only hear their voice on the phone. They rarely knew how to correct people about it either, especially authors or anyone older than them, really. The truth was, Nico thought, they were a coward who couldn't stand up for themself or, by extension, other queer people.

Okay, enough self-flagellation. They needed to get through this call without having a full-on anxiety attack.

"Yes, I believe Janet spoke with you about the twentieth-anniversary edition of *The Unified Theory*, and we'd need about twenty percent more text"—God, but Nico hated the word *content*—"for that. I was wondering how you would like to go about creating that. I don't suppose you have anything written already or—"

A hearty laugh on the other end of the call cut them off. So there was the answer to that question.

"I sure don't!" he said, unnecessarily. "Brent said you'd be taking the lead on that. I'll be needing your help there and am ready to hear ideas."

There was silence—a long, ugly silence. What were they supposed to say?

"Well, we've been discussing conducting more audio interviews, so perhaps we could—"

"Now that's a bright idea. You're always welcome up here at the cabin."

To hell with panic attacks, they'd be lucky if they got through this without vomiting. "That would not be necessary. We could do this remotely, or I believe Brent might be seeking out studio space for such—"

"Oh, but where's the fun in that? Nick, I say cabin, but we've got running water and heat, the works. And electricity for all your fancy recorders," he said. The rustic act that Glenn put on truly was grating. He was a very, *very* rich man who had grown up in Seattle.

Plus, being called Nick repeatedly made them feel like they were being worked over with a hammer and chisel.

"Perhaps," they said, if only to placate him. "I'll get answers regarding recording space and equipment on Monday, and we can go from there."

"Alright, alright, and I'll put in a word with Brent. You deserve a little vacation, I'd say," Glenn said.

Nico didn't want a "little vacation," and if they did, the last place they wanted to take it was at Richard Glenn's remote cabin.

"You're a good guy, Nick. Talk soon," Glenn said, and the line went dead.

After a moment of disorientation, Nico put the phone back on its cradle. Then they sighed, took off their glasses, and buried their face in their hands. There simply wasn't enough air in the room to make them feel better right now. Outside their window, however, it was a perfectly clear day. They dragged themself out of the desk chair and stumbled onto the front porch.

The sidewalks were busier than they were during the week. Portlanders soldiered through rainy days without umbrellas (umbrellas were for amateurs). However, on days like this, they left their rain jackets at home in favor of puffy vests, tunics, and the odd pair of Tevas. There were fewer and fewer of those these days, as neighborhoods like these had fewer hippies and more yuppies pushing strollers or walking purebred dogs.

In fact, there was a familiar dog walking up the street in their direction right now with a familiar man at the end of its leash. Jasper's ice-blue sweater was already becoming commonplace to Nico, and at the moment they were amazed at what a welcome sight it was, how they felt their chest unclench. They wondered for a moment whether Jasper would notice them huddled on the front steps.

They would have to continue wondering if he would have, because of course Lady found them first. By now they were old friends—Meera often walked her by UTP on weekends and chastised Nico for being at work. It was a routine that had become rather comforting, in fact.

Lady veered away from Jasper and trotted up the stairs as if she had a checklist of important business and saying hello to Nico was at the top of it.

"Hello, Lady," they said softly as Jasper caught up.

"Nico! What are you doing here?" he said, a little more surprise in his tone than Meera usually had by this point.

"Ah...just, had to make that phone call to Richard Glenn," they said. The tremble in their voice was irrepressible, like a rose petal being slowly ripped away from the rest of the bud by a strong wind. Nico hoped Jasper would let it slide.

He didn't. "Was it...are you okay?"

Lady scrabbled with both her little paws at Nico's thigh, and they relented and pulled her into their lap as Jasper moved closer to give the leash slack.

"I've been better," they admitted. "I just..." *Don't have a clue what I'm doing? Barely know who I am anymore, if I ever did in the first place?* They settled on "Getting called 'Nick' over and over wore me down a bit."

"Oh, that motherfucker," Jasper said, then clapped his non-leash-holding hand over his mouth. Then, just as quickly, he lowered it. His mouth and eyebrows were both set in angry straight lines across his face. "Well, he's definitely on my shit list."

Nico's laugh was loud enough that Lady twisted her head around to look at them in puzzlement. "You probably shouldn't say things like that about our company's bread and butter, Jasper." They said it to try and counter the grin on their own face, which Lady was now trying with all her might to lick.

"I don't care," Jasper said, emboldened. They were looking at Nico with more conviction than they'd seen from him before now, except perhaps during his outburst at them yesterday. It felt very nice to have that energy be on their behalf rather than against them.

"Well, I appreciate it," they finally said. They looked at him as long as they could manage, finally refocusing back on the dog in their lap. The sound of traffic from a couple blocks away mingled with the susurration of bike wheels and the breeze through the branches overhead.

"Do you need anything, or…?" Jasper said, more reserved than before.

A part of them wondered what would happen if they went inside and got their bag, locked up, and joined them on their walk. But no. As much as they might like to, it was an unprofessional thought. Dangerous, even.

Nico shook their head. "No, please just enjoy your weekend. You don't need to worry about me," they said. They set Lady back on her feet and stood, attempting another smile but not feeling successful. Lady shook herself off as if Nico's hands had dirtied her somehow.

Jasper looked at them, obviously unconvinced. All the same, they guided the dog back down the steps.

"Don't stay too late, okay?" he said, giving a wave and a final look before following the corgi as she headed for the next item on her agenda.

Nico stood on the porch, watching them until they turned the corner at the end of the block. With every step Jasper took away from them, the fist in their chest tightened. They sighed and headed back inside, refusing to interrogate what that meant.

SECRETS OF THE SUCKER

On Monday, Jasper was ready for the presentation Brent had asked for, having spent the previous night preparing. There was no reason to be nervous about this, he told himself. No reason at all.

Except, the only reason Jasper even knew any of this stuff in the first place was because of the big fat secret he was trying to hide from everyone in the office. If someone started following that badly covered path, they could walk it straight back to the fact that Jasper had lied about almost everything on his résumé.

His laptop was hooked up to an overhead projector, and naturally they all waited for a full ten minutes before Brent appeared.

"Nice of him to show up," Nico said under their breath, just loud enough for Jasper to hear. Jasper's chest spasmed with a badly muffled laugh.

A lightning bolt of white teeth shot across Brent's otherwise blank face, in what was probably supposed to be a smile. "Wanna share what's so funny with the rest of us, Jasper?"

"Um...n-no, but I do have that presentation you asked for on Friday?" Jasper covered. Pretty smooth transition, if he said so himself.

Brent's flash of teeth was gone and replaced with a blank look. "I didn't say anything about a presentation."

"I..." Jasper was gobsmacked.

"You did, though," Nico jumped in. "He spent all of Friday afternoon on it to the exclusion of all other tasks." Okay, that last bit felt a little like a dig on Jasper, but at least Nico was standing up for him.

Brent shook his head. "No, I don't think so. Anyway, I want project updates. Who's got 'em?"

Suddenly, the presentation that Jasper had most certainly not wanted to do was something he was just as upset to have taken away from him. He could have done something that was for *him* last night, not for this wannabe cult leader and his ugly tunic and shitty beads.

Jasper's anger was interrupted by the ghost of a touch on the back of his arm. He looked down just in time to see Nico's hand retracting into their own lap. Had they just touched him? Why? And why did they stop?

Evan was talking, and Jasper tried to redirect his attention without spiraling.

"...marketing meeting about Skip's book this afternoon. Before you say anything, yes, it's already written and the contract was signed a while back, right, Nico?"

"It's in design right now," Nico said. "With Jack."

Jack jerked upright as if he'd just woken up in the middle of roll call. "Yes! Yeah, yup. With me."

"And we've got Sparkle Sanders at Blossom & Crow tomorrow night," Evan continued. "And I think that's all set, right, Clara?"

"Yeah, Andie's got enough seating there, and a PA system in case we need it, so we don't have to worry about that. They've also been helping me gather the art contest winners. I may need someone's help with setting up all that, um...Evan," Clara said.

"You got it," Evan said, winking at her. Jasper barely managed to keep his eyebrows from rising. "Anyway, the social media numbers have been mostly level, because I've been a little tangled up with other projects and have been relying on autoposting. Either we could talk about that now, or you and I can talk one-on-one about maybe getting a Jasper for the marketing department."

"Don't be greedy," Brent said.

Evan flinched as if someone had blown a spitball at him. "I'm not sure what that means."

"You already have an assistant," he said.

The bright look Jasper was used to seeing on Evan's face had gone completely dark. "I don't have an assistant. Who did you think my assistant was?"

"Clara, obviously," Brent said in a *don't be stupid* tone.

"And why," Clara said, stony, "would you think I was his assistant?"

"Oh, don't make this a *feminism* thing." Brent rolled his eyes. "It was a simple mistake to make. And I don't think we're hiring anyone new right now. Jasper can probably make you a couple extra posts here and there."

"I can't spare him," Nico said quickly. Jasper looked over at them with surprise. Part of him had believed that they weren't truly serious about their offer to train him in different aspects of the editorial job, but apparently they still intended to. He tried not to blush, but it was already too late.

All the fake cheer drained from Brent's face at this as well. He stared at Nico, and Nico stared back just as hard. It was...

Really hot.

Hrrrrgh.

"Fine," Brent finally said. "Let's move past all this old stuff and onto the new. Specifically, getting Nico ready for hi—getting Nico ready to go up to Uncle Ricky's house."

Nico's posture was already good, but their spine went fully rigid at this. Clearly, it was news to them.

"Excuse me? I didn't agree to that. There has to be another option. Plus I have no experience with sound recording or mixing or—"

"That's where *he* comes in." Brent nodded toward Jasper. "Jasper, you've got a podcast, right?"

"I'm working on an audio drama," Jasper said quickly. Because it was *true*, dammit. "I just haven't posted it yet." Hopefully throwing out that red herring meant nobody would go looking for anything.

Wait. Shit.

"A-are you saying *I'm* going too?" Jasper said. There was always an embarrassing shrillness to his voice when he was stressed that no amount of training had helped him undo.

"I'll need to run it by Uncle Ricky, but yes. That's what he's for, right?"

That second bit was directed at Nico, and once again Jasper was stung, resentment spreading through his veins like venom. He wasn't a child. The fact that he made himself smaller so as not to come off as intimidating, the fact that he looked soft and actually shaved his face unlike half the rest of the fake lumberjacks in this city—that didn't make it okay for people to be condescending.

The second sting he got was the shocking realization that he and Nico were supposed to go *together*. Resentment was replaced by excitement, then quickly replaced again with mortification. He looked over to see Nico giving the tabletop a thousand-yard stare. Clearly they didn't want to be in that close proximity to him for such a long time. Of course, why would they? Jasper was dead weight at best, a nuisance at worst.

Maybe he should just quit now and go back to doing what he was doing before, all alone in his silent house. He could live like a monk, if a monk were allowed to spend their day making paywalled erotic bedtime stories. It certainly wouldn't keep him from remaining celibate.

The rest of the meeting passed in a blur.

When it was all done, Nico couldn't manage to say anything to Jasper. They should have assured him that they'd do what they could to make sure he wasn't exploited. Maybe they would, but it would have to be later. Right now, they could barely form words in their own head.

Instead they went for a walk. The homes in the neighborhood were lovely—so many Victorian or craftsman-style with wraparound porches. In the last year or so, a number of them had been knocked down, though, and in their place were split properties with tall, skinny homes out of an Escher print.

Richard Glenn lived at one of the northernmost points in the lower forty-eight states, right on the border of Washington State and Canada. They would have to drive for upwards of six hours to a remote area to stay with a man that was essentially a stranger. People who looked and dressed like Nico tended to keep out of the countryside in the Pacific Northwest, or at least keep a low profile. Once you left the cities, you often faced less *tolerant* people (although there were also plenty of that type *in* the city).

And it wasn't that they thought Glenn would try to physically hurt them for being queer or not being white. However, the oblivious rich white man was his own type of threat. Nico might as well go back into the closet for this whole thing. In fact, they would probably have to. In that case, at least it would be their own decision rather than a constant battle to correct and assert.

On top of that, they would be making the drive with Jasper. It wasn't as if they could do anything to keep him physically safe. Perhaps he wouldn't need it. He cut a rather intimidating figure if you didn't count the sweet, bashful way he had about him. On the other hand, he'd had trouble managing Hannah Hodge. How would he be able to assert himself against the power of Richard Glenn?

And how will you manage so much time in such close quarters with him, feeling the way you do? The thought came unbidden, and as hard as Nico tried to bat it away, they couldn't seem to do it.

Definitely not the ideal time for this realization.

They walked and they walked until they reached the footbridge over Interstate 84. Only then, when the crosswalks were not worth the danger of dodging cars who took yield signs as suggestions, did they turn around and go back to the office.

When they got back, their office chair was full of a tall man with a potbelly, wearing deck shoes and a wrinkled Hawaiian shirt. It was Skip Stewart, author of *Secrets of the Sucker*. (Evan was a fan of the title, Nico less so). He must have been there for his meeting with Evan and Clara.

Skip's ideas had been interesting enough. Most people were somewhat unsettled by the specter of the giant squid or the alien genius of the octopus. Over the years, Skip had harassed enough people into sharing stories of their supernatural encounters with multitentacled monsters so he could collect them into a book. Nico had been confident it would do well with an audience of fictional and nonfictional monster lovers.

However, the man himself was as slimy as the skin of one of his writing subjects. Nico wished they'd realized this sooner, but Janet seemed to have an existing relationship with him. Also, once she'd plucked an idea from Nico's hands, there wasn't much they could do to dissuade her.

Plus they hadn't really noticed how much they hated him until they saw him talking to Jasper.

"I believe you're in my chair," Nico said in lieu of a greeting. "You'll find this isn't the marketing department."

The cheer on Skip's face made Nico want to tie his leather shoelaces together and dump him out of their chair.

"My mistake, Mister Senior Editor!" Skip said.

"Th—" Jasper cut off quickly as he turned around to Nico, eyebrows questioning.

For a moment, Nico was puzzled, unsure what it was they were supposed to be doing or saying. Then they realized it—Jasper had wanted to correct Skip, but he didn't want to out Nico. Nico wasn't the best at reading people, but it was fairly clear. For a moment, they felt so grateful they could have melted. However, there wasn't time for that. There was still a garbage man in their desk chair, and Jasper didn't look happy to be talking to him.

"Thanks," they said, in the way one does when one assumes someone is already going to do what they want.

Much too slowly, Skip rose to his feet. Then he stepped forward until he was towering over Nico, looking down his disproportionately small nose.

"Brent says you and Jasper here are taking a little trip up north soon," he said. His tone had an uncanny cheer to it, as if that were the only way he knew how to speak, no matter how sour his mood.

"Has he?" Nico said. They still hadn't fully accepted that this was really happening, but the belief that it was inevitable was slowly sinking into their bones.

"Well, Rick's an old friend. Might take a trip myself and see you there." He grinned as he turned toward Jasper. Nico's fists tightened at their sides.

Thankfully, Evan chose that moment to appear.

"Skip! Ready?" he said, clipped and clear words pulling Skip's attention from Jasper.

"Yes, sir." With a nod to Nico, he followed Evan into the other room. When Nico shut the door behind him, the glass rattled.

Nico reclaimed their chair, adjusting it so their feet touched the ground again. They started to turn back toward the desk, then froze. Jasper was pointedly not looking at them, but Nico wasn't sure what he could have been working on right now. Chances were, Jasper was deliberately not speaking to them. Why should he want to? Taking someone to lunch wasn't sufficient to win back their goodwill.

They cleared their throat. "Jasper," they said, and Jasper turned toward them. At least he gave them that much. "I don't know what your responsibilities are outside of work, but this project would likely involve traveling a few hundred miles and being out of town for over a week. Is that something you could do? Or that you'd even want to do?"

Jasper looked down at his hands, and Nico's eyes followed to the long, thick fingers clutching his knees. They cleared their throat and looked up at his face again.

"If you're going"—Nico held their breath to brace for the rejection—"I don't want you to go alone."

Oh.

"Are you sure?" they said. "Apparently I don't have as much power here as I thought, but I can push harder for you to stay here."

"Do, um, do you not want me to come?" Jasper finally looked up at them, then blinked and shook his head, as if he'd phrased it wrong. "Er, to not come up there with you?"

"No! I do. If that's what you want, that is."

"Yeah, yeah, definitely," Jasper said, finally smiling again. Nico felt the corners of their mouth twitch and realized they were smiling too.

"Oh, well, in that case..."

They had both been assigned a project, without permission, that they didn't get paid nearly enough to do. A smile shouldn't have made Nico feel better about this. But for some reason, at least in this moment, it really did.

CHAPTER THIRTEEN

HOW WAS THAT?

Jasper was surprised that he'd passed this place on his commute to and from work and had barely registered it. Walking into Blossom & Crow was like walking into a Victorian-style apothecary, but instead of bottles of the crumbled remains of looted graves, there were books. The types of books would have to be examined later, however, because the art pieces on display for Sparkle Sanders's event were clamoring for attention.

The first thing he saw as he walked through the open door was a full-sized carousel horse covered in iridescent bursts of metallic paint. Braided pastel "horse tails" dangled from the end caps of each shelf. A photorealistic image of a human body with the head of a dead-eyed unicorn was placed behind one of the front display tables. That one may have fit in more with the darker vibe that seemed to usually define the place underneath all that color.

In addition to the over-the-top art pieces, the entire shop was full of people dressed like unicorns. Some wore rainbow-colored outfits; others were draped in fringe and even wrapped in shimmering paper. There was more than one uncanny rubber unicorn mask, which set Jasper a little on edge.

His eye was drawn to a person with dyed black hair pooled like a fine dark shawl over their right shoulder, eyes and lips blackened by makeup thick as charcoal against their pale skin. Their shoulders were pushed back, giving them very cocky energy as they looked sidelong at…holy shit, that was Nico.

Tonight, Nico looked like a completely different person. They were wearing eyeliner, too, along with a dark-red-and-silver button-up over a crepey black ankle-length skirt. Cool, another thing Jasper didn't know he was into. Add it to the list.

Just then, the black-haired person caught Jasper's eye, and they held eye contact as they leaned over to murmur something in Nico's ear. Before Nico could look up, Jasper ducked his head and slunk away toward the events space. It was framed by two interior pillars that had probably once offset a dining room back when this was a house.

"Jasper!" Evan called. "You made it!" Evan was wearing a deep pink shirt and a dark-blue-and-purple tie. Jasper wondered if he was intentionally dressed like a walking bisexual flag.

"Oh! Yup! Wouldn't miss it." He skirted around the rows of folding chairs in front of a central podium. There was a table beside it covered with hard-backed books with glossy jackets, the title reading *Hay Is for Unicorns!*

"I'd introduce you to Sparkle, but she and Clara are in *the green room.*" He said that last bit with a hand wave, as if he were an amateur illusionist who hadn't nailed the "sleight" part of "sleight of hand" yet. Under his jolly tone, there was something hard in his voice and on his face. A divot was etched between his eyebrows.

"Everything okay?" Jasper said.

"Yeah, sure," he said, craning his neck a little to look over Jasper's shoulder. "Just been a long day. I'm going to grab something to drink before the Sparklers take it all."

As he walked briskly away, Clara approached from behind Jasper. "Dammit. Almost caught him," she muttered, then perked up. "Good to see you here!"

She almost always wore bright colors and patterns, but she'd gone all out today. Her dress was dotted with tiny unicorns, two rainbow ice cream cone earrings hung from her lobes, and she'd topped it all off with a hot pink wig styled into a blunt bob.

"What's his problem?" Jasper asked.

"He's just mad at me about something and being dramatic"—she lowered her voice—"he's a Leo. Anyway, would you mind helping me set up this speaker? The art took so long, we didn't manage to hook this up yet."

"Sure!" Jasper said, relieved to have something to do. It would keep him from continuously looking over at Nico, their very flattering outfit, and the annoyingly hot person who he was desperately trying not to be jealous of right now.

For events like this, Andie always insisted on dressing Nico up the way they used to before they went out to shows. Nico's abuela, who had taken care of them since their parents had died in a car accident, might not have minded whether Nico got home late, but she certainly would have minded seeing them going out in a skirt. Fortunately, Nico didn't swim too much in Andie's clothes, despite their sturdier frame, and they were a very enthusiastic sharer.

"You can just have this," Andie had said earlier that evening as they'd changed in Andie's shed-turned-tiny-house in the backyard of Blossom & Crow. "I don't really wear fem stuff anymore."

There was an initial impulse to refuse, but Nico pushed back against it. Why shouldn't they wear it? Andie certainly would understand. Plus, it wasn't too ostentatious, and it looked quite good on them. They realized that they really wanted to feel good about how they looked today.

"Nico?"

"Oh! Yes. Thank you," they said.

Andie nudged Nico until they sat down on the corner of the bed and submitted to their eyeliner pencil. While this was (so far) the sort of thing Nico saved for special occasions, Andie wore this type of makeup every day. They were dressed in the usual pair of faux-leather pants and a local band t-shirt with the sleeves cut off, featuring a cartoon of a crescent moon with a screaming skull inside of it.

"So...," they said. Nico set their teeth against the sly tone of their voice. "You've complained plenty about your boss, but how's the new assistant?"

Nico inhaled sharply, and Andie pulled their hand back. "Sorry. Did I hurt you?"

"No! No, you're fine," they said.

Andie grinned. "I know I'm *fine*, but did I hurt you?"

"Shut up," Nico laughed. "No, you didn't. Just..." They sighed.

"Jesus, why are you sighing so much? Is he that bad?"

"He's not bad at all. That's the problem," Nico said.

Andie gasped and pulled their hand back again. "Nico! Do you *like* him?"

A third sigh from Nico, and Andie made a strangled, gleeful noise. "The *scandal*! The *power imbalance*! Nico, I had no idea you were so problematic. Do you get how hot that is?"

"If you say anything else like that, I'm leaving right now," Nico said.

"No, you won't. Not when I've only done one eye," they said. Grinning now, they leaned back in to make up the other. "Am I going to meet him tonight?"

Something lurched in Nico's chest, something bigger than their heart could possibly be. They wanted Jasper to be there tonight, actually. In fact, it was mortifying how much they wanted that.

"Niiiico...," Andie sang, sitting back and putting the cap back on the pencil. "If he's there tonight, you better introduce me."

Nico sighed again. "I will, I will." They stood up from the bed and resisted the urge to do a 360-degree turn in front of the mirror (not a twirl, never a twirl). That would certainly draw some snarky words from their friend.

But unexpectedly, Andie leaned back on their hands and gave them a thoughtful look. "You know, I'm proud of you," they said. "Compared to hating the guy, this is a pretty positive move for you."

"There's no need to be rude." Nico scowled at them in the mirror. They'd always had a magical ability to make a compliment sound like an insult.

"I'm serious! You can get so 'aaaaah it's the end of the world' about everything, and seeing you actually liking someone like this seems kind of optimistic," they said. "Also I'm proud that you're doing the whole gender expression *thing* at a work event."

Jumping to their feet, they leaned against Nico's back and gave them an aggressive hug around the shoulders. It was just a little too tight, but Nico knew they meant it affectionately. They patted Andie's hand indulgently.

"Well, thank you. I appreciate it," they said. "Are you ready to go in?"

Later, they stood behind the front counter of Blossom & Crow, watching people dressed in garish colors and diaphanous fabrics stream through the front door. Sparkle Sanders had a dedicated social media following who called themselves Sparklers (so far no one had tried to set off fireworks during an event, and hopefully tonight would be no exception). While some did dress as actual unicorns, most of them simply matched the exuberant rainbow colors and glittery hair extensions of their favorite author.

Andie's shop had never been so bright, and Andie's eyes were manic as they stood back with their arms crossed over their Dead Moon shirt.

"You know you don't have to hang out with me the whole time," they said to Nico. Before Nico could ask them if they were trying to tell them to go away, they leaned closer to their ear. "That guy is looking at you, and he seems like your type."

"Oh god," Nico said, following their eye line to where Jasper was retreating. They jerked their gaze away as if they'd accidentally looked straight into the sun. "Dammit, Andie, why?"

Andie gasped. "That's him, isn't it?" They hummed appreciatively. "I can see the appeal. Well, for you at least. Ooooo, he could throw you around like a rag doll."

"*Andie!*" Nico brimmed with indignation, and an embarrassing amount of heat spread down their face as if someone had spilled warm tea on their cheekbones. In spite of themself, Andie's laughter infected them, and they stifled their own snicker with their hand.

They were interrupted by a very unwelcome, yet familiar, voice.

"Hate to interrupt," Brent said, leaning across the counter. He was wearing a more deeply plunging neckline than usual, his many strings of wooden beads embedded in a tuft of chest hair. He gave Nico a grimacing nod, then focused back on Andie, eyes sweeping over them from head to chest. Slimeball. "I was wondering if you rented out your space over there for seminars."

Andie was no longer laughing, nor were they smiling. "Seminars?"

"For entrepreneurs. I've got a mentoring group together and we're hoping to do a speaker series. Might even be able to get a very high-profile men's fitness influencer in here—I've got a line on a guy." Brent wiggled his eyebrows, as if he truly believed he'd said something impressive.

Never one to be diplomatic, Andie wrinkled their nose. "Nope. We don't do that here."

Brent narrowed his eyes. "Could you get your manager, then?"

"Wait, let me go get him," Andie ducked under the counter, then came back up with their hair tucked over the other shoulder. "Did you have a question? Because if you're looking for more anal beads you're going to have to go across the street."

Brent gave them a closed-mouth smile, eyes narrow and poisonous.

"Funny," he said. "You know, your jokes would land better if you smiled more."

Nico winced. There had been a night in high school where they'd had to climb out of the window of a bar bathroom because Andie had knocked out a guy's tooth for saying something similar.

Instead of sudden violence, there was a pause. A smile spread in slow motion across Andie's face until it was stretched ghoulishly. Nico looked from Andie to Brent, whose own face was pinched. Behind him, Evan stood with his head cocked in fascination.

Then Andie started to laugh, a real supervillain laugh, one that grew louder until someone in the crowd of Sparklers joined in. Soon Andie's laugh was drowned out by a crowd of unicorn cosplayers delivering whinny after full-throated whinny.

"Alright, alright!" Brent's terse voice cut through the braying.

"How was that?" Andie said with exaggerated energy. A couple more hoots rippled through the group as Clara started corralling them into the event space.

"I get your point," he said. "Also, I forgot I had to meet someone. Just..." There was no follow-up before he turned and stomped out past the carousel horse and into the night.

Nico's shoulders fell as they let out a breath.

"Holy shit, that was *amazing*!" Evan said, approaching the counter and raising his hand for a high five. Andie looked at his hand, unmoved other than a single raised eyebrow. Apparently not torn up over the rejection, Evan put his hand down again. "Thanks for that, dude, you're a legend."

The corner of Andie's mouth twitched. "Dude" may not have been gender-neutral in Nico's opinion, but Andie certainly seemed to respond to it more favorably than they did.

"What can I say? I'm good at taking the garbage out," they finally said.

"Hell yeah, you are." Evan shook his head as if adjusting to his own disbelief. "Damn. Well. I guess it's showtime." He downed the last of his drink, set the empty cup back on the table, and shot Nico and Andie both finger guns before walking away.

When he'd gone, Andie turned to Nico, who was still reeling from all the noise from earlier.

"What's his deal?" Andie said sotto voce.

"Oh, he's always like that," Nico said.

"No, I mean—" The dull thud of a microphone switching on interrupted them. Andie shook their head too, but more like they were trying to evict an unwanted thought. "Never mind. You heard the man. Showtime."

CHAPTER FOURTEEN

JUST GO FOR IT

There is a reason certain people get into publishing, and it isn't usually because they want to go to loud, glitter-filled events. Nico, in particular, was looking forward to the opportunities to sit quietly and become absorbed in written words when they started working toward a job as an editor. They were very sensitive to noise, which they had learned the hard way after spending years of their youth in tight spaces with loud guitars.

Sparkle Sanders had the high, resonant voice of someone trained for theater in an age before microphones. It worked well for her, but it had always been something that sucked energy from Nico when they'd worked through the editorial process together. As much as they were happy to be there, happy to be with their best friend, and (*dammit*) happy to be in the same room as Jasper, they were quickly losing steam.

After about forty-five minutes of speaking and reading about lessons learned by using the "Unicorn Mindset," the

Q&A began. After the second "more of a comment than a question," Nico gave Andie a meaningful look. Without a word, Andie handed over the key to the shed, and Nico slipped out the back door, feeling the cool night air chill some of the sizzling wires of their overheated mind.

For a moment they stood staring at the sky. The moon was full tonight, and its yellow edges were blurred by a thin wisp of cloud. Nico's ears still rang with the memory of amplified voices echoing through a room, but they tried now to acclimate to the relative quiet of the Portland evening.

"Nico?" Another voice cut through their reverie, and they flinched as they turned to see Jasper coming down the back steps and along the pavers toward them. "Are you okay? You looked a little rough in there."

They were having trouble deciding what was more striking about this—the fact that Jasper had been watching them, or the fact that he'd noticed that Nico was having a hard time just from their mannerisms.

"I could have just been looking for the bathroom," they said peevishly, foolishly.

"Well, you went the wrong way," Jasper laughed. "Plus it's not like you haven't been here before. You're friends with the owner, right?"

Doubly observant, then. Might as well stop playing coy. "Yes, they're my oldest friend, actually." They held up the key ring as if revealing their mediocre hand at cards. "Just needed a break, really."

"Yeah, Sparkle's got quite a voice, doesn't she?" Jasper grinned.

"I feel guilty thinking that way. It's a bit misogynistic, isn't it?" they said, immediately wishing they hadn't. It came off as if they were asking Jasper's permission to say something inappropriate, and of course Jasper seemed to be accommodating them as usual.

"If it bothers you, it bothers you. It's not like you're making it someone else's problem," Jasper said. He stood with his arms at his sides, the moonlight diffused over him in combination with the warm yellow light from the bookshop windows. The striking shadows made him look like something cinematic. Nico bristled a little at the inadequate poetry of their own thoughts.

"Um, so I guess I should get back...," Jasper said, turning toward the back door of the shop.

"You don't have to," Nico rushed to say. They felt the blood rise in their face, and they hoped it was dark enough that Jasper didn't notice. "You can come with me, if you'd like. Andie said they wanted to meet you anyway."

Jasper's eyes opened wider. "They did?"

Nico coughed. Maybe they shouldn't have said that. Too late now. "Yes. So, okay..."

"Okay," Jasper said, more enthusiastically.

Nico turned and led him toward the repurposed shed, forcing themself not to turn around and look at him every few steps. Bringing him here felt like a step toward taking him to their own home, and that was an idea that sent a chill down their spine. They hadn't allowed themself to think about such a thing before, but they could feel the thought taking root right now. Hopefully it wouldn't be too hard to pull up and discard later.

The room wasn't terribly clean, and a part of them felt guilty that they'd allowed them into Andie's space like this. However, there was nothing too intimate in sight, and Andie was never one to be ashamed of themself. Nico moved a pile of clothes onto the nearby tabletop and perched on the corner of the bed. Jasper's eyes swept over the room, falling first on the tiny booth seats that were on either side of the table, then the empty space on the bed.

"You can...I'll just...," Nico said, sliding even further over until they weren't even fully sitting on the bed anymore.

Jasper was about as flushed as Nico felt, and Nico hoped that it wasn't something they'd done. He sat down and rested his hands on his knees. When he finally looked up after a moment of staring at the ground, there was a slight bow to his lips, and it somehow set Nico at ease.

"So, how did you two meet?" he asked.

Ah. Something they could talk about, and oddly, a story people rarely asked them to tell.

"We were just the two kids nobody wanted to hang out with in middle school. One day they came and sat with me and, you know...were themself about it. I was, well, a little scared of them at first," Nico laughed. "But they eventually wore me down, and we've been friends ever since."

"Did you two go to OSU together as well?" Jasper said.

"No, they didn't go to college, just moved here to take over the shop right after high school. It was a family business. I came and visited a couple of times, but we sort of fell off for a couple of years until I started working at UTP." The office was *right there*, after all. It would have been callous of Nico not to come by and visit on a regular basis.

"And...are you two, like, you know...?" Jasper's voice had suddenly climbed into an unnaturally high range.

Nico cocked their head. "Are we what?"

"Sorry, that was rude of me," Jasper said.

"No, what were you going to say?"

"I just...you seem really close, and I wasn't sure whether you two were, like..."

"Oh!" Nico felt their adrenaline spike. Jasper thought they were dating, and that was unacceptable for a whole host of reasons. "No, no. We, well...I guess you could say *tried* when we were sixteen and it didn't work. Too much like dating a sibling. Or, you know, I assume. Neither of us have one."

Tried was a bit of an overstatement. They'd kissed a few times, but Andie was a lot more...well. Let's just say their enthusiasm levels didn't match up when it came to that sort of thing. As much as Nico cared for Andie, they just weren't made for that type of relationship.

"Ah—okay. Good. I mean, sorry," Jasper laughed painfully and put his hands over his flaming cheeks.

Good. Nico swallowed a dry lump in their throat. This was getting too blatant for even them not to notice. But there wasn't a hell of a lot they could do about it. Jasper was their assistant. If anything, they should be discouraging him from this. Desperately, they cast about in their head for some safe topic of discussion.

"So, um, how's the podcast going?"

After an initial jolt of fear that he'd been found out, Jasper was glad that Nico had changed the subject so quickly. The question about them dating Andie was way too personal, and it just made him sound like a dork.

Good. Christ, Jasper, way to lay it all out on the table.

He couldn't say he wasn't deeply relieved Nico was definitely not dating Andie. He shouldn't have been nurturing this stupid hope, but at the same time, he dreaded the moment when it was finally and totally disappointed. The longer he could put that off, the better.

Even though the topic of a podcast danced on the edge of something Jasper definitely did not want to share, he was just comfortable enough with Nico to share ideas about his writing projects. In fact, he sort of lost track of time until he realized he'd been going on for several minutes, Nico fixing a very serious gaze on him the whole time. They listened actively, the same look on their face that they'd had when they were absorbed in editing Hannah's book earlier today.

It made Jasper feel important, like he mattered. That wasn't a feeling Jasper was used to.

It seemed only a few minutes later that there was a knock on the door, then it slowly opened to reveal Andie, holding several partially full wine bottles.

A sly grin curled their lips when their eyes landed on Jasper. "Am I interrupting something?" They wiggled their eyebrows in a way that made Jasper think of Evan at his most inappropriate.

"No idea what you're talking about," Nico said, withering. Jasper couldn't help but chuckle.

Andie stuck their tongue out at them. "Very ungrateful to talk that way to the person who brought the party back."

"Are you really done cleaning up already?" Nico said, dropping the acerbic tone. "I thought it would take longer."

Andie gave a single, barking laugh. "It's been over an hour, and you came out here when the event had almost wrapped up already." They set the bottles on the table and took down three mugs from their cupboard. "Anyway, who's this *guy* you brought to my room, Nico?"

Before Jasper could start apologizing, Nico waved a perfunctory hand and said, "Sorry, this is my friend, Jasper. Jasper, this is Andie."

Friend. Jasper felt his chest squeeze, but Andie was the one who actually said it.

"Friend, huh? Thought he was your assistant." They handed Jasper a mug with a big picture of something that he recognized from his horror-related research as the sigil of Baphomet.

With a nervous glance toward Jasper, Nico shrugged. "We'd just been having a lovely conversation about Jasper's podcast," they said, by way of nonanswer. Jasper wondered if they could hear his heart pounding. How were they acting so cool right now? Probably because they didn't feel the same way about him that he felt about them.

Andie scrunched up their face like they'd just taken a big whiff of expired yogurt. "It isn't, like, 'observational comedy' or 'social commentary,' is it?"

"No," Nico said, sounding insulted on Jasper's behalf. "It's a horror narrative."

"It's an audio drama," Jasper said at the same time.

"Oh! Well, you should have said that first, Nico, that's completely different," Andie said. "Sorry, Jasper, I always assume a man with a podcast is going to try to get me into crypto or to read Marcus Aurelius."

"Nah," Jasper said. "They don't let fat guys be stoics."

Nico looked at him with a raised eyebrow as Andie burst out laughing.

"Yeah, they don't like people who like to fuck either, so that counts me out," Andie said, holding out their mug.

"*Andie*," Nico said, scandalized, over the clinking ceramic. Jasper laughed and took a drink, because at this point he knew it was impossible for his face to get any redder.

"Sorry, Nico has delicate sensibilities, but this is my house," Andie said with a wink. "Now, tell me your life story."

⌒⌒

By the time they'd finished the leftover wine, Jasper's eyes were half-lidded, and Nico was yawning every few minutes. Even Andie was much more subdued than usual. It felt nice, though, companionable. Jasper was even better company in this more social context than he'd been before, and Nico was rather proud of the way he got along with Andie. Frankly, if Andie didn't like Jasper, that would be that. Even if nothing ever happened between the two of them, which it *shouldn't*, it would still probably lead to years of obnoxious teasing.

Jasper's audio drama project sounded fascinating. It wasn't something that Nico knew much about, as Brent's misguided audio obsession was proving, but the way Jasper explained it, it was a very versatile form of storytelling.

Nico had even found themself offering to read the scripts to offer pointers, and they weren't just saying it to be nice (they were very careful never to even hint that people could get free editorial services from them, or else they'd never get a moment of peace).

Secretly, Nico did love reading fiction, mostly speculative, sometimes sci-fi or fantasy, and even a little horror sometimes. Talking to Jasper was making them want to go home and dust off their Edgar Allen Poe short story collection. Perhaps they would. Who knew whether they would feel as sleepy as they did right now after going home? Very likely they'd be preoccupied with thoughts about everything that had happened tonight.

"Okay, I love y'all, but you've gotta get out," Andie said, popping up from the bench where they'd been perched. "You don't have to go home, but you can't stay here, etc., etc."

Nico had only had one glass of wine, intent on not making the same mistake they'd made after happy hour a couple weeks ago. They offered Jasper a ride back home, and he nodded, actually rubbing his eyes with the back of his hands. It was frustratingly cute.

When Andie hugged Nico as they were leaving for the night, they leaned in and whispered. "I like him. Fuck propriety. You should just go for it."

Pulling back, Nico shot daggers at them with their eyes.

Andie winked. Bastard.

The ride to Jasper's was quiet, but not in an awkward way. For as awkward as Nico almost always felt, that should have been disconcerting.

"I guess I'll see you tomorrow, then?" Nico said. They wondered whether it was obvious in their tone how sad they were about the night ending. By now the sleepiness had worn off, evaporated by the energy thrumming through them after their evening together. They'd definitely have trouble sleeping tonight, with the gnawing feeling that had already taken up space in their stomach.

"You could come in if you'd like," Jasper said.

Nico inhaled sharply, and it couldn't have been more obvious. The sound of it practically rattled the car windows.

Jasper's gaze was glued to the tops of his hands, but he hadn't stammered when he'd made the invitation. The softness in his voice told Nico that he expected the answer to be no.

But Nico didn't want to say no.

It puzzled them that there were things that they could hear in Jasper's voice that they couldn't decipher from anyone else. They wondered whether there was any significance to that. All they knew was that they were both disturbed and fascinated by it in equal measure.

This was a terrible idea.

But no. They'd just go inside, maybe have some tea, then go home and stay up reading until their eyes crossed. At least that was what they told themself as they shut the driver's-side door and followed Jasper up the front walk.

CHAPTER FIFTEEN

OUT OF MY DEPTH

The inside of Jasper's house was not what Nico expected. In fact, Nico hadn't really expected a house at all. It was modest enough, in a slightly run-down neighborhood but still surrounded by other quaint single-story homes. The inside was sparse, and the decor dated back to the '70s.

"Have you lived here long?" Nico asked.

Jasper hummed. "Most of my life, actually. It's my mom's house."

"Oh!" Nico lowered their voice. "I'm sorry, is she sleeping?"

"Ummm, kind of? She's over on the shelf, actually," Jasper said, gesturing to a heavy oak cabinet on the far wall. Nestled in between two lines of books was a familiar-looking square tin; Nico had collected more than their fair share of those at this point in their life (three, to be specific).

"Ah, my mistake," they said, trying to tamp down on their horror. "How long has it been?"

"Wow, um…" Jasper looked around the room as if he'd posted the date on the wall somewhere. "God, it'll be a year next month."

Fresh, then.

"Do you have other family?"

Setting his bag on the floor, Jasper turned his back to Nico and led them to the galley kitchen. "Only child. Never met my dad. So, no, not really," he said. "But you didn't want to hang out to hear a sob story."

If anyone knew a deflection, it was Nico, and they didn't want to harass Jasper into talking about something so emotional. Not when he'd been so accommodating already. On the other hand, they also didn't want to seem to be minimizing his feelings.

"I wish I could say I don't understand what that's like, but unfortunately I do," they said. "If you ever want to talk about it…"

There was a clunk as Jasper nearly dropped his electric kettle on the counter. He turned around. "God, I'm sorry, I didn't—"

Nico waved it off. "Don't worry."

For a moment, Jasper didn't move, and Nico wondered how they were going to dig themself out of this. It would be them, walking into a man's house for the first time and finding the most upsetting thing possible to bring up.

"Maybe another time?" His smile couldn't have been genuine. "I probably should talk about it at some point with someone, but, um…yeah, that's a rabbit hole."

At first, Nico balked at "someone," but the truth was, they hadn't exactly been forthcoming with their grief over the years either. Instead, they simply nodded. Jasper opened another cupboard that was stacked with tea tins and little boxes. Nico could tell that several of them were the same brand of tea that they had at work.

"Any requests?" Jasper said.

"If you have Meadow, I'll have that, please," Nico said.

Jasper gave them an odd look. "I think that one's kind of old."

"Well, it's tea. That's normal, isn't it? I mean, except for people who are deeply interested in tea," they said with an awkward laugh.

Jasper pulled the box down from the cupboard and gave it a shake. "Ah, well," he said. "There's one more bag in here."

"Oh, well, if you want it instead—"

"No!" Jasper said sharply. "I mean, no problem. Sorry. All yours."

Soon after, he placed the bag in a glossy blue ceramic mug and poured hot water over it, setting a timer without even checking the instructions on the back of the box. Nico was never very good about that sort of thing. Usually they'd throw out the wrapper first, and sometimes forget they'd left the bag to steep at all. However, Jasper was very thoughtful about details like that.

He was thoughtful in general, Nico mused.

It wasn't long before they were sitting side by side on a multicolored green couch upholstered with worn corduroy. Normally, Nico would balk at the texture, but for some reason tonight they didn't mind so much. Their attention was so focused on the man sitting next to them, they couldn't find it in themself to care.

⸺ele⸺

Oh god. Nico was in his house. His house where he *lived*. Fortunately, Jasper was a pretty clean guy, and also it was Tuesday. Things didn't usually fall apart until a little later in the week. But still, what if he'd left out something he didn't want them to see?

God, he needcd to relax.

Jasper wasn't sure what he had done to make this happen, why Nico had said yes when he'd asked them to come inside. But then, the night had been going well, and Andie seemed to like him, and getting the best friend to like you was kind of a big deal, wasn't it?

Here he was thinking about this as if it were actually happening. Nico could just want to be friends.

Yet, the fact was, *something* was happening. They were sitting on the couch beside him, sipping tea and looking at their nails, eyes occasionally flicking upward to sneak a look at him.

"So do you know when we'll be heading up north?" Jasper asked. He didn't necessarily want to talk about work, but the silence was starting to make him nervous. After all the progress they'd made tonight, he didn't want to ruin it by being a bad host. He'd already almost messed it all up by being weird about the tea.

Nico sighed with resignation. "Probably sometime in the next couple of weeks. I don't imagine they'd do anything so considerate as giving us time to adjust."

Setting his cup of tea down on the table, Jasper turned his body toward Nico. "You're probably right. But you might have guessed, I don't have a lot of other things to do, so it's not like they'd be interrupting anything."

God, way to make yourself look like even more of a loser, Jasper.

"It's the principle of the thing," Nico said, then sat up straighter as if they'd just remembered something they'd left in the car. "Hold on, we haven't even spoken about equipment. Brent hasn't assumed—has he assumed that you'd volunteer yours?"

That hadn't occurred to Jasper, but the idea annoyed him. However, at this point he was just as resigned as Nico. "I guess I don't mind. Although, I think we should hire an engineer to help us. There's someone I know in Olympia who might be able to help."

MixerKing was pretty talented, but he was having trouble finding gigs right now. Hopefully his schedule happened to be clear for whenever this trip happened (and Brent would agree to it). Plus it would be cool to finally meet him in person.

"If he'll pay for it." Nico rolled their eyes and slouched against the back of the couch. "I feel very out of my depth, honestly. If I'm supposed to be hosting this or asking questions or...I don't know. I'm not exactly a performer."

"Yes, but you have a very good natural speaking voice," Jasper said before he could hold the words in. "It's a lot better than mine, to be honest."

Visibly flustered, Nico shook their head. "No...that's not true, you sound—" They cleared their throat and turned to set their mug on the coffee table as well. "You should really be the one doing this, but I don't want to pile work onto you that's above your pay grade."

"I can give you a little voice crash course if you'd like," he said. "Not tonight, but..." Yeah, definitely not tonight. He was feeling far too worked over for that at the moment. "We'll make sure you're totally confident, and I'll be in the room with you if you need pointers. Or, you know, if I need to kick some old bastard's ass for you."

Nico didn't laugh. They didn't make any move, in fact. For a moment, Jasper was afraid he might have overstepped and offended them. But then, they turned, tucking one leg under them as they sat sideways on the couch.

"Why are you so kind to me?" Their voice was thin, as if the air had been sucked from their lungs.

Jasper furrowed his brow. "Because why wouldn't I be? Because you deserve it."

"But I don't," Nico said, shaking their head. "I really don't—"

"Stop that," Jasper cut them off. "You deserve kindness as much as anybody, and I"—*fuck it*—"like you a lot. And it's not hard for me to be kind to you because of, well, that."

Now Nico stared at him, mouth open as if they were searching for words. It was Jasper's turn to feel like the wind had been knocked out of him. Then, it all came back, and naturally, he started babbling.

"I-if it's awkward for you, and if you don't like that, I get it, and I can never bring it up again. A-and you can put me in a different office, and I'll try to get over it, and I'm so—"

Before he could go on, Nico kissed him. It was like he'd blinked and missed them springing onto their knees to cup his face with both hands.

It didn't take long for Jasper to return the kiss, and there was no time for him to doubt his own reaction before Nico was straddling his knee. Now that they were on the same level, Nico became bolder, pushing Jasper's shoulders against the back of the couch and their tongue artlessly into his mouth. They pulled back briefly, panting a little before swooping in to press kisses against the side of his neck.

"God, Nico," Jasper gasped. It was surprising and a little aggressive, but he definitely wasn't complaining.

"I-I should, I-I'm sorry, I—" They started to pull away, but Jasper wrapped his arms around their middle and held them in place. "Ah," they said, sounding at once disoriented and desperate.

Jasper's heart was pounding, and there was no way Nico couldn't feel it. He could certainly feel their heart doing the same. Through the thin fabric of their skirt, he could also feel that they were hard. And probably it was because of that transparent desire, but it emboldened him.

He pulled back, slightly, holding on to their face before they could chase his lips. Their eyes were glazed, lips kiss-bitten red, and their breath shuddered as they held still within his grasp. As his thumb slowly ran across the side of their jaw, their eyes fell closed and they sighed.

"Do you want me to help with that?" Jasper said, their voice falling into that low, slow cadence that was so practiced it felt like second nature.

"With...," they said breathlessly, eyes still shut.

Jasper reached down between their legs, and they shivered.

"*Oh. Please.*"

It never would have occurred to Jasper that Nico would be such a wreck, that they'd sound so helpless in a moment like this. Jasper shifted them over until they were sitting across his lap. They nestled into the crook of his neck and Jasper had never felt such a strange sense of purpose and authority before.

He reached under their skirt and felt the shape of them through the microfiber of their underwear first.

"What do you want me to call this?" he asked, barely above a whisper.

A shaky, broken sound, and then Nico said, "It's...you can...I don't care what you call it."

"Is cock okay?" Jasper said.

Nico made a weak sound of assent as they nodded against him, their hair tickling at the side of Jasper's face as they turned to brush their mouth against his jaw. He met their lips as his hand dipped beneath their waistband. They made a desperate noise into his mouth as he tightened his grasp around their cock. The tip was already dotted with pre-cum, and he swirled his thumb around the head of it.

"Thank you for letting me touch your cock, sweet thing," he said softly against their lips. "I love how wet you are for me already."

A guttural noise rumbled from the back of Nico's throat as Jasper's hand slid to the base of their cock. They separated from his kiss and burrowed into his shoulder again.

The thing was, they were trembling quite a bit, and it set off a tiny alarm inside Jasper. Was it that they were that turned on, or were they having a problem? He hoped it was the first one but figured it was a good idea to ask anyway. Nico was so reserved normally, and this was a lot of control they were giving up.

"Is this okay?" Jasper said. If he were the one being touched, he knew that the lazy strokes he was giving wouldn't be nearly enough to make him shake like this.

"I can't," Nico gasped.

Immediately, Jasper pulled his hand out from under Nico's skirt. Nico, however, didn't release their hold around Jasper's neck. He froze, not sure how to react.

"Do you want to get down?" Jasper said, still quiet, but free of the cajoling tone he'd had earlier.

"No, uh, I..." Nico growled in frustration.

"Okay, just breathe for a second," Jasper said, hesitating before encircling them with his arms.

"I'm sorry," Nico finally said. "It's just. Sometimes it's too much? Too much feeling, I mean. The sensations..."

Jasper tried to meet their gaze, but they clamped harder around his neck. He settled for rubbing their back, up and down.

"That's okay," Jasper said. It surprised him that he wasn't panicking, but this freakout didn't really seem to be about him. "We can stop. No problem."

"No," Nico said emphatically. When they finally released their hold and sat back, their face was set with determination.

"No?" Jasper cocked his head. He wasn't sure he was comfortable continuing just because Nico was feeling stubborn. "You don't have to prove anything. If you're uncomfortable, or if you've changed your mind, or..."

There was pressure against his arms as Nico sat back and slipped out of his lap. Jasper tried not to let his disappointment show, and tried not to think about how, if last time they'd kissed, Nico had been weird afterwards, this time they'd be even weirder.

But then, Nico was on their knees in front of him. When they set their hands on his knees and looked up at him, eyes rolled up and shaded by their brows, Jasper knew that could only mean one thing.

"Oh, you don't have to do that. You don't have to, like, make up for it if—"

"I want to," they said, lifting their chin to look up at him fully. "Please?"

Jasper groaned and let his eyes fall shut for a moment. "How can I say no to that?"

Nico answered with a breathless laugh as they fumbled with the buttons of his jeans. He changed his position, leaning back to make it easier on them, giving them space and trying not to feel self-conscious as the air hit his embarrassingly hard dick.

There wasn't a hell of a lot of time to be self-conscious, though, because Nico took him into their mouth almost immediately.

"*Christ.*"

With all the time he spent writing and narrating explicit material, he hadn't been able to get out and meet people, so Jasper didn't have a hell of a lot of experience. Being a caretaker didn't really allow for much dating, and since his mother's death, he'd only had a few Grindr hookups. None of them had felt this way.

Watching Nico's head bobbing on his cock, their hair falling out of its elastic...nothing could beat this. Maybe Nico wasn't taking him too deep and their movements were arrhythmic and a little sloppy, but this was perfect.

"You're incredible, Nico," Jasper said, letting the sentence take as long as it wanted to take. "Your mouth feels so good."

There was a harsh puff of breath, then Nico doubled down. Heat coiled in Jasper's pelvis, and he knew this wasn't going to last long.

"Oh fuck," he said. "*Good girl.*"

Nico gasped.

For a moment, Jasper was absolutely mortified. It'd just slipped—he'd used it so often that the phrase was second nature. But misgendering them while they were doing this for him? They were going to stop, and he couldn't blame them.

But they didn't stop.

They *moaned.*

It was a deep, pornographic moan that vibrated around Jasper's cock, and it was the hottest thing he had ever heard in his life. He dug his nails into the upholstery of the couch as he came hard and without warning.

Dick move. The thought mocked him, floating in the air unheeded as he caught his breath.

"I'm sorry I forgot to—ah!" He yelped as Nico licked up the side of his overstimulated cock, catching the last drops of semen. "Forgot to warn you."

Nico wiped their mouth with the back of their hand and looked up at him with heavy lids. "That's okay," they said, half smiling.

Jasper readjusted and buttoned himself back up as Nico sat back on their heels. Completely drained of all shyness, Jasper leaned forward and scooped them off the floor into his lap again. When they kissed, he could taste himself on their lips.

"Thanks for that," he said as Nico hummed and leaned their head against his shoulder. "Um..."

"Um?" Nico echoed.

"You're not..." Jasper was glad for the face tucked into his neck, because as much as it would have been a good idea, he was afraid to look Nico in the eye right now. "This is going to be okay tomorrow, right? Like, I really like you, and I feel like if we just pretend nothing happened..."

He stopped talking as Nico tightened their hold around his neck. Suddenly, it was like all the confidence he'd had evaporated with his orgasm, and he desperately needed this reassurance.

"We won't," Nico said softly. "I really like you too."

CHAPTER SIXTEEN

BOTH OF THEM

It shocked Nico how normal they felt about this whole situation. In maybe their only act of contrition, they woke up far earlier than normal to go into the office. They didn't do much work, though. For a while, they sat in front of their desk; they decided to get up and make a cup of Meadow tea, then they took the tea back to their desk, sipping on it and thinking (very inappropriately) of what they'd been up to just seven or so hours ago.

There was a part of them that couldn't believe what they'd done. They'd never been terribly interested in sex; they didn't hate it, per se, just didn't feel driven to seek it out. Last night, though, they'd been seized by such a deep desire to make Jasper feel good, that feeling had overridden all others. The experience didn't leave behind any of the residual ickiness they'd felt after previous sexual encounters. Considering their problematic relation to one another, it probably should have.

Maybe it was just because their professional life had been thrown into such chaos that Nico seemed to have dropped their professionalism altogether. Surely the guilt would creep in at some point.

Or maybe it wouldn't. Maybe they would just continue to feel happy, if not a little sleepy.

The front doorbell rang, undoubtedly heralding Meera or Clara, and Nico blinked a few times to try and refocus on the screen in front of them.

There were footsteps on the wooden floor, then a familiar voice said, "Good morning."

Nico felt a flutter in their chest as they swiveled to face Jasper. "Good morning," they echoed. God, they must have looked like a sloth, or one of those baby dolls that closed its eyes when it was laid on its back. Nico had plucked the eyelashes out of one as a child, and they'd never fully closed again, just made the thing look sort of dull.

"You look like you've been hanging out with Jack," Jasper teased.

"You know exactly who I was hanging out with," Nico said. A flush washed over Jasper's face. Nico wanted to lay their cheek against it to see if it felt any warmer than the rest of him.

Jasper sat in his chair. "So you're not, um—" He cleared his throat. "You didn't get scared off?"

Nico shook their head. They briefly wondered why their face was starting to get so sore, and they realized it was because they had been smiling since they'd woken up this morning.

"Did you?"

Jasper shook his head as well. "I was actually wondering if, um..." The burn in his cheeks hadn't lessened at all. It was adorable. "I was wondering if maybe I could take you to dinner tonight? Like, on a real date?"

"Oh! Yes." Nico blinked. They hadn't even thought ahead to lunchtime, much less all the way to tonight. "That'd be really...nice."

They'd have liked to be more eloquent, but they were much too sleep-deprived and distracted for that. If someone had told them they'd be this mixed up over a man—particularly *this* man—a couple of weeks ago, they would have run screaming into traffic. There had to be something that would flip Nico into feeling nervous about this. It probably said something about them that they were searching for what that thing might be.

"I'm still your boss, you know," they said.

"I know. I know that nothing's changed there," he said.

"Good. In that ca—"

"Morning!" Evan's voice filled up their office. He was looking a bit worse for wear. His candy-striped button-up shirt, normally perfectly pressed, was as wrinkled as if he'd picked it up off the floor this morning.

Both of them jumped. Had the bell on the door even rung, or had Nico just been that caught up in talking to Jasper?

"How are you two—" He abruptly stopped talking and narrowed his eyes. They volleyed from Jasper to Nico and back. "You two are plotting something."

"Ha! Well, this is editorial," Jasper said with forced jollity. His entire face was beet red now and Nico tried to wipe their own smile away.

Evan's jaw twitched. "Got me there, I guess," he said with a weak laugh. It was strange, as they would have expected Evan to have made a silly joke like that in the first place. "Nico, can we chat a little later? I have some calls to make first."

"Of course," Nico said. "I've got nothing on my calendar"—*except a date with my assistant tonight*—"so any time works."

"Great." Evan slapped a loose palm against the doorjamb, then strolled toward his desk.

Jasper let loose a breath. "Yeah, well, yeah, so...we can talk about this later, I guess," he said.

"Right. Later," Nico said, staring at him just a little too long before finally turning back around and trying to force themself to work.

Jasper left the room to the two of them and headed down the hall. After that awkward encounter this morning, it was probably better that they not be in the same room together with Evan right now. The guy had just a little too sensitive of a social antenna not to notice something was going on between them.

Jasper was certain he'd had the best sleep of his life after Nico had gone home the night before. He hadn't asked them to stay the night; that seemed like it would have been tempting fate. Seeing them in the office, sleepy-eyed and smiling, was a less stressful morning-after scenario. Even though he'd stayed up far too late, he'd felt like he had all the time in the world to get to work this morning.

Clara was in the kitchenette when Jasper arrived. They exchanged pleasantries, and Jasper leaned back against the counter and yawned indulgently.

"Do you want to know something interesting?" Clara said as she set her lunch in the fridge.

"Hm?" Jasper said, only half listening.

"That discussion about ASMR the other day kind of sent me down a rabbit hole," she said.

Jasper's skin went the temperature of a car windshield in January.

"And I came across this whole genre of, like, people with sexy voices who do guided meditation type things. Well, meditation is obviously a euphemism, but you know..." She snickered. "Anyway, does the name Dante Stone ring a bell?"

"Don't see why it would," he said, switching on the kettle. Maybe if he didn't look her in the eye, he could survive this conversation without revealing himself. Probably not, though. Fuck.

Clara sniffed, and Jasper heard the sound of her chair scraping over the floor. "Yeah, okay," she said. "Anyway, I listened to some of his stuff. Very sexy. Except the last episode he did. He obviously really phoned that one in."

"Maybe he was just tired that week," Jasper said before he could stop himself.

"Doing what? Fantasizing about kissing his boss?"

Jasper whipped around and met Clara's triumphant gaze.

"Clara, who told you—"

"*You* just did!" she said gleefully. "Oh my god, I was right. I can't believe it. I saw your Patreon numbers and they're ridiculous! What are you even *doing* here?"

"Please, Clara, please don't tell anyone," Jasper said, ignoring her question. It was really none of her business what job he took or how much money his Patreon was making. He wasn't a publicly held company. She didn't have any stock in what he did.

"Of course I won't," she said. "But I really am impressed. That's fuck-you money, you should just get out while you can."

"Health insurance, Clara," he said flatly.

She bit her lip, obviously chastened. "Right. Sorry."

He was about to storm out of the room when he remembered that Nico and Evan were having a conversation in their office. With a heavy sigh, he sat at the table across from Clara. She was suddenly looking significantly less impressed with herself.

They were silent for a while, other than Jasper swearing under his breath when he accidentally splashed hot water on his hand.

"Here's the truth," Clara finally said. "I'm miserable here, and I got a little jealous of the fact that you could leave anytime you wanted. And it may have made me a little salty. So again, I'm sorry about that. But I can trade you for my own secret."

"I'm listening," Jasper said, sitting back in the chair and crossing his arms.

⁓ele⁓

"So in short, I'm kind of fucked right now," Evan said. "Clara's going to be gone in about a week, and I'll be saddled with both publicity and marketing. And Brent doesn't even know the difference between the two."

Normally Nico would have their back up over the favor that Evan was asking, but the man seemed like he was at risk of coming apart at any moment. It was unsettling for a person who was normally so good-natured to look the way he did right now. If lending Jasper out for some marketing tasks was what it took to get him back on an even keel, then they were willing to sacrifice some of Jasper's time for the cause.

"Perhaps we can make it easier for Brent to hire someone quickly to replace her," they tried, knowing that would be laughably out of character for their so-called boss.

Evan dragged both hands over his face. "Yeah, well, I'd agree with you if he weren't about to throw a bunch of money at you and Jasper going up to Bigfoot-landia."

Nico sighed. "Look, I'll ask Jasper and I'm sure he'd be willing to help you out. But as you said, we're going out of town soon, so it's probably not an ideal solution."

"Fuck, I know," Evan muttered, eyes falling to the ground. "Thanks, though, I guess?"

"Sorry I can't do more."

"Yeah, I know," Evan said, still not looking up at them. "Sorry to be so..." He waved a hand in the air. Nico was apparently supposed to know what that meant.

In any case, Evan seemed to be doing badly. But if Clara was leaving to work for Sparkle Sanders, that would leave everyone at Unified Theory doing quite badly. Well, except for Clara, of course. She would soon be making more money and having a lot more fun.

After Evan trudged out of the room, Nico figured they'd go find Jasper. They should have just waited until he got back, but they were sort of grasping for any chance to see him right now. It was a little pathetic, but Nico had read that these sorts of feelings usually made people act very pathetically.

As they approached the break room, they heard Clara saying something in a low voice. They hesitated, remembering how Evan had looked at them and Jasper earlier. Waiting until she was gone might give her less cause for suspicion.

Then they heard Jasper say, "Thank you so much for keeping this quiet."

"Your secret's safe with me," she said. "Both of them."

Their stomach seized. At first they were incensed at the idea that Jasper might be talking about them to someone else. But "both of them"? What was Jasper hiding that they didn't know about?

Then again, what did they actually know about Jasper? They hadn't even known he was getting hired before he showed up. They hadn't even seen his résumé.

They turned and hurried back to their office, heart pounding. There was research to be done.

CHAPTER SEVENTEEN

ONE OF THEM

When Jasper came back from lunch, Nico barely looked at him before sending him straight over to Evan's desk. He tried to tell himself that it didn't mean anything bad. After all, the two of them had a very positive conversation this morning, and they'd already agreed to go out together after work.

Everything was fine—great, in fact. That terrible sense of foreboding Jasper was feeling was an illusion his low self-esteem had conjured. He refused to let that side of himself win. In the meantime, he was stuck with another job he'd never signed up to do.

Jasper *hated* social media. He'd always had so much trouble figuring out what to post, and the way that people who made the sexier stuff—artists, writers, and people like him—had to jump from platform to platform was exhausting. Even a creator as big as he was had trouble not getting buried without paying a lot of money for the attention.

He asked Evan whether Unified Theory used paid social posts, and he'd just laughed. "I wish they'd give me the budget for that. It took me long enough to get Janet to do Amazon ads," Evan said.

"But, um, isn't it a bit like screaming into the wind without it?" It *was*. Jasper knew it was.

Evan shrugged. "Yeah, but I'd at least like something up there, so if people research us, we don't look like we're out of touch."

Jasper shoved his opinion to the back of his mind. Who cared about the way the marketing department did their stuff? At least this was something just to get him through the day. He was already impatient for the end of the workday, when he and Nico could spend some more time together.

It was a little disconcerting that Nico had shut their office door and pulled down a little shade that Jasper hadn't noticed before now. He wasn't sure why they'd done that, but maybe they wanted to get some work done without Jasper distracting them. It didn't really sound like a sustainable technique, but then, it was early in their relationship. And maybe he was kidding himself about whether it was even a relationship in the first place.

Stop being so negative, Jasper.

He settled down at an old computer, waiting for Canva to open, scrolling through a shared drive full of unedited photos, and glancing at the closed office door from time to time.

An hour passed, then two, and Nico still hadn't opened the door or brought up the shade. Every once in a while, he'd hear their voice, straining to make out the words and failing. Finally, after Jasper had filled out UTP's content calendar for the next few weeks, he stood up.

Evan looked up from his screen, blinking. His eyes were still as bleary as they'd been this morning.

"How's it going?" he said. When Jasper didn't immediately answer, Evan popped out of his chair and came to look over his shoulder.

"Wow, you're really good at this! I might steal you from Nico, actually," Evan said, tone brightening. He crossed his arms and stood back as if admiring a piece of art. "What do you think? Come be *my* assistant?"

Jasper laughed uneasily. "Uh, thanks but no thanks?"

"I know, I know, you're devoted to shaping the written word. Well, and I guess the spoken word too, right?"

Jasper twitched a little, wondering if Clara had told Evan about what she knew. Then he remembered his cover story and took the subtlest deep breath he could through his nose. He really had too many irons in the fire with these secrets, and dating Nico—if it got to that point—could be the drop of water that made all of them finally overflow. Maybe once he was more settled in here, he could be more honest.

"Anyway, thanks for that," Evan said. "You have no idea how helpful it is."

He stepped out of Jasper's way as he mumbled the kind of nonsensical response one gives when one doesn't know how to take a compliment. His mind had already fixated on knocking on his office door to be let back in. He was nervous as hell, and he thought he had the right to be. Two hours? That couldn't be a good sign, could it?

Evan called one last thank-you after him as he slowly opened the door.

There was a squeak as Nico turned around in their chair, eyes narrowed, spine straight. Behind them, he caught the words "Office of the Registrar" on their computer screen, and his stomach dropped. He couldn't quite see the logo from across the room, but he recognized the orange-and-black school colors of Oregon State University.

"Sit down," Nico said.

Jasper hadn't even had the time to think about how he was going to handle *this* particular lie, now that the way he interacted with Nico had changed so much. In fact, he'd almost entirely forgotten about it. He couldn't guarantee he would have told them the truth in a timely way, but he would have had to eventually, right? Clearly, the option to keep it hidden forever was gone.

"Did you do a major or a minor in English literature, Jasper?"

Dammit. He'd said both of those things, hadn't he? He really sucked at this, and now it was about to torpedo his life. Jasper didn't speak; he only glared down at where his hands were clenched in his lap.

"Because I just spoke with the records office at OSU," Nico continued, their volume rising, "and you weren't there. So due to that, and the fact that I don't remember seeing you at all while we supposedly were there at the same time, I can only assume you've been lying to me."

It hadn't even been three weeks since Jasper had gotten this job, and it hadn't even been twenty-four hours since Nico had confessed that they liked him. For the first time since he was a little kid, life actually seemed like it might be starting to get good. Of course he'd already ruined it.

***

To say Nico felt betrayed would be an understatement. They were humiliated—violated, even.

Jasper's face did something complicated at Nico's accusation, and if it had been even an hour ago, they could have deluded themself into thinking they knew what it meant. Now they were starting to realize their supposed intimacy had been built on sand. It made them sick to their stomach. It made them want to go home and crawl under their bed.

So, instead they yelled at someone they had never wanted to yell at again.

They sat there and wished that Jasper would tell them that he actually had another name that he'd used as a student. *Something.* Even if that meant they'd have to apologize for the half-dozenth time, it would be better than the way they felt right now, better than the truth.

Finally Jasper looked up.

"You're right," he said. "I didn't go to OSU. I didn't go to a four-year at all. I took community college classes, but I don't even have an AA. I lied on my résumé."

Dammit.

"Why?"

"I needed a job. Why else? I needed health insurance, and I'd been all alone in my house for nearly a year," he said, sounding strangely calm, like a criminal who knows their punishment is inevitable. This made Nico feel even sicker.

"But—you could have told me sooner," they said.

"When? You only really started being nice to me on Friday," Jasper said. His voice didn't rise to Nico's level; instead it was cold. "Is that why you decided to look into that? Didn't like the idea of actually liking me?"

Oh, *the nerve*. It made their skin prickle, but they felt a stab of guilt too. They really had been looking for something like this, hadn't they?

"I overheard Clara say she was going to keep both of your secrets," they said. "So what's the other one?"

Jasper laughed and leaned his head back against his chair's headrest, staring at the ceiling. "That wasn't even one of them, ironically enough," Jasper said.

"Well?" Their indignance whistled through them like steam through a tea kettle.

"One of them you know already. It was that I liked you," he said.

Liked—past tense—rang in Nico's ears, and their twisting guts were closer than ever to bursting.

"The other one has nothing to do with work, and it's none of your business." Jasper stood, picked up his bag, and slung it over his shoulder. "I'm not feeling great, and I assume you don't want to see me right now, so I'm going home."

Nico didn't stop him; they only vibrated with adrenaline and a cocktail of confused emotions. Jasper didn't look over his shoulder as he left the office, closing the door behind him. Under the ring in their ears, Nico heard the garbled sounds of him exchanging clipped words with Meera, followed quickly by the front doorbell ringing as he left.

With the door closed, they folded their arms on the desk and sank their face into the tiny cave they created. They weren't much of a crier, but at that moment, they really wished they were. There was so much bad feeling inside them that it felt like they'd been poisoned.

This hurt so much worse than anything Brent had thrown them in the last couple weeks. They couldn't believe they'd been so gullible, and so foolish to think that someone might actually care about them without there being some horrible catch.

There was a knock at the door, and they sat bolt upright. It wasn't a moment too soon, as Brent shouldered open the door without waiting for an answer.

"Heeeyyyyy," he said. He sounded almost as unhappy to see them as they were to see him. "Where's Jasper? I needed to talk to both of you together."

"He went home sick." Nico repeated Jasper's lie. *The irony.*

Brent didn't bother to hide an irritated look, as if being ill was some kind of intolerable weakness. As angry as they were at Jasper, Nico still bristled as Brent paused in the doorway.

"Your friend was kind of rude last night, you know," Brent said.

"Is that what you wanted to talk about?" Nico said. They barely had energy left for this conversation, but they were sure they could rally some anger on Andie's behalf if pressed.

"No," Brent said. "I wanted to tell you that Uncle Ricky chose a date for you to go do your thing. You'll be leaving next Wednesday."

"Wednesday, as in a week from today?" That was hardly enough time to get things straightened out.

Brent looked confused at the quick rise of Nico's vocal pitch. "Yeah? Anyway, it'd be great if you could text Jasper. You need to get your equipment"—Nico *knew* he would be relying on them for that—"and transportation and everything straightened out pretty quick. He's the one who has all that stuff."

Nico barely knew whether Jasper had just walked out of the office expecting never to return or was only leaving for the afternoon. They'd had no time to think through the implications of what had just happened before Brent had blown in like the hurricane he was. Now they were just supposed to call Jasper and fully coordinate some silly project that neither of them wanted to do anyway?

They still weren't even sure which of the two of them had fucked up worse.

"Is there anything you'd actually planned out in advance or is that—"

But Brent was already gone, leaving Nico to, again, figure it out on their own.

CHAPTER EIGHTEEN

MORE WORK FOR YOU

J asper didn't have it in him to go back to work on Thursday. He felt like he had a flu, limbs and joints radiating with an ache that couldn't possibly have been in his imagination.

When he woke up on Friday morning, he didn't feel much better. Rather than stew in his indecision until right before he had to leave for MAX, he called Meera and told her that he was still sick. It wasn't hard. Few people were less intimidating than Meera. She just fussed and tutted and told him that he better not come back until he was sure he wouldn't give everyone his germs.

Lady the corgi really would've taken the edge off all this heartache. He'd get a dog if he had the least amount of faith in himself not to fuck it up, like he fucked up everything.

He wasn't in as much physical pain as on Thursday, unless you counted a very itchy restlessness from having so little to do. Writing a new script was off the table. Every lousy TV show made him want to throw the remote control against the wall. Finally he stood up and decided that today was the perfect time to scrub his floors and blast one of his comfort podcasts.

He was on his hands and knees, starting to think maybe this was a terrible idea, when the doorbell rang. Like most people his age, he went still as an opossum hit with the sudden glare of a patio light.

Whoever was outside rang the bell again, and Jasper started to get a little pissed off. It was the sort of neighborhood where sometimes people would knock on the door and bug you for stuff. They were usually harmless, but it didn't seem worth the risk, or the irritation, to get involved.

Then the person knocked, and a familiar voice called his name from the other side of the door.

Fuck.

Jasper rushed to turn down the volume on his speaker. It was obvious he was home, and Nico was a person he was already involved with, whether he liked it or not.

"What are you doing here?" Jasper called through the door. He didn't relish the idea of Nico seeing him in sweatpants-Cinderella mode. And dammit, he missed them, but the whole deal from Wednesday afternoon still sat in his stomach like bad sushi.

"I need to talk to you," Nico said.

No shit. Jasper mouthed it, but he knew better than to say it out loud. "Give me two minutes," he said. Jasper was going to put some actual clothes on before he let Nico see him. They could wait until he'd given himself at least a little bit of dignity. Without that, Nico wouldn't have anything to tear down, would they?

Ugh, it was so unfair how that thought hurt *him* when it was meant to insult *them*.

Finally, once he was wearing a pair of jeans, slippers that *kinda* looked like shoes, and his favorite t-shirt with a neon green eye design on the front (also comfort podcast-related—don't worry about it), Jasper opened the door.

In Nico's hand was a bouquet of flowers wrapped in cellophane, very likely bought from the Trader Joe's a few blocks from the office. Nobody had ever bought flowers for Jasper before, not even his mother. Of course the first flowers anyone was giving him were *I'm sorry* flowers. It was just too on brand.

"I'm here to apologize," Nico said.

They didn't speak for a moment, instead clearing their throat as if they were about to testify in front of Congress.

"So apologize," Jasper said. Maybe it was mean of him to throw them off like that, but he was just passive-aggressive enough to enjoy the flash of extra-strength unease he caught in their expression.

"I'm sorry," they said. "I should have just talked to you about what I heard like an adult instead of sneaking around behind your back."

Nico tipped their head back to meet Jasper's eyes. Their hand that didn't have a death grip on the poor flower stems was fidgeting so wildly at their side that it looked like it had its own nervous system. When Jasper didn't immediately reply, they seemed to check themself and shoved the hand into the pocket of their corduroy blazer.

"And I'm sorry for the harsh way I spoke to you as well," they said.

Jasper nearly bit through his lip to keep from forgiving them immediately, and he nodded slowly as he processed the words. Then he stepped back to let them inside. Half a very loud breath escaped Nico's lips, and the other half came out when Jasper finally accepted the bouquet. It was a cluster of yellow-and-white daffodils, much like the ones that were growing under his window already. Nico had been there at night, though, so there was no reason for them to remember that.

They slipped off their buckled leather shoes when they came in the door. "I also wanted to see if you were coming back. There's been some news about the trip to Richard Glenn's that you probably want to know if you do."

"Great," Jasper said, unable to hide how little he cared about that right now. To keep Nico from seeing his scowl, he started going through his cupboards to look for a vase. Did he even have one?

"We've, um...got a date, and it's much, much too soon," Nico continued. "I probably should have contacted you earlier to help with planning, but, well..."

Unlucky so far, Jasper got down on the ground to look under the sink, even though he'd just been in there to get out the cleaning supplies. As he took mostly empty bottles of cleaner and ancient plastic bags out from the large cupboard, he felt Nico looming over him.

"I've just created more work for you, haven't I?" they said with a sad half-smile.

Jasper continued to rummage even though he was pretty sure there was no point. "Haven't had much need for a vase, haven't really gotten flowers before," he said.

"Not even when your—" They stopped short. Jasper looked up just in time to catch Nico's eyes darting back from the other side of the room. They looked mortified, like they'd just really fucked up that testimony they were giving to Congress. Jasper couldn't help but laugh.

But once he started, he couldn't stop.

"No," he said through gasps. "Not...even...then..." He leaned (well, more like knocked) his head into the wooden lip of the cabinet and let it rest there as his lungs heaved with laughter.

"Jasper..." Nico knelt on the floor next to him, and Jasper registered their touch light on his shoulder. Good thing he'd just cleaned in here, he thought hysterically.

Then he realized he wasn't laughing anymore. It was the way the tension dropped from the top of his lungs to the bottom, like his breath was a sinking lifeboat. Now he was sitting on the floor sobbing into his hands, and he couldn't think of a worse way this could have gone short of Nico coming over just to yell at him some more. On the other hand, at least then he could have yelled back. *And* he wouldn't have been alone.

"Jasper, breathe," Nico said, their hand tightening on his shoulder. He couldn't stop his hand from flying to hold it before they could take it back, before they could leave him too.

Instead of leaving, they moved closer, and Jasper really wished it were under different circumstances than him having a breakdown on his kitchen floor. But then, he couldn't remember the last time he'd let anyone see him cry either, and in some perverse way, that felt good too.

Finally, his breathing started to even out. He wiped the slowing tears from his eyes, finally letting go of Nico's hand. Without breaking contact, they rubbed slow circles over his back. It made Jasper wish he could sleep, that they'd sit there and do exactly that until he was unconscious and couldn't humiliate himself any more than he already had. He didn't have the energy to feel shy about how intimate that would be.

⸎

For as wonderful as Tuesday had been, the rest of the week had overcorrected to total shit. Wednesday and Thursday, Nico had thought it best to give Jasper space rather than obey their so-called boss by texting him. If they were going to message him while he was off the clock, it would have been something that wasn't related to work. But as the days wore on, that seemed like it would be less and less of an option.

And *of course* the first thing Nico would do when they saw him again was throw him into a full crying jag. They'd realized long ago they had the emotional intelligence of a gnat, but that didn't mean it was fun to be reminded.

But how the hell had *no one* sent the man flowers when his mother had died? If Jasper gave them another chance, Nico resolved, he'd never suffer from a lack of flowers again. Nico didn't have the patience to be afraid of how earnest that thought was.

At last, the sobs quieted, and Nico gently petted Jasper's back. "I'm so sorry, I didn't mean to make you cry."

They weren't prepared for Jasper to turn and engulf Nico in his arms. Without hesitation, they leaned into the soft give of his chest and belly, closing their eyes and letting the relief spread through their veins. They weren't sure how much of the full-body warmth they felt was from him and how much was radiating from inside of them.

"I'm sorry I lied on my résumé," Jasper croaked. "I didn't do it to hurt you."

"Of course you didn't," Nico said. "It was incredibly arrogant of me to think so." It was so much easier to be honest in this position, they thought as Jasper's arms tightened around them.

Unfortunately for them (but fortunately for their knees), Jasper finally let go and sat back.

"I forgive you," he said. "And, I mean, I'd understand if this ruined things for you, and I'm fine to go back to just being your assistant if that's what you want."

Nico tensed. "Well, not—not necessarily? Although, maybe we should slow down and get to know each other a little better to avoid similar...upheaval."

Jasper's poor eyes were red and puffy, but his smile still stoked the furnace in Nico's chest.

"Guess we're even now," he said. "One for one on crying fits."

The internal furnace spared a little heat for Nico's cheeks. "Oh god, I forgot about that."

Now they both laughed, and if Nico had been as brave as they were the other night, they would have kissed him. Unfortunately, part of the barrier that had been between them before had rebuilt itself. There would have to be a lot more than this single reconciliation to take it down again. The safest thing they could do now was move on to work topics (which would probably make them cry again at some point soon, so they had that to look forward to).

"If you're coming back to work...," Nico said.

"Yeah, I'll come back," Jasper said, and Nico felt a part of themself that they didn't even know was tense relax.

"Well, then, I've been told we're due up north next Wednesday," they said.

Jasper blinked as if he had been shaken awake. "Next week?"

They could have said something snarky, but they resisted the impulse and nodded.

"Fuck," Jasper said. He leaned his head back against the cupboard, wincing when he knocked it a little too hard. "Okay, well, I need to call my guy and see if he can help with production. I don't care what Brent says, and who even knows if we can get him so last-minute. Oh, and I guess he wants me to use my own equipment?"

Nico nodded again, and a part of them felt guilty for not warning him on Wednesday, emotional upheaval or no.

"Okay, I'll do that now," Jasper said, pulling himself up off the ground with a small groan. Nico followed, echoing him. "You probably want me to come back to work with you?"

"You don't have to," they said. "But it is Clara's last day, and we're going to get drinks after work to celebrate. I'm sure she'd love to see you there, and I'd be happy to give you a ride home afterward."

"Oh, good for her," Jasper said emphatically. "Bad for everyone else, but good for her. Let me go get some shoes and my bag, then we can go."

As he disappeared down the hall, Nico wondered what Jasper's other secret was. He'd said it was none of their business. Maybe if they ever earned his trust back, he'd feel comfortable enough to tell them. In the meantime, they wouldn't bother him about it.

CHAPTER NINETEEN

NOT COMMON KNOWLEDGE

When Jasper and Nico came through the front door of Unified Theory, Meera snatched the hand sanitizer bottle from beside one of her many snow globes. She held it out in front of her like a taser.

"What are you doing back, Jasper? I thought you were sick!" she said in a much more aggressive tone than Nico was used to hearing from her.

"He's feeling much better now. Don't worry, Meera," Nico said.

Meera glared at them both dubiously. "I'm going to my cousin's wedding this weekend, and I cannot get sick."

"W-what I had wasn't, um, wasn't contagious," Jasper said.

Lowering the sanitizer, Meera continued to glare. "I've been telling all of you that you should be more careful about these food carts. Anyone can just put one up around here."

Nico knew that wasn't quite true but decided not to argue. They and Jasper had bigger issues to deal with than a case of mistaken food poisoning. Barely giving Jasper time to set down his bag, they started up the stairs to Brent's office.

By some miracle, the man was actually there to-day—Nico could hear muffled voices on the other side of the door. When they opened it, they revealed Brent seated on his medicine ball with Skip Stewart across the desk bouncing on one of his own like they were kindergartners in PE class. The two looked at them as if they were interrupting their planning session for the wrongfully rich asshole summit (although Nico wasn't sure whether Skip was actually a rich person or was just very good at latching on to them).

"Hi," Brent said, making his eyes bigger in what Nico guessed was an attempt to menace. He raised his chin as Nico became aware Jasper had caught up to them. "What's, uh...what can I do for you?"

"Jasper's secured the services of a sound engineer to help us create a quality recording at Richard Glenn's house next week," they said.

Skip twisted around at the shoulders, his cap crooked on his head. Brent's eyes were still wide. Nico wasn't used to exercising this type of authority with superiors, but having Jasper behind them like a bodyguard made them braver.

Nico continued, keeping their voice steady. "His name is Eddie Walker, and he's a professional contact of Jasper's. We'll be taking care of his transportation, and I'll make arrangements for payment with Meera, then bring up the paperwork for your signature. Then we'll need the next several days cleared of other responsibilities in order to—"

"Fine, fine, I don't care. Do whatever you want," Brent said, agitated.

"Great," Nico said. It was a surprising lack of friction, but they'd take it. Without a thank-you, they turned to head back downstairs, leaving the door open just to make life a little more difficult for Brent.

When they got back to their office, Jasper stood for a moment in the doorway. His lips were parted as if he were about to say something.

"What?" Nico said, worried they'd done something wrong. Should they have let Jasper present their case instead?

Jasper shook his head, shutting his mouth and taking a visible deep breath through his nose. "N-nothing, just, that was..." He cleared his throat. "You can be very impressive."

Nico cleared their throat as well, a little shocked by the buzz that shot through them at Jasper's words. They weren't sure anyone had called them impressive since they'd defended their master's thesis. Part of them wanted to reject the compliment, but it was far too nice to hear, and they didn't want to discourage it for the future (oh god, they were already thinking this way again).

"Well, thank you," they said, then shoved themself back into business mode. "You'll need to take the lead on planning these scripts, I'm afraid, because I have no idea how they work. We should try to get as much done as possible before the end of the day."

Jasper was seized by a desperate desire to touch Nico as they locked up and headed to the bar. It would be nice just to put his hand on their back, or hold their hand, but he restrained himself. In the car on the way back to the office, they'd agreed to slow down. Nico had described it as a "probationary friendship period," and they'd been so emphatic about it that Jasper hadn't wanted to argue. To him, it seemed like self-flagellation on their part.

Then again, there was a lot they still didn't know about each other, and Jasper suspected his own issues were still more likely to be deal breakers.

"You're late!" Clara yelled at Jasper and Nico from the opposite side of the bar. It was one of those divey places with lottery machines and no windows, filled with the sorts of characters you don't see at brewpubs. There were balloons attached to her chair and a tiara on her head. She was dressed in vintage-store splendor as usual, wearing a candy-apple red dress with frills at the sleeves and neckline.

"You're drunk!" Evan yelled, pointing at her accusingly.

"So are *you!*" Clara shouted back. Then they both grinned and clinked their lowball glasses.

Evan appeared to be drinking straight whiskey. He'd been a little bit shaky-looking the other day, and his manic energy seemed as forced as the last bits of toothpaste squeezed from a tube.

"Sorry, lots of preparations to make, unfortunately," Nico said wearily, just begging to be comforted. Man, this urge to touch was going to be a bitch, wasn't it?

"So you'll be leaving on Wednesday, already? That's far too soon," Meera said, brow wrinkled. She was drinking what was either a gin and tonic or, more likely, a glass of soda water.

"It certainly is. I'll need to stay over the weekend to make sure you don't get into any editorial emergencies while the two of us are away," Nico said.

"And who will take care of that if it happens?"

"I vote Jack," Evan said.

"Huh?" Jack, as usual, jumped to attention at the sound of his name, head snapping up from where it was leaned over the lip of their table. A cloud of vapor rose up around his shoulders.

A woman with curly black hair wearing an army jacket was sitting at the end of the table between Evan and Clara. Jasper had never seen her before, but she smiled at him.

"Hey, I don't think we've met!" she shouted across the table over Evan and Clara's loud bantering.

"Oh! I'm Jasper," he said.

"What?"

"Jasper!" Nico flinched a little at Jasper's increase in volume. "Sorry," he murmured and squeezed their shoulder before he could stop himself. To his relief, Nico accepted it without tensing up.

"I'm Bethany! Clara's roommate!" she shouted back.

Clara's attention jumped to their conversation from whatever Evan was saying. Noticing, he stopped talking too, looking suspiciously at her. Her mouth twitched as she looked from Jasper to her roommate.

Bethany's eyes narrowed. "Why does that sound so familiar?" she said. "Have we met before?"

It was hot in the bar from the Friday night crush of people, but Jasper's skin went cold all the same. When Clara's hand dropped to grip Bethany's wrist, the cold sensation turned fully into a cold sweat.

Deflect! Deflect!

"Uuuum…I don't know? Did you go to Parkrose, maybe?" he said.

"Oh! Oh! I know what it is!" she said, ignoring where Clara's grip had become a claw. "You're the porn guy!"

Welp. Now Jasper was all out of secrets. Did that mean a portal to hell was about to open and swallow him up? At this point he would have welcomed it. His eyes darted to Nico, whose lips were pressed together so hard you'd think they didn't even exist, though their eyes had doubled in size.

"*Bethany.*" Clara smacked her arm with the back of her fingers and Bethany's hand flew up to grip the place she'd been hit. "What the fuck?"

"What, what, what?" Evan had half leapt from his chair. Then he settled back, one knee tucked under him. "Jasper, are you…what?"

"Oh shit, was that not common knowledge?" Bethany said.

Jasper shot to his feet, hands shaking as he lifted his bag from where it hung on the chair. "Well, um, well, congratulations on the new job, Clara. See you—sometime—"

Before he could say anything else, his feet carried him out of the bar as fast as they could.

Nico's ears were ringing as they tried to catch up to what had just taken place.

Evan was shouting after Jasper's disappearing figure, "Wait! That's so cool! Jasper, it's okay!" He lowered his voice, but only slightly. "Should I go after him?"

"Bethany, I told you that in confidence," Clara hissed.

Ah. The other secret.

"Was Jasper a *porn star*?" Evan stage-whispered at Clara. He looked back up to the doorway where Jasper had just escaped. "I can see it, actually."

Nico shook a very inappropriate image out of their head and stood, slinging their own bag over their shoulder. "I'll go talk to him," they said. After everything, they owed him that much.

"Tell him I'm sorry!!" Bethany yelled after them. They didn't respond, irritated that she'd done this to Jasper after it had been so hard to get him out of his house in the first place. But then, what right did Nico have to be annoyed after how they'd acted toward him?

Emerging from the bar, Nico scanned the street. An old man with a mustache so gray it looked blue was leaning against the wall, smoking a cigarette. Finally, Nico spotted Jasper halfway down the street that led to his MAX stop.

"Jasper, wait!" Nico called. The man with the blue mustache shot them a look, but they couldn't care less. They ran after Jasper, dodging a woman riding her rusted bicycle down the middle of the uneven sidewalk. It was the most athletic thing they'd done in years, but they didn't want him to get too far ahead of them.

They were out of breath when they finally caught up, and when Jasper turned around, he looked like he'd been running from someone carrying a large knife. Fully throwing out their earlier discussion about taking it easy on the touching, they grabbed onto both his elbows to hold him there.

"Nico, I swear I was going to tell you eventually, but—" Jasper started.

"Wait," they cut him off. "You don't need to tell me anything you don't want to. Just know that whatever it is, it's your personal business and it doesn't change how I think of you."

Some of the fear had gone out of Jasper's eyes. Instead, he looked doubtful.

"And if you do want to tell me, I'm always glad to listen, even if you think I can't handle it. I can." They might have said this too fiercely. Yes, Nico could be persnickity about sexual topics, as Jasper was surely aware from how they'd acted Tuesday night, but they were a full-grown adult and didn't need to be treated like they were made of glass.

Jasper hung his head, perhaps saddened, undoubtedly stressed. It needled every sympathetic cell inside Nico. Their hold on his elbows loosened, and they kept one anchoring hand on his upper arm, waiting for him to choose to look at them again.

"O-okay," Jasper finally said. He took a shaky breath, still looking at the ground. "So, first you need to know that my mother was sick for a very long time, and I was the only person who could care for her."

Nico nodded, but then they figured Jasper couldn't see it. "Okay," they said softly.

"A-and, I needed to find *some* way to make money. And it's not like I could go somewhere and get a job with benefits when I had no experience either, so..." He sighed heavily. "So at first I was doing some—well, I guess it was kind of like, phone sex stuff? L-like, through the internet, but obviously it was just audio—I mean, look at me."

"Jasper..." Nico didn't like the insinuation he was making about his looks, but they figured now wasn't the time to affirm him that way.

"T-that's the part Clara doesn't know about, that it wasn't just the recordings. Whatever, anyway, um... so, eventually when subscription services started coming out, I decided to set up something where I could do recordings instead of live calls. So, I finally started making money with it," he said, then laughed humorlessly. "And it couldn't have happened at a better time, because that's when she really started going downhill and I needed the help."

For a moment Nico waited, not wanting to interrupt Jasper if he wasn't finished. Finally he lifted his eyes from the ground to meet Nico's. Nico did their best to hold on to that contact, and they squeezed his upper arm.

"Is that it?" they asked.

"What do you mean, 'is that it?'" Jasper said, a shake in his voice. "The only work experience I've ever had was as a sex worker."

"Sex worker *and* entrepreneur," Nico corrected him.

There was a pause, and then Jasper gave something between a laugh and a sob, lifting his free hand to his eyes. "Jesus, how are you so funny?"

"It's mostly by accident," Nico said. "So that's where your audio experience comes from too, isn't it?"

Jasper nodded.

Nico shrugged. "Sounds like you're more qualified than you think you are, then. Especially for the nonsense you're having to do here."

He put his hand down and let it dangle at his side. Nico, feeling much more confident that they were doing this right, took both his hands in theirs.

"Yeah, and the money was much better, actually." Then the smile dropped from his face. "But you should probably know that I haven't quit doing it, and I don't really plan to. I've just sort of reduced the amount of content I'm releasing."

"Better than driving for Lyft as a side job," Nico said.

Jasper laughed again. "Jesus Christ, Nico," he said. He sniffed. "C-can I give you a hug? Is that okay?"

Without hesitating, Nico wrapped their arms around the middle of his chest, leaning into him. It was still a move that a friend would make, right? Something someone would do to comfort a friend who was in emotional distress? As Jasper's arms encircled them, pulling them closer, they weren't sure they cared.

CHAPTER TWENTY

AHA! A DEGENERATE!

The evening had gone so much better than expected. Eventually, Nico had coaxed Jasper to come back into the bar. There, Bethany had apologized profusely, and Clara had rushed to buy him another drink.

"Dude, I mean this totally platonically, but I think you're cool and sexy and I have nothing but massive respect for you," Evan had said, lifting his glass to him, then quickly draining it.

"Evan," Nico said, putting on the stern tone that Jasper was realizing he was hopelessly into. Evan winked at them.

"Um, thanks, I guess," Jasper said. "Just...don't—if you listen to it, don't tell me. I'd rather not talk about it after this, if that's okay."

"Well, I certainly won't," Meera said. "I'm going to pretend this conversation never happened, no offense."

"None taken at all," Jasper said with a relieved laugh, followed by a long sip of his beer. His cheeks were still burning, but he felt like an enormous weight had been lifted.

The only concerning thing was that Nico had started giving him a very strange look, and it made Jasper think they were starting to actually understand what they'd gotten themself into.

On the way home, Jasper distracted himself from fretting about it by looking through Nico's sleeve of CDs.

"Do you have an aux or Bluetooth or something in here?"

"I don't," Nico said. Jasper couldn't tell whether they were proud or ashamed. "It's mostly just a lot of what I listened to when I was a teenager. It's been…a while since I had the energy or desire to try new music."

"I bet Mixer, um, Eddie still has CDs," Jasper said, almost to himself. "I just have, well—"

"What?" Nico said.

A laugh was expelled from Jasper's chest, almost against his will. After their conversation earlier, so many things seemed way less embarrassing. "All I listened to in high school was musical theater soundtracks," he said.

Nico started laughing. "Among the two of us, how were you the bigger dork in high school?"

"Hey! I branched out afterward. And I didn't have a cool best friend to carry me through like you did," Jasper said.

"I suppose that's fair," Nico sighed, then went quiet. The smile slowly drained from their face until that strange look from the bar had returned. "Jasper, could I ask something?"

Jasper couldn't help the stab of terror after the highs and lows of the past week. "Okay."

"Can I...?" Nico grumbled, as if there were a gremlin inside them that didn't want the words to come out of their mouth. "Would you mind if I listened?"

"To...?" For a second Jasper thought they meant one of the CDs in the folder, but then it dawned on him. "Oh. Um. Now?"

"No, no, not now," they rushed to say. "A-and I know you told Evan and everyone else you didn't want them to listen, and if you don't want me to I won't, but...I just, I sort of want to know? If we're trying to...you know..."

There was heavy silence in the car (aside from the sound of a woman wailing on the stereo). Jasper wasn't sure what to say. Was he okay with this?

"First, you should know that my audience is mostly women," he began.

"Okay..." Nico gave a single nod.

"Yeah, so I usually use feminine terms." A memory of the way Nico had moaned when he'd accidentally called them a good girl flitted through his head, getting scrambled in the wires for a second. "And I don't know if that would be uncomfortable for you."

"I'm not doing it for titillation, Jasper," Nico said, a sneer in their voice, and Jasper couldn't help but laugh at their use of the word. "Oh, stop it, you. Anyway, pornography doesn't really do anything for me. I just want to...I guess I just want to know more about you and what you do."

You really don't, Jasper thought. It would just challenge something that was already so fragile if Nico were to listen.

"Well, no offense, but video and audio tend to push different buttons for different people," he said. "Trust me on this."

"To put it bluntly, Jasper, it's been, um…" Nico sighed. "It's been suggested that I may be asexual. I don't know if I fully identify that way, but I don't relate to sex the same way others seem to."

"But the other night—" Jasper started, then his stomach dropped. Shit. "Did I pressure you into something you didn't want?"

"No," they said emphatically. "I-I liked it. In fact I believe I initiated, didn't I?"

Jasper cleared his throat. "I think so." (As if he didn't remember every second in vivid detail.)

"Anyway, the point is, I'm favorable enough that I'm not disgusted, but it takes a lot for me to be interested, or for it to even occur to me to want, frankly. So I'm confident I'll be able to listen to this fairly objectively."

Jasper couldn't help but be a little flattered by the "interested" bit, but he was still too nervous to preen over it. He took a lot of pride in his work, but in the end, it was erotica—very explicit erotica. And as much as Nico seemed to try to be using it as a reassurance, the fact that they'd brought up asexuality made Jasper self-conscious that he was going to come across as, well, a perv.

But on the other hand, fuck it. If they were going to do this, he might as well start being honest. Every lie had been revealed. It was time to get real, and if this was the thing that made it fall apart, he'd give up. And maybe quit his job.

Hush, Jasper.

"Okay." Jasper nodded, taking his phone out of his pocket. "Fine, I'm texting you a link to the Patreon, and a free coupon code so you don't have to pay." The only other person who had that link was Eddie, and that was for work. He couldn't think of any other reason it should exist, but here they were.

"Great," Nico said, their voice a little higher than usual. Jasper wasn't sure whether they were just overly pleased with themself or whether they were nervous about this as well.

"A-and, look, you can listen to whatever you want, but definitely read the tags first. Some of them are just erotic stories, and, *yes*, some of them are in second person. I won't take an ounce of shit from you on that," Jasper said, and Nico snickered. He was aware that he was talking very quickly, but then at least this would all be out of the way and into Nico's hands. "But some of them are like...um. Well. Some of them *aren't* narratives, they're more like...act-outs almost?"

"Goodness," Nico said, eyes opening wider. If Jasper weren't slightly mortified by all this, he'd think it was adorable.

They both sat in silence for the rest of the ride until Nico put the car in park in front of Jasper's house.

"I hope you aren't disappointed if I don't, um, you know...," Nico said, nodding across Jasper toward the house.

"Not a problem. Probably a smart move." Yes, he was disappointed, but he understood. The two of them looked at each other for a few awkward seconds before Jasper opened the door, then stopped. "Oh! Also, listen to whatever you want, but I'd really rather you didn't listen to the latest one. I sound like total shit on it."

"I promise," Nico said, and the way they smiled made Jasper feel much better about this whole bizarre situation.

The two or three times Nico had tried watching porn in their apartment, they'd spent the whole time looking over their shoulder as if someone were about to walk in, point at them, and shout, "Aha! A degenerate!" Needless to say, they were too nervous to even try to enjoy it. The sight of other people having sex didn't do much for them anyway. They always just ended up bored or judgmental about the poor acting or the way the rooms were decorated, or fixated on some odd sound someone was making.

But this was a big part of Jasper's life, and they liked Jasper. They liked him a lot, actually, and they found that they wanted to know as much about him as possible.

Having always had trouble sleeping, Nico had a white noise machine, a weighted blanket, and several large pillows. (One of these might or might not resemble a large tabby cat, but not so much that it would be considered a stuffed animal—or at least that was what they told themself.) They had never tried guided meditations, much less erotic ones, but as they settled into bed with their headphones, a part of them wondered idly if it might actually help them sleep in some way.

But that was a dangerous way to think. They were listening for reconnaissance only, not enjoyment.

Dutifully, they scrolled past the most recent post. They had resolved not to go nosing around when Jasper had asked them not to. The next one in the feed, titled "Dante's Home," seemed as good as any. It was tagged such that Nico knew it was one of those "act-outs" Jasper had referred to. Despite his obvious self-consciousness, Nico was quite curious about how that might sound.

(And if they realized that one of the things that made them behave so recklessly around Jasper was his voice, well, that wasn't something anyone was going to *force* them to acknowledge.)

They pressed play and immediately could hear Jasper breathing straight into their ears; not as if he were blowing into the microphone, but as if he were actually there, lying on their bed next to them.

"Thank you for waiting up for me, sweetheart. I'm sorry I'm so late. My flight was delayed," Jasper, or *Dante*, Nico supposed, said.

Ah. So "Dante's" wasn't possessive—it was a contraction of "Dante is." Apparently this was intended to simulate a character coming home from a trip and finding the listener in bed, not to be a tour of Dante's home. Nico wasn't sure they would have chosen such an awkward title, but they could forgive it.

"Oh...," Jasper said after a pause. Nico cocked their head curiously. His voice was low, almost reverent. "Darling, did you wear that just for me? You're beautiful. But you know I think you're beautiful no matter what you wear. Especially when you don't wear anything." He said the last bit with his familiar bashful giggle, except with none of its usual nervousness and twice its fondness.

God, that was cheesy. This certainly wasn't literature.

If it's so cheesy, why is your face hot? Some demon inside Nico taunted them. They shouldered it further back into their subconscious as they sunk deeper into their nest of pillows.

Jasper—*Dante*, rather—stretched time between each of his sentences. His unhurried voice sounded as if his lips were grazing the microphone with every word. There was a gentle rustle of fabric that Nico supposed was meant to simulate him removing his own clothes.

"God, all I've been able to think about all day is touching you like this," Jasper said. "How does that feel, my love? Do you like that? Oh, I think you do. I can tell by how wet you are for me."

When he gave that same warm chuckle, Nico realized their mouth had gone dry. They rolled onto their side and clutched their largest pillow, as if making themself smaller would help them regain control of their shallow breaths. The shuddering noise Jasper made next undid all that work, as a memory of the way he'd whimpered when Nico had had him in their mouth flashed through their mind. It wasn't quite the same, though, and Nico's cheeks burned at the thought that maybe that sound had been just for them, had been the *real* Jasper.

"Ah," Jasper gasped, "you're so good to me, darling. I love the way you touch me. Such a good, good girl."

At this, Nico's hips bucked against the pillow they were holding like a piece of driftwood in a storm. Their paranoia dissipated a little when they realized how satisfying it was—the combination of the friction between their legs and Jasper's gasps of praise in their ears. They gave in to their own body and did it again, then again, then again, to the crescendoing desire in Jasper's voice.

"You want me inside you? Of course, sweetheart."

Nico pressed their face into the pillow, for a moment feeling like they'd disconnected from reality. How the hell had they gone from listening to something out of curiosity to humping their pillow like an animal? It was like their will had been hijacked by some invisible creature that wanted nothing more than to laugh at how pathetic they were. Whatever that creature was, good for them. They'd won.

The beginning of the recording had seemed almost innocent, but at some point Jasper's voice had transformed into something textured with intensity and purpose.

"Will you touch yourself while I fuck you? I want to feel you come on my cock."

Nico made an embarrassing noise as they gave in and did what Jasper's voice asked them to do. Still curled up on their side, they added their hand to the stimulation on their cock. Everything in them contracted into a vibrating ball of nerves as Jasper's breath quickened, and they moved to match its rhythm. They weren't sure how long the recording would last, but they were torn between craving release and never wanting it to end.

It went on like this for just enough time to be satisfying, passing in a blur of murmured praise. The things that came out of Jasper's mouth were like incantations, while the sounds Nico made into the bedspread sounded much, much less professional.

"I'm getting close, darling," Jasper said with a languorous sigh, which sounded a lot more composed than Nico felt. How did he have just the right amount of tremble in his voice to sound so affected, yet still in control?

Before they had time to think much more about it, they gasped as the force of their climax hit them like a truck running a red light. Their body jolted as they bit down hard on the fabric of their poor, unexpectedly used pillow.

Vaguely, they were aware of the almost musical sound of Jasper's simulated pleasure, and along with the wash of pleasure was a tinge of smugness. Nico knew what the real version sounded like.

There were more soothing whispers in Nico's ear as they caught their breath, keeping them steady as they faced down complete surprise. That had not been anything like what they'd expected. A little embarrassed, even with nobody around to see, they peeled off their underpants and the pillowcase and chucked both toward the hamper. Normally a neat person, they still found themself far, far too tired to get up and change.

They slept better than they'd slept in months, without a single concern over how this might shake them up in the morning.

CHAPTER TWENTY-ONE

A THIRD THING

Wednesday morning saw Jasper and Nico in the office, belongings and sound equipment packed into the back of Nico's Subaru. They were just at the office to make final preparations, and Jasper tapped his ballpoint pen as they reviewed a printed-out spreadsheet together.

"Tentacle monsters?" Nico said.

"All scheduled, narration and questions finalized," Jasper replied.

"Mothman?"

"Same."

"Bigfoot?"

"Same."

They ran through the entire list of cryptids featured in Richard Glenn's original text, determining how much was still left to do for each. There were glaring white gaps when it came to recording, editing, and in some cases narration and scheduling as well. Jasper had a copy of Glenn's book littered with Post-its in all colors of the rainbow. He had kept his head down for the last several days (including his whole damn weekend), reading, internalizing, and typing as much as he could before they left for Northern Washington.

"You'll have to do the remaining ones on the fly," Nico said. "Hopefully you'll have the privacy and space to do so. If I recall, Glenn has an irritating habit of droning on and on, and he actually expects you to listen to him. I've yet to meet one of these cultists who wasn't the same."

Notably, Nico hadn't called any of these people cultists in front of Brent. Then again, Brent had been scarce over the last few days. During the Monday morning meeting, he'd brushed off Evan's concerns about hiring a new PR director and then immediately disappeared. As far as Jasper could see, he had been spending two hours max per day in the office and sometimes never showed up at all.

"Oh, I know. I met Hannah, remember?" Jasper snickered, and Nico gratifyingly joined in. He worried he was becoming addicted to making Nico laugh. It was never something he'd thought he could do the first few days he'd worked at Unified Theory, but it had become kind of a fixation since that first time after happy hour.

The pleasure of making them laugh was quickly soured by the unspoken question he'd had since Friday. With all the work he'd been doing, he had barely had time to obsess over whether Nico had listened to any of his Dante Stone recordings. If they had, they were certainly keeping quiet about it, and that fact threatened to send him into an anxiety spiral. It wasn't just sexual anxiety; he was also worried that Nico thought he was bad at the job itself.

To *hell with it*, Jasper thought. If Nico was as unaffected by erotica as they said, he should be able to ask them what they thought. All this uncertainty was a bad way to start a business trip, much less a completely batshit one.

"Hey, Nico," he said, fighting through his dry mouth. "You didn't happen to listen to any of..." The rest of the words clung to the back of his throat like a glob of peanut butter he couldn't quite swallow, but he assumed Nico got the message.

It was as if they were hit by a cold gust of air. "I did," they said in a voice that was frosty at the edges.

"Oh," Jasper said. The following silence wasn't encouraging. "You don't think I'm some kind of hack now, do you?" The desperate thought that Nico would not have allowed him to write these scripts if they thought he sucked clung to his brain stem. Then again, what options did Nico have for this project other than Jasper?

Nico shook their head emphatically. "No, of course not. You did... well..."

Jasper waited, but he was only met with more silence. "I did well? Is that it?" It wasn't the worst evaluation, but Jasper's professional pride demanded more feedback. How that took over from his sexual anxiety spiral was a mystery to him, but it had.

"You did very well." A reluctant laugh slipped from them as they fixed their eyes on the floor. "I, um, I liked it more than I thought I would."

"Liked it?"

Nico nodded, eyes still avoiding him. "Yes. I, um...it engaged me, you could say."

Oh. Invisible hands squeezed Jasper's stomach like it was a sand-filled balloon. Now in emergency mode, Jasper started trying to think of the unsexiest things he possibly could to fight back the unavoidable horniness triggered by the phrase *it engaged me.* The glass of ginger ale that Hannah Hodge had given him. The squirrel carcass that had been lying by his MAX stop for the past month. Brent, full stop.

Fortunately, Jasper was saved by a jarring shout from outside their office door.

"You can't be serious!" Evan's voice, completely drained of the pretentious cheer he'd been attempting since Brent had arrived, boomed through the office. "This cover has been approved for months. All our promotional materials have it. Skip likes it, your mother liked it—not that you care—and most of all I'm pretty sure we've already sent it to print. You're putting us at a huge disadvantage if we change it now."

"Calm down. It can't be that big of a deal." Jasper could hear Brent roll his eyes. "There's no need for the drama."

Evan started a sentence, then stopped, then said, "I'm not being dramatic, I'm being realistic. We all know you don't know shit about publishing, but you obviously don't know anything about business either, and you're going to run us into the ground. What's it been, a month? And you've already fucked it up this much?"

Meera gasped as Jasper felt his jaw go slack. He and Nico shamelessly hung in the doorway. The only person who didn't seem affected was Jack, who was still wearing the gigantic cans over his ears.

"Wow, man, this is some seriously toxic behavior." Brent's voice was like flavorless poison in a bottle of kombucha. "The truth is, you're not the one in charge—I am. So you can do one of two things: what I tell you to do, or what I tell you to do."

Evan set his arms akimbo and took a step back. A smile slowly lit up the lower half of his face, but his eyes were mean.

"Nah, there's a third thing," he said. "I can leave right now. Good luck selling books with no marketing or PR."

With that, he turned his back on Brent, scooped up his jacket from his desk, and swept out of the room. The slamming of the front door and the clanking bell were followed by thick, uncomfortable stillness. Brent looked like he'd suddenly slid off a mountain trail and was holding on to the edge by one hand. He turned toward the doorway where Jasper and Nico stood.

" Jasper—" He cut himself off. "Nico... do you..."

Repressed glee trembled in Nico's voice. "Sorry, Brent. We'd love to stay and help, but we're already due to be on the road. Good luck."

The two of them waited until they were safely inside the car to start cackling.

Nico was both glad and frustrated that they had to leave the office directly after Evan's exit. They had worked with him for years now, and in spite of all the chaos, they still wanted to help him. But how?

Then, an idea bloomed in their mind like a firework against a dark sky.

"I need to make a call. Do you mind?" Nico said as they pulled onto the freeway.

"Not at all," Jasper replied. Nico enlisted his help dialing Andie's number and setting the call on speaker.

"Have you fucked your assistant yet?" Andie said by way of greeting.

"You're on speakerphone, Andie," Nico cringed. "Jasper and I are in the car headed north."

"Jasper? Have they fucked you yet?"

This time, Nico couldn't stop themself from glancing at Jasper, whose face was beet red. "Uuuum...," he said. Very smooth, the both of them.

"That's not why I'm calling," Nico sighed.

A raucous laugh shook the interior of the car. "I'll take that as a yes, then," they said. Nico suppressed a groan. "So, what can I do for you?"

"Well, you know how you've been working yourself into the ground with no help for the past ten years?" Maybe it was blunt to speak to Andie that way, but they didn't much feel like extending grace. Plus, the bluntness was received with more laughter.

"You got me there. So what?"

"I might have a solution for that. Evan Brooks has had enough of our new overlord and unexpectedly quit today."

"Which one's Evan?" Andie said. "Oh! Was he the hot one?"

"I'm sure I wouldn't know," Nico said. Jasper's hand flew to cover his mouth, and his shoulders shook. "Anyway, I wanted to give him a glowing endorsement to handle your marketing and events, and perhaps bookselling as well. I can have Jasper send you his number when we hang up."

Andie made a thoughtful sound, which to the inexperienced ear might have sounded mocking. "Wow, so business-y, so network-ish. I guess I can conduct an impromptu interview today if he's around."

"He's probably wandering the streets, considering he just walked out a few minutes ago. And also, I want to go on record that my endorsement is purely professional."

"Yeah, yeah, I know," they said. "Don't worry, believe it or not, I am capable of keeping business and shenanigans separate. I'll call him after Jasper sends me that number."

Nico wasn't so sure they believed that, but it was really none of their business. They'd done what they could. It was out of their hands.

"Have a great trip, you two! And don't forget to wear protection!"

They hung up before Nico could protest. As if this weren't already a deeply uncomfortable experience. Christ. Fortunately the drama of Unified Theory's precarious situation was still overshadowing it.

A few weeks ago, Nico would have been horrified by the idea of leaving the office after the sort of disaster they'd just witnessed. However, a few weeks ago, they wouldn't have been forced to drive six hours away to do a task that had almost nothing to do with their job description. They felt a little guilty leaving Jack and Meera alone with Brent, but it wasn't as if they had a choice.

They had already hit traffic waiting to cross over the I-5 bridge to Washington (seriously, at almost noon on a Wednesday?). Jasper stared out the passenger window at the expanse of the Columbia River, white-capped and gray in the windy spring gloom. They felt a deep pressure to speak and figured if they couldn't address one awkward topic, they would bring up another.

"I'm going to have to ask you a favor," they said. Jasper turned away from the window to look at them. "It might seem like it's going against everything we've talked about before, but I've been thinking about it a lot."

They heard Jasper inhale sharply, and they realized that might have come off as ominous.

"It's not about you. It's about gender-related issues," they clarified. They took a deep breath, and they would have closed their eyes if they weren't in stop-and-go traffic. "I'm afraid I'm going to have to go back into the closet for this trip. I have no energy to explain myself, and I don't know how safe I would be if I tried. Better not to risk it."

"Understood," Jasper said. The painful sympathy in his voice was almost unbearable. "I'm so sorry. But also... the thing is, we're going to have to tell Eddie as well. Because, before I knew that you two would ever meet, I told him about...you. That I liked you. *Like* you, honestly."

A cocktail of emotions stirred inside Nico. One ingredient was the pleasure of knowing that Jasper did, indeed, still like them. The second was apprehension over the fact that they were about to meet a stranger who probably knew more about their relationship than even their best friend did.

"I'm so sorry," Jasper rushed to repeat, and Nico felt a twist of reluctant affection added to that cocktail.

"It's alright. I understand. I suppose we'll have to have a conversation between the three of us. But we should probably keep the whole..."—*relationship*, Nico—"thing with us... on pause until we get back to Portland."

"Yeah, that's probably for the best," Jasper said, subdued. He didn't look at Nico as he pulled out the CD folder from the center console and silently flipped through it.

They passed the final exit for the city of Vancouver before either one of them said anything again.

"Sleater-Kinney?" Jasper held up a CD he'd removed from one of the sleeves.

"Please," Nico said, as relieved as they could be under the circumstances.

Chapter Twenty-Two

Sound Man

The Subaru idled in front of a sign with the number of a towing company in large, bold print. As Jasper checked the address on his phone, a young Black man with several layers of braids haloing his head emerged from the condo to their right. When he spotted the car, his face broke into a dimpled smile, and he trotted toward them. Jasper got out and walked straight into a handshake that transformed into a one-armed hug.

"What's up, Jasper?" Eddie's voice cracked a little as he slapped Jasper's back.

"So good to finally meet you," Jasper said. "Sorry we didn't do this sooner."

"Same, man, and here we've got..." He leaned his head down to peer at Nico.

"Eddie, this is my... boss, Nico Juárez." Jasper tried not to show the anxiety on his face as his mind flipped through the catalog of things he might have told Eddie about them.

Nico hadn't asked how far the sharing had gone, and the truth was, Jasper couldn't quite remember.

Eddie leaned across the passenger seat to shake Nico's hand. Once he emerged, he gave Jasper a mischievous grin, wiggling his eyebrows.

"Let me help you get the stuff," Jasper sighed. He was hoping to get Eddie alone for a second to get that whole awkward conversation out of the way.

"Cool, cool," Eddie said. "Imani wants to meet you, so brace yourself."

Jasper followed Eddie inside to where a pile of black nylon bags—undoubtedly full of mics, cables, and other equipment—lay waiting. The walls were covered with framed concert posters, most of them signed with thick black marker. A glittering red electric guitar rested on a stand in the corner amidst a cream-colored living room set, furniture draped with handmade throw blankets.

"Is that him?" A woman's voice echoed from the back of the condo.

"That it is," Eddie called back.

A woman approached, wearing a red patterned sweater, jeans, and house slippers, her hair tied in a bun on top of her head. Technically, she only came up to Jasper's shoulder, but she vibrated with short-person energy. It was a vibe that Jasper had come to respect (and fear a little) over the years.

"So you're taking my husband out into the sticks? With all those hillbillies and right-wingers?"

Jasper wasn't sure if he was supposed to answer, but he gambled. "Uh…we probably won't be seeing a lot of hillbillies. Staying with the rich guy and all."

"Worse, then." Imani gave a skeptical hum. "Well, we're glad for the work. *However*"—she put heavy emphasis on the word—"if there is a hair out of place when you bring him back, they'll never find your body."

"Don't worry, we'll be safe," Jasper said, keenly aware of how high his voice had gotten. He hoped he was correct, but the truth was, he had no idea how weird Richard Glenn might be. If there had been some kind of unsolved crime in his past, he imagined someone would have told him about it by now.

"Alright, woman," Eddie said affectionately, "show him your sweet side now."

Imani rolled her eyes, leaning over to the side table to pick up a plastic bag stuffed to the gills with light brown cookies. "For the road," she said.

"There's a little rum in them, but Nico seems like they're a pretty safe driver," Eddie said.

"It's not *that* much rum," Imani insisted, giving Eddie's arm a playful smack with the back of her hand.

Perfect opening. "They're going to use 'he' on this trip, actually," Jasper said. "And at the moment we're not…you know…a couple."

"Aw, sorry, man. That sucks," Eddie said.

Imani bit her lip and looked sidelong at Eddie. "Now you've got me worried again," she said to Jasper. "If y'all don't think you can be yourselves…"

"It was their idea, and they're kind of a cautious person," Jasper rushed to say.

She looked at him dubiously, but after a short delay, she nodded. "Probably smart. Well, I've got to get to class, and you should be getting on the road," she sighed. "Come here." She pulled Eddie into a kiss, then murmured something in his ear. Jasper focused on the dried flowers sitting in a vase over the white-painted brick fireplace.

He nearly jumped when he felt himself being hugged. He was getting more hugs in quick succession today than he'd gotten in a very long time.

"Remember what I said." Imani's words were firm as she gave Jasper a parting pat on the back. She stepped away and held the door as the two of them gathered up the equipment.

The next three hours were relatively comfortable, even as the highway narrowed and became curvier and overshadowed with trees. For as anxious a person as Nico was, they weren't an anxious driver. Eddie was even more gregarious in person than he was over text. In spite of the fact that there wasn't *that* much rum in the cookies, Nico seemed more at ease than when it had been just them and Jasper. Jasper tried not to take it personally, or feel jealous.

"Wait, your wife is *Doctor* Imani Walker?" Nico said. Their voice had shot up several decibels louder than Jasper had ever heard it. "As in, *the* primary expert in Afropunk in the United States?"

Eddie grinned. "That's the one."

Nico shook their head. "My god. I suppose I should have come in to help with the equipment."

"With those stick arms?" Eddie said. Jasper's jaw clenched at the comment, which was very weird of him given Eddie was not a competitor for Nico's affection. "Nah, you're good being the driver. You can meet her when we're all done."

They listened to the CDs Eddie had brought at Jasper's suggestion. He and Nico chatted about bands Jasper had never heard of as they climbed higher into the mountains. Jasper couldn't help but imagine the opening scene from *The Shining*, the ill-fated family heading up a steep road to the remote, haunted hotel. The sky had started to darken when they finally arrived at a solid wooden gate held up by stacked timber walls. Nico took their phone out and drew up their notes app.

"Well, are we ready?" They finally turned to look straight at Jasper.

Jasper nodded gravely, and Nico punched in the gate code.

⁓ℓℓℓ⁓

The "cabin," as Richard Glenn had called it, could only be called a cabin in that it appeared to be built out of logs. The fact was, the place was a classic mansion with a rustic facade that likely made Glenn feel more like he belonged out in the woods. Nico lazily wondered what his net worth was. Probably they could get an answer down to the dime if they asked him, but it seemed like too much of a concession.

A small man in designer jeans and a flannel shirt answered the door—Glenn's personal assistant, Leonard. Behind him, the entryway had the look of the kind of lodge Nico had seen on television and in lifestyle magazines. It was full of glossy wood and natural-edged tables that made the whole place seem hewn from the inside of a gigantic old-growth tree.

Leonard looked first at Jasper.

"Nick Jarez?" He pronounced it like the name Jared, and Nico felt their back go up. Jasper looked at them sidelong, undoubtedly wondering if they'd correct his pronunciation *and* who he should be addressing. If they were going to make so many other concessions, they thought, they owed themself the right to their actual name.

"It's Nico Juárez, actually," they said coldly. Leonard's head snapped from Jasper to them, seeming to realize he'd miscalculated.

"Wah-rez, waaaah-rez," he said under his breath, as if committing a clue from a game of charades to memory. "And these two are..."

"My production crew, Jasper and Eddie," Nico said. They wondered if it was obvious how much adrenaline pumped through them already, both from having to deal with Leonard's ignorance, but also at the words "my production crew." It was almost like an unexpected promotion, one that they didn't truly deserve or really want.

"Nick! There you are! I was hoping you'd get here in time for supper." Nico suppressed a grimace as Richard Glenn sidled into the entryway. He was also wearing expensive jeans and a button-up shirt with an unsettling lack of shoes or socks. His body had the same rustic affectation as the design of his home; it was clear his tan came from a bottle, not from spending time on horseback.

"And who are your compadres here?" Glenn said, with an artificial drawl.

Nico was now certain they would die up here somehow, if not from murder, then from embarrassment.

Everyone was introduced, and Leonard tried to help them carry in the equipment (Eddie, understandably untrusting with the tools of his trade, roundly rebuffed him). They were instructed to place it in a separate room with two leather armchairs centered in front of a wide river rock fireplace. An elk's head was mounted over it, and a stretched animal hide, likely from a cow, sat at its base.

Eddie's gaze swept the room from its vaulted ceilings to its hardwood floor, fixing for a moment on the elk's head. He grumbled something to Jasper. From the little Nico knew about recording, they assumed it would be difficult to avoid echoes in a room like this. They'd see if they could conduct the interviews in a smaller room once they had their bearings.

For all Glenn seemed to be laissez-faire about animal death, dinner was vegetarian chili. They ate from heavy ceramic bowls as they surrounded another natural-wood table that must have cost more than Nico's master's degree.

"And how long have *you* worked in publishing...?" Glenn trailed off, squinting at Jasper and wiping his mouth with the backs of his knuckles, in spite of the perfectly good cloth napkin sitting beside him.

"Jasper. I-I'm pretty new to it, actually," he said, which Nico knew to be both the truth and an understatement. Nico was a terrible liar, so they looked down, trying their best to stay out of the conversation. They poked at one of the red kidney beans in their bowl. Was that normally an ingredient in chili?

"Ah yes, Jasper. Janet told me you were mainly a sound man," their host said.

Before they could stop it, Nico's head snapped up. "When did you speak with Janet about him?" Jasper froze with his spoon halfway to his mouth.

Glenn gave a disproportionately loud laugh. "Couldn't tell you the exact day, but in the last few weeks. Janet and I do talk, you know."

"But she's been—" Nico began, then stopped. The man seemed to gloat about the slightest advantage, and Nico didn't want to give him any more ammunition. "Well, she's correct. Jasper is an experienced, um, podcaster."

Oh, that was cruel of them. They looked over at Jasper and tried to telepathically apologize as Jasper glared back at them. Eddie was the only one who snickered into his bowl.

"You're in for a treat, Jasper. Nick here is familiar with my unified theory of the paranormal already, but I've become pretty damn good at spreading the word, even without all the wonders of new technology." Fortunately, Glenn didn't seem terribly interested in the sound of anyone's voice but his own. "Haven't listened to any podcasts myself, but I hear it's the best way to reach the new generation. Well, other than Click-Clock."

Eddie made another stifled sound beside them, disguising it with a cough.

"Whoa, whoa, whoa there, son. It's your first night here, don't make my insurance go up that quick," Glenn said with another booming laugh. Eddie's cough stopped as abruptly as it had appeared.

"So, um, you haven't listened to any podcasts?" Jasper said. "None at all?"

"Nope. I'll be coming to this fresh as a newly sprouted snowdrop," Glenn said.

Fantastic. They doubted Richard Glenn would be a very teachable person.

"I hadn't realized snowdrops were known for their freshness," Nico said dryly. They couldn't help themself.

"Ah well, Nick, sounds like you don't know much about the climate here in the Pacific Northwest," he said, apparently assuming Nico hadn't been born and raised in Oregon. With that, he launched into a description of all the different types of foliage on the property, which took up the entirety of the rest of dinner, and then some.

For several hours after dinner, they retired to what Glenn called "the study" (despite it being fully devoid of books). Eddie had hurried to take one of the armchairs, leaving Nico and Jasper to the remaining two-seater couch. One would think it would be a solace to sit next to Jasper through this ordeal. Instead, they spent the whole time wishing more than anything that he would wrap an arm around their shoulder, and they could relax against his side instead of trying to keep a strip of cushion between the two of them.

After an extensive, rambling monologue, Glenn yawned at last. "You'll each have your own room for now," he said. "That is, until our other guests get here."

For now? Nico's breath stopped, and they felt Jasper tense beside them. They caught Eddie giving Jasper a bright-eyed look, the corners of his mouth twitching.

Something told Nico that nothing, and nobody, was going to make this experience easy for them.

Chapter Twenty-Three

Bigfoot or a Bear

When Jasper opened his eyes, there was a man in his room. He bolted straight up in bed.

"Sorry, sorry, Richard sent me to wake you up," said the man. Leonard, Jasper remembered. His name was Leonard—the one who butchered Nico's name. "It's time for your morning walk."

Jasper didn't move, self-conscious about the amount of soft fabric between himself and this awkward stranger. He couldn't remember agreeing to a walk, but then again, he hadn't followed the conversation too closely last night. For one thing, it had been tedious, and for another, he'd been too focused on not making Nico uncomfortable with how close they were sitting.

"Sure, right," Jasper finally said. Leonard lingered in the doorway, looking as if he were ready to march Jasper downstairs himself. Call Jasper uptight, but he wasn't into the idea of the man seeing him in sweatpants. "Could you um, just, like, give me a minute?"

"Oh!" Leonard hopped as if he'd been startled out of a reverie. "Yes, of course." The words were barely out of his mouth before he was gone.

Downstairs, Nico and Eddie were standing in the foyer, both looking like they'd rather be anywhere else. Maybe he shouldn't have been surprised that Glenn hadn't bothered to come downstairs yet. It seemed to be a habit with Unified Theory people to demand everyone hurry up and wait for them. However, to his credit, there was an insulated mug full of coffee waiting for Jasper on a side table.

"Damn, you look like hell," Eddie said, both hands clasped around the cup, shoulders hunched as vapor wafted toward his face.

"Yeah, well, you don't look so hot yourself," Jasper said. He took a sip from his cup and almost dropped it as the liquid burned his tongue. "What are we even doing here?"

"You forgot? He asked us if we wanted to go for a walk and one of you cocksuckers said yes," Eddie said, then his bloodshot eyes opened wider as he realized what he'd said. "Aw shit, my bad."

Nico made a sound like a dog getting up from a nap. Jasper didn't have time to parse whether it was a snort of laughter or offense before there was a call from the staircase.

"Top of the morning to you all," Dick Glenn said in a horrible Irish accent. Was he supposed to be a cowboy or a leprechaun? Jasper supposed he was rich enough to play at both without anyone arguing. "Hope you're ready for the wonders of the natural world."

Nico grunted and Eddie said something in a voice too low to be understood. Glenn raised his eyebrows at Jasper, who felt a sudden rush of obligation to speak for the group.

"Great! Yeah, the early bird catches the worm and all that." Jasper masked his internal screaming with a self-emasculating giggle. Eddie wore a look Jasper recognized as amusement at his expense.

"Wagons ho!" Glenn said, striding through the open door.

There was much more land here than Jasper could believe belonged to a single person. The inside of the log cabin was much more house than he'd ever seen, too. He knew voicing anything like that would just make him seem like a bumpkin. There were plenty of reasons to look down on Jasper without him adding one more to the pile.

The three of them trudged across a field of long, wet grass behind Glenn, Nico closer to the front and Jasper and Eddie lagging behind them. Either it had rained overnight or the place was perpetually muddy. Mist hung over the tops of trees that stretched out as far as Jasper could see. They were similar to the ones back home; Jasper had learned the names of them in elementary school, but then he'd immediately forgotten.

"I'm sure you Oregonians recognize your old friend, the Douglas fir, over here," Glenn said, gesturing. "One of the most common coniferous trees, used heavily in the logging industry. It's also named for the man who discovered it in 1820, a Scotsman named David Douglas."

Nico scoffed. "Before the Scots arrived, the population of Douglas fir lurked in underground caverns, I'm guessing."

Eddie shot a wide-eyed look at Jasper in response to their snark. Glenn laughed the laugh of a man who knew he was being mocked but refused to give over any power.

"You know who the elusive resident of these woods actually is," he said. "Don't you, Nick?"

Anger flared in Jasper's stomach on Nico's behalf, but he kept quiet. They did too.

"What about you, Eddie? Who do you think might be hiding in the woods up here?"

Eddie shrugged. "Ted Bundy?"

Another laugh rang through the woods, and whatever was hiding in there must have known to retreat further into its lair. Jasper didn't really like how hard the guy who had them all at his mercy was laughing at the serial killer joke.

"You're over thirty years too late, but very funny," Glenn said. "I was referring, of course, to our friend the Sasquatch."

"Like, Bigfoot?" Eddie said. With an inward grimace, Jasper realized he hadn't told Eddie much about the actual content of this podcast. Then again, for all Eddie had listened to Jasper's sexy moans over the years, he figured this was a welcome break.

"Right you are," Glenn said, taking long steps up a rocky incline into a cluster of trees. "In fact, I believe we're scheduled to be discussing him today, right, Jasper?"

"Yup. Think so." He didn't have the schedule on him at the moment, but by now he had it (with all its many gaps) memorized. "With Morton Sanderson."

"Two last names, huh?" Eddie said out of the corner of his mouth. Jasper shot him a dirty look.

"Some call them skunk apes, but that's more of a category than a title. In different areas of the country, they have different names, but Bigfoot is definitely preferred up—"

Suddenly, Glenn froze, lifting up his hand like a crossing guard against a line of cars. Everyone else stopped, too, and Jasper's breath caught in his throat. There was a crackling in the brush nearby, and Jasper's first thought wasn't *Bigfoot*, it was *grizzly bear*.

Then, a tall, hairy-faced being crashed out of the brush from the side of the trail. The group descended into chaos as Jasper and Eddie crashed into each other. Eddie rushed down the path toward the house, yelling something that sounded like, "Fuck this, fuck this, fuck this!" Jasper grabbed for Nico's arm as they protested, and the travel mug flew from their hands.

Cutting through all of it was Richard Glenn's booming laugh.

"Boys, boys, please! You'll offend our guest," he called after them.

Jasper took a breath and a better look at what had come out of the bushes. Rather than a Bigfoot or a bear, it was a man with a long, unkempt beard and about two inches more height over Jasper. Dew clung to his facial hair and his bushy eyebrows. He looked like an Ent ready to march to Isengard.

There was a tug at Jasper's arm, and he realized he was still gripping Nico's elbow. He released them and fetched the discarded travel mug from where it had landed upside down in the bushes.

"This is Morty," Glenn said, gesturing toward the puzzled man. "Let's go inside. I think we could all use a fresh pot of coffee."

⸺⸺

Nico had convinced Glenn to relocate to a smaller room, which, to their chagrin, had ended up being the guest room where they were staying. A true professional, Eddie had set up the equipment so smoothly that it was almost like it had appeared on its own. He and Jasper were crammed into the corner, as Jasper looked down at his copy of the script.

Having heard Jasper's narration, Nico was stressed about how they would sound on the recording. In fact, when they looked at their own script, they noticed their hands were shaking.

"Nico." Jasper's gentle voice snapped them out of their trance, "You, um, may want to tie up your hair. It tends to brush against the mic if you leave it down."

Nico nearly dropped their stack of papers as they obeyed. The two larger men seemed to be ignoring them as Glenn carried on a one-sided conversation about his scant knowledge of podcasting. Morty the Bigfoot specialist gave Nico an unnerving stare, even as Glenn monologued.

"Oooh-kay," Eddie finally said, clapping his hands. Glenn's mouth slammed shut, and he looked at Eddie as if he'd just noticed he was there, despite the fact that the man had just been adjusting his microphone stand. "Are we ready to go, Nico?"

"Um, yes," they said. The "um" probably wasn't a great sign for the confidence of their narration, but they supposed there'd be a certain amount of on-the-job learning. It wasn't their favorite way to operate, for sure, but there didn't seem to be another option. They cleared their throat, and when Eddie gave them the signal, the interview began.

Four hours later, Nico was still on the bed, now with their arms wrapped around their shins and their head between their knees. Glenn and Morty had left for God knew where, slapping one another on the back over a job well done. In Nico's opinion, they hadn't earned the self-satisfaction. Of course, neither had they.

"You did fine," Jasper said. The bed sank slightly as he sat down next to them, and he rested a hand on their hunched back. They fought hard against the urge to put their head in his lap and cry.

"Yeah, man, er, buddy," Eddie said. "Not your fault those guys are crazy as hell."

If Nico's throat weren't raw with how much they'd spoken already, they'd have said something sarcastic. Maybe something about how Sanderson had gone on an entire rant about how Bigfoot was persecuted and hunted because humankind was "racist against tall people." Or maybe something about how Glenn talked over the end of each of their sentences, to the point that they'd likely have to re-record their entire half of the conversation.

"Jasper, you want to see if you can grab us some beers or something?" Eddie said.

The bed creaked as Jasper stood up again. "Yeah, sure." The door opened, then clicked shut again as Jasper went to find Leonard.

"I don't know if I can do this," Nico whined into their knees.

"Don't be a pussy." Eddie sounded bored, and the nonchalance was even more irritating than if his tone had been abusive.

Nico sat up with a surge of indignation, legs unfolding until their feet (nearly) touched the floor. "Excuse me? A *what*?"

"Heeey, there you are!" Eddie said with a triumphant grin. So, it had just been a ploy to uncurl them from their ball of misery. Ingenious, really, but still obnoxious.

"Asshole," Nico muttered, and Eddie chuckled at his own wit as he zipped up the small nylon bag holding one of the microphones. "Anyway, it doesn't make sense for me to be doing this if Jasper has so much more skill and experience."

This time, Eddie laughed outright, pausing his bag-zipping. "Skill and experience, huh? Have you actually heard his shit? I'm not saying it isn't good shit, but it doesn't exactly translate to this."

Nico bowed their head but didn't resume their pill bug posture. Their face heated and they made a useless attempt to clear their dry throat. "I, um, yeah," they said. "It is, er, it wouldn't."

"Oh my god," Eddie hooted. "You *loved* it, didn't you?"

"Shut up," Nico hissed. "That's inappropriate."

"Naaaah..." Eddie started to wind up one of the microphone cables. "Life's short and y'all are only human. Might as well have a little happiness. Plus I know for a *fact* that he's super into you."

Maybe Nico's skin would be too hot for the rest of their life. Maybe they'd forever raised their body temperature, and their dry mouth was a permanent casualty. Eddie rolled his eyes at the lack of response, and Nico stayed silent until Jasper had returned with several bottles of Heineken in a bucket of ice.

"Well, day one's a wrap, right?" Eddie said, holding up his beer.

"Yup, now to spend the rest of the day banging out these ridiculous scripts." Jasper raised his as well.

Nico clinked bottlenecks with the other two begrudgingly and ignored Eddie when he gave them a conspiratorial wink.

Chapter Twenty-Four

Won't That Be Fun

Richard Glenn seemed to have gotten bored with his podcast production crew, and Nico was in no way complaining. If the Bigfoot aficionado (who seemed to be very annoyed with Nico for being short) was more interesting to him, that was just that much more time they could focus on more important things. Those things mainly consisted of being finished with this entire nightmare of a project.

Dinner on the first night was the only time they'd eaten at the big, fancy table, and now they were relegated to a small breakfast nook off the kitchen. It sat bolted to the floor and set into wood-paneled walls like a booth at a country diner. Nico was crammed in beside Jasper, trying to enjoy his warmth and proximity without being too obvious about it. Their throat was still raw and tight from all the speaking they'd done the day before, and they hunched over the hot vapor rising from their cup of coffee in hopes it would soothe them back into working order.

"What's on the schedule for today?" Eddie said, pronouncing it "shed-ule" like a caricature of a posh British man. He took a sip from his coffee mug, pinkie up.

Not glancing up from his spreadsheet, Jasper let loose a yawn. Likely, he had as much difficulty sleeping as Nico had, given that an awkward man had burst into all of their rooms the previous morning to awaken them. It hadn't set a precedent for comfort and privacy, that was for sure.

"We're starting off with Boyd Bodean," Jasper said, scanning from one column of the spreadsheet to the next with his finger. "And he's here to talk about...frogmen, then we've got Mothman tomorrow, and then we've got dogmen on Saturday."

Hearing these things listed out always brought the silliness of the whole venture into stark focus. These were three creatures in a row that were just humanoid animals. It made a unified theory of the paranormal seem more like a unified theory of man's self-centeredness.

"Frogmen. Dogmen. All I'm seeing around here is *log* men, you know what I'm saying?" Eddie laughed. "Like with all the flannel?"

"Eddie, that sounds pretty gay," Jasper said without looking up from his clipboard.

"I don't know, I kinda got a vibe from the Bigfoot guy, didn't you? Wouldn't he be a bear or whatever you call it?"

Jasper's only answer was an exasperated sigh.

"I think he'd prefer Sasquatch to any other"—Nico cleared their scratchy throat—"moniker." They had never been a fan of the categories queer people were supposed to muscle themselves into to somehow make their sexuality valid. "You *did* write that script already, didn't you, Jasper?"

The words came out too clipped, too accusatory. A pang of guilt shot through them at the sight of Jasper's purpled lower lids, and the depth of the lines around his eyes. Eddie shot them a glare of disapproval, which they certainly deserved.

"Sorry, I wrote it on Monday, and I've done like six more of them since then," he sighed. "I've still got to schedule someone for the fae, aliens, and...shit, did we decide we're doing the Loch Ness monster, or...?"

"I think Skip Stewart was going to be our interviewee for anything having to do with water monsters. And he's apparently just going to show up when he shows up," they said. Jasper groaned, undoubtedly remembering the day Skip had invaded their office like a badly dressed pirate. "How has scheduling the rest of them been?"

"Fruitless? I tried to make some calls yesterday, but nobody would pick up for me."

It was logical that the authors wouldn't pick up the phone for an unfamiliar number. Frustrating, but logical. But the longer they held off scheduling the rest of the interviews, the longer they'd be stuck in this off-putting place, and the longer Nico would have to keep up the charade of being a man. The solution stood out in their mind like a bold line of text in a book Nico hated.

"I'll do it myself," they sighed, and Jasper's voice cracked in wordless protest. "I edited most of their books. They'll probably think I have news about their royalties or new editions."

"Tricky, tricky," Eddie said. "You could always do them back in Portland, or over video calls or something."

If Nico had any filters before, they were all gone. "Do you think I didn't think of that? Do you think I didn't do everything I could not to drag you two up here?" they snapped.

"Sorry, m—sorry," Eddie said, more quietly. Now Jasper was staring at them too, and his expression sent a syringeful of guilt into their veins.

"I'll take care of this myself, Jasper. You just focus on your writing." They stood, leaving their oatmeal barely a quarter eaten. They held out their hand for the clipboard. It was past 9 a.m. on a Friday morning; might as well get to it. Perhaps it meant the unpleasant task of making phone calls, but it would produce the welcome side effect of not having to look at anyone's face for a while.

~*~

Once Nico left the room, Jasper slumped over the space where the spreadsheet used to be. "They hate me," he whined. He'd long ago given up on having any sort of dignity in front of Eddie, particularly where vocalizations were concerned.

Eddie shrugged. "I was the one they got mad at just now, and they *definitely* don't hate you."

"You're just trying to make me feel better," Jasper said, purposefully breezing over the suggestive undertones in Eddie's voice.

"Jasper, when have I ever lied to make you feel better?"

He had a point—Eddie had only ever been honest with him about when he'd made a mistake, or when he could do better. There wasn't really any reason he should stop doing that when it came to Nico. Then again, he'd only just met Nico, and he was turning out to have an optimistic view of love in general. Another hopeless romantic. Who knew there were so many?

"How would you know if they like me or not?" Jasper allowed himself to say.

"Other than the way they cozy up to you like you've got magnets under your sweater?" Eddie scanned the room like he was looking for hidden cameras and leaned into the table as if to get closer to Jasper. "They basically admitted they listened to your stuff, and they obviously jerked off to it."

Coffee siphoned up Jasper's sinuses and he slapped a napkin over his face as it all came leaking back out. Eddie snorted, but at least he didn't make a mess. Bastard.

"First of all, I *know* they listened to it," Jasper said, once they'd recovered. "But did they tell you that they...?"

"They didn't have to." Eddie shrugged. At least that part was a relief.

It engaged me, Nico had said when Jasper had asked them about the recording. Of course, that had to have been what it meant. Jasper's sweater was suddenly much too warm.

"But I thought they were—but then again, we—" He cut himself off. It would be awful to out Nico as ace (especially since they seemed unsure), and it would also be rude to kiss and tell. But Jasper knew his face had betrayed him on that second point when Eddie's smile widened. So much for being discreet.

"You gave them the D already, didn't you?" he whispered in a way that carried far too well. "I knew you'd already been canoodling that first week, but you didn't tell me—"

"Shh! Why would I tell you? That's private!" Jasper hissed back. "*Canoodling.* Seriously?" Eddie laughed out loud, regarding Jasper's crankiness like he was a little boy who needed a nap or a juice box.

"So you *did*! Y'all are ridiculous. Just date already," Eddie said at full volume. "As far as I can see, this is a nonproblem."

"I could list several ways that it actually *is* a problem, not the least of which"—Jasper gestured around the room, stopping on a taxidermied lynx on a shelf above the window—"we don't exactly know if this guy is down with the LGBT, but we *do* know he has guns. Then there's the fact that we're all stuck here together, and if something goes wrong it's going to make this even more uncomfortable, and then there's the fact that they're still my *boss*, and—"

"Hey, I know you!" A cheerful masculine voice rang from behind him like a gunshot. Jasper leapt halfway out of the booth, and his head whipped toward the source of the voice. Skip Stewart stood in the doorway, a heavy black leather jacket layered over his pathetically thin Hawaiian shirt. "Good ol' Yes-per! Who's your friend?"

Jasper's eyes darted toward Eddie, whose face had gone cold as stone at the sight of the tacky stranger. "This is Eddie. He's doing sound production for us."

"Eddie, what's up, my man?" Skip stepped forward, holding out his hand for a fist bump. Jasper bit his lip in vicarious embarrassment. Giving Skip a slight nod, Eddie kept his hands folded on the table, and Skip withdrew, as if slowly moving backward could reverse his gaffe.

Dry coughing and angry footfalls sounded from the hallway, and Nico was talking before they were even in the room. "Well, they aren't picking up for me, either, so I'm not exactly sure how—" They stopped short at the sight of Skip, and the lines of frustration on their face deepened.

Skip turned away from Eddie and Jasper. "Nick! Great to see you," he said. Eddie scrunched up his face as if he had just got a whiff of a dead skunk, and Nico seemed to smell it too. Jasper was starting to wish he and Eddie weren't crammed into this booth as everyone was beginning to hover over them.

Before they could say anything, Richard Glenn and a short, stocky man entered the room as well—Boyd Bodean, Jasper assumed. The man was wearing exactly what Jasper imagined an expert in a random Midwestern monster would wear—a hospital-blue button-up, tucked into jeans faded to nearly the same shade, and (for some reason) a bolo tie.

Glenn looked about as surprised as everyone else to see Skip.

"Skip," Glenn said in a flatter tone than Jasper had heard him use before now. At least there was one thing that he had in common with this guy—neither of them was happy to see the slimy guy standing in the kitchen. "Didn't expect to see you yet."

"Well, I had some extra time and thought I'd head on up," he said in a chipper voice, completely oblivious to the fact that no other face in the room had a smile on it.

Can't show up early if you aren't even on the schedule in the first place, Jasper thought bitterly.

Glenn clucked his tongue a couple of times, then called out, "Len!" The name ripped through the air like a hatchet. Glenn already set Jasper on edge; this harshness made his mistrust even worse.

Leonard came scurrying into the room and started at the sight of Skip.

"So we have two more guests for the night?" His brows came together beneath his receding hairline as he literally wrung his hands. "I'm, um...I'm not sure we have the room."

"What a shame. I suppose...," Glenn began. With a jump in his chest, Jasper wondered if he might be kicking Skip out for the night. "I suppose someone will have to share a room."

"Why can't someone sleep on the sof—" The end of Nico's sentence was cut off by a coughing fit. Jasper knew they'd woken up with a sore throat from talking so much the day before, and he cringed with sympathy pain.

"Well, I suppose one could, but it does get awfully cold down here at night," Leonard said, still looking ready to flee into the woods. "Maybe two of the crew wouldn't mind sharing?"

"I'm good," Eddie said, face impassive. Only Jasper could see the self-satisfaction hidden behind his lopsided smile. "Nico, Jasper, you don't mind, right?"

Nico continued to cough, and Jasper stuttered, trying to regain his composure and not make himself completely obvious. "Well, as long as Nico doesn't mind sleeping next to a furnace," he said, tacking a nervous giggle to the end of his sentence.

"Great, then it's decided," Glenn said before Nico could calm his lungs enough to respond.

God, this wasn't good. Jasper didn't want to force Nico into anything they didn't want to do. He'd tell them he could take the couch when the time came. The idea of sharing a bed with Nico was so, so tempting, but the idea of doing it when Nico didn't want the same thing was too horrific to consider.

It was impossible to tell whether Nico was reacting to the idea of their being forced into bed with Jasper, or if they just weren't feeling well. He'd have to wait until later to find out. In the meantime, he'd sit with his discomfort like he was waiting to find out whether he'd flunked a final exam.

"Well, Nick, you get to do two interviews today. Won't that be fun?" Glenn said, clapping a hand onto Nico's shoulder. Nico gave Jasper a pained look, and Jasper could only pray that he wasn't just giving them one more thing to dread.

CHAPTER TWENTY-FIVE

JUST ABOUT EVERYTHING

The sun was still out, but it was cold enough that they were lighting a fire in the center of Richard Glenn's stone patio. Normally the combination of sunlight and crisp air would put Nico in higher spirits than this, but they were much too broken from the past six hours, which they'd spent recording two separate interviews. One was with Boyd, who couldn't seem to speak into the microphone, no matter how much he was coaxed. He had chosen instead to mumble into his own shoulder like a shy child. Eventually Eddie became too irritated to correct him, and Jasper had to take over.

Then there was Skip, who pontificated enough to rival even Richard Glenn. Glenn had treated him like a rival, too, to the point that Nico had wanted to just hand over the script to the two of them and make their escape. By the time they finished for the day, Nico wasn't sure they could manage to speak at all.

They would have to, though, because when they looked at their phone, there were four missed calls from Meera.

Possibly they should have felt a sense of foreboding, but instead they just looked forward to having a moment away from the crowd of men by the edge of the fire. Nico plodded all the way across the field to the edge of the forest and held their phone in the air, checking the screen. The signal showed one bar, occasionally flickering to two.

Might as well try.

"Meera? What's wrong?" they said when the call connected.

"Just about everything," she said with a laugh that made Nico feel like a ghostly hand gripped the back of their neck. "But currently we've lost track of a—" The call cut out for a second. "—and they're saying tha—and Bre—and the tracking codes are actually f—"

The line went silent for a moment, then three aggressive tones beeped in their ear as the call was dropped. They cursed under their breath and tried again. Nothing. After a few useless minutes, they put their phone in their pocket. They gazed ahead, down the overgrown path rising into coniferous trees and bright green underbrush. Part of them wanted to walk into it with no plan, and the other wondered whether Glenn had other friends lurking out there like the bizarre creatures that he was so hell-bent on honoring.

They turned around and headed back to the patio. When they finally got close enough to hear what was being said, they wished they'd walked in the other direction.

"What I didn't talk about was the inherent eroticism of the giant squid," Skip said. Christ. "I'm not sure folks are ready to talk about that. Not in America, at least." He said that last bit with the sniff of a man who considered himself cosmopolitan but who was terrified at the idea of thinking beyond his tiny corner of the world.

By now, Eddie was giving the fire a thousand-yard stare, and Jasper was looking nervously from speaker to speaker as if he would receive a quiz at the end of the night. They could only imagine what kind of offensive talk had been going on in the few minutes they'd been away from the group.

This was all Nico's fault. If only they'd had the courage to say no to all this, to insist on doing things in a more sensible way. Instead they'd denied any of it was happening until it was too late.

"Nicky! Come have a beer! One of the lead tenors at the Seattle opera once told me it's good for the voice," Glenn said. "Grab the man a beer, Boyd."

Even as they tamped down a flinch at being misgendered, Nico marveled at how quickly Boyd moved to obey him. They were noticing the strange influence Glenn had on the people around him; it was unsettling given how long-winded and boring he was. It was his money, though, wasn't it? It was always money.

The bottle was open and in their hand before they could protest.

"Actually, I need to take this inside. They're trying to get in touch with me back at the office, and I think there have been some issues with a shipment," Nico said. Every word was like sneakers squeaking on a gym floor. They had no idea how they were supposed to continue working tomorrow.

"Look at him. This is a man who is dedicated to his work," Glenn said. Nico wasn't sure whether he was being sincere or not, but that hardly mattered at the moment. What mattered was finding out what sort of disaster was going on back at Unified Theory.

They would have taken the steps two at a time, but they weren't a frogman, no matter how disappointing that might be to Boyd Bodean.

They woke up their laptop, which hummed with the same sort of exhaustion Nico felt themself. They were backing up everything on an external hard drive, but the machine had still been put through a lot of recording in the past couple of days. That, combined with the spotty Wi-Fi, meant logging into their email took a lot longer than usual.

Meera, bless her, had emailed them with an update that hardly surprised them—a shipment of books bound for a Sparkle Sanders event was missing and would very likely not make it. There was very little Nico could do about that. There were also orders that needed a signature from someone in a senior position, and Brent was (unsurprisingly) nowhere to be found. Ever proactive, Meera was valiantly setting up an e-signature system, but she needed approval for that as well.

It was strange she didn't have the power to do things herself, but that actually couldn't be blamed on Brent, Nico realized. Even before Brent had arrived, Unified Theory had been held together by metaphorical spit and duct tape. It was Janet who had failed to set them up to run smoothly without all the onus landing on one person. One person who was never where they were supposed to be.

Whereas for the last few weeks, Nico had only been concerned about their ability to do their job, now the scope of their despair widened. Evan was right. There was no way the business would survive at this rate. At the end of that spectacular failure, where would they all land?

Nico shut their laptop and curled into a fetal position on the bed.

Standing outside with the other men was excruciating. Jasper had never been good with the sort of good-old-boy banter. It was always just someone bringing up X name he didn't know and then talking about how they were doing Y thing he didn't care about; then X person (a man, always a man) was being held back from doing it "right" by Z person (usually a woman or a liberal). It was the same old thing, but referencing a bunch of rich guys and their investments. Maybe he should have listened; maybe it would have taught him something about the other authors he might meet, but he just couldn't bring himself to care.

What he cared about was the fact that, even after the sun sank behind the western treeline, Nico didn't come out of their room.

Both of their room, he reminded himself. Shit.

Jasper was about to go upstairs to try and get them to come down when he heard Glenn say, "Eddie, why don't you go see if Len needs help setting up for dinner?"

"Why me?" Eddie said, voice even flatter than it had been after the tenth time he'd told Boyd to speak into the microphone. His eyes had narrowed, and his fingertips splayed as he clenched the empty bottle tight in his hand.

"Oh, don't play the—" Skip started.

"I'll do it!" Jasper interrupted, and Eddie's eyes darted to him, not softening in the slightest. He realized that meant leaving Eddie alone with these guys, and that wasn't great either. "I-if anyone wants to come along or..."

Eddie didn't look at any of the men around the fire. He set his bottle down on the ground, as if daring any of them to tell him to throw it away, then followed Jasper into the house.

"I'm sorry...," Jasper whispered.

"Why are *you* sorry?" Eddie snapped back, without bothering to lower his voice. "I'm surprised they didn't do it sooner. I'm just going to go back to the room."

"I'll bring you something later?" Jasper offered.

"Whatever," he said. "Don't trust the food here anyway. Probably drug me and I'll wake up tied to a gurney or some shit."

"Not interested in Imani killing me, thanks," Jasper said. "I'll test everything first."

That brought the corners of Eddie's mouth up just a little bit, but only until they were in a straight line. He gave Jasper a nod as he veered up the stairs. The sound of the door slamming rattled the house a few seconds later, with only Jasper to hear it.

Dinner passed with a torturous conversation about how everyone was so sensitive these days, as they choked down mediocre beans and rice.

～ele～

When the door opened, Nico sat straight up on the bed. The room was pitch dark except for a spill of yellow light from the hallway, shadowed by Jasper's form. They had fallen asleep in front of their computer, which whirred in front of them. Stupid of them to let that happen. That was how fires started.

"Sorry," Jasper said softly. "Can I turn on the light?" He was wheeling his suitcase in behind him, and his hair was already wet, presumably from the shower, as they couldn't hear any patter of raindrops on the window.

Nico closed their eyes to prevent the unpleasant flash, rubbing them with the heels of their palms. "Go ahead. What time is it?"

"Like, ten thirty?" Jasper said. "Are you hungry? I could go get you something if you want."

The thought of food nauseated them right now. They shook their head. It was slowly dawning on them that they'd be spending the night with Jasper in a queen bed—just small enough that there might be accidental contact. To this point, they'd worked so hard to keep things profession-al and platonic. How were they going to survive this when they already felt so weak?

As if reading their mind, Jasper hesitated on the other side of the room. "I'm fine to sleep on the floor if you'd be more comfortable," he said.

Maybe it was a safer idea, and maybe it was what Nico should be offering to do. However, Nico's back would complain, and it was rather cold. The added discomfort would probably kill them tomorrow.

Plus they were both adults. They should be able to control themselves instead of acting like silly teenagers about all this.

"No, no it's fine. Just let me actually..." They trailed off as they crawled down from the rat's nest of blankets they'd made for themself during their fitful five-hour nap.

When they returned from the bathroom, Jasper was pressed nearly against the wall, leaving as much room for Nico as possible. Unfair indignance shot through Nico. Of course Jasper was just trying to be respectful, but their lizard brain was reading it as him being disgusted by them. They shook it off, got into bed, and switched off the light.

They lay in silence for a few minutes, and Nico was hyperaware of Jasper's breathing—very much not falling asleep. After sleeping the whole evening away, Nico was positive they'd have the same fate.

"Are you okay?" Jasper asked in a small voice.

Nico's harsh laugh was a shock even to them. "Are any of us?"

Jasper sighed, and he shifted onto his side, facing Nico. "If you want, I can do the interview tomorrow instead," he said. "I don't mind. If I have a script I won't, you know, trip over my words like I did."

It was a testament to how difficult they were that Jasper's self-deprecating offers to help only annoyed them. They didn't say anything in response, because anything they could have said would be too mean.

But Jasper didn't stop talking. "You've been doing really well, but you've been pushing yourself so hard," he continued, in that soft, sweet voice that enflamed and melted Nico from the inside out. "It's okay to ask for help. There's so much more I could be doing for—"

"Stop using that voice on me," Nico snapped.

This time he felt Jasper recoil. A toxic silence filled the room like sewage from a broken pipe.

"Nico, this is just how I talk. I'm not trying to...*trick* you or something," Jasper said, his hurt palpable. Nico wanted to disappear more than ever. "Do you want me to leave?"

"No, it's fine," Nico said, and they couldn't seem to silence their exasperation. "Just. Just stop."

There was a sigh and a rustling of fabric as Jasper turned over on his other side to face the wall.

"I don't seem to be very good at making you happy," he said.

Then he was silent, just like Nico had asked, for the rest of the night. Nico had never felt so miserable about being respected.

Chapter Twenty-Six

Kooks

Just like Jasper thought they would be, Nico was much too hoarse the next day to interview anyone. Every time they tried to speak, they would start coughing.

There was no satisfaction in watching Nico suffer, despite the fact that they had, once again, made him feel so small. Of course he knew it was because they were deeply uncomfortable and probably worried about whatever disasters were going on back at Unified Theory Press (not that they would tell him what those were).

It was clear from their face that they had slept just as badly as Jasper had as they silently tidied the room together and prepared it for the interview. They were doing their best not to make eye contact with him, and Jasper wondered whether that was due to shame or being unable to tolerate his presence. Happy to have a distraction from these lines of thought, Jasper dragged another upholstered chair out of Eddie's room as three pairs of footsteps plodded up the stairs.

A short Black man with a potbelly and white hair at his temples had joined them in the bedroom. His name was Dr. Alasdair Parks, and he was the only participant so far who was actually a scholar rather than a self-appointed monster expert. He had traveled all the way from Virginia for this interview. It was this final fact that convinced Nico to let Jasper record, rather than inconvenience Dr. Parks by making him wait another day. Jasper was fairly certain they wouldn't have done the same for Skip.

"Will we be needing to re-record the others?" Richard Glenn said. Eddie was tightening the microphone stand in front of him, not acknowledging how his elbow nearly caught him in the solar plexus. "Boyd went back to Ohio, and it might be hard to find Morty—he's already gone out into the woods again."

Jasper didn't want to ask where "the woods" were, afraid that it might mean he permanently camped out on Glenn's property. The idea of him lurking in the shadows every night was about as scary a scenario as an actual sasquatch being out there.

"No," Nico rasped, not wasting a painful word. "We'll record a new intro in Portland."

"Alright," Jasper said. His eyes tracked Eddie as he sat back at the laptop and cracked his neck. "Are we ready to go, then?"

"Yes, sir," Glenn said with a little too much emphasis. Eddie kept his eyes on the computer as he nodded in Jasper's direction.

Jasper cleared his throat, then waited a second before launching into the introduction he'd written. The story of Mothman had always given him the creeps (no self-respecting horror writer would not have at least read the Wikipedia page for it, if not watched *The Mothman Prophecies*). He was actually hopeful that this would be a bright spot in this miserable project. After last night, he could really use the boost.

Parks ended up being well versed in the folklore of Mothman, the history of Point Pleasant, and even the biology and habits of sand cranes and herons, which were often mistaken for the Mothman. The subject was studied much more extensively than frogmen, so it made sense that a Mothman scholar would need to work extra hard to set himself apart from other people claiming to be experts. The hour-and-a-half-long interview flew by, and when he caught Nico's eye at one point, they seemed to be fascinated by the conversation.

At least Jasper was doing something right.

"Have there been Mothman sightings outside of West Virginia?" he prompted. Parks's face lit up like a child who'd been asked to talk about his favorite dinosaur.

"That's been the subject of our most recent studies, actually," he said. "Other survivors of disasters have reported seeing creatures with large wingspans and glowing eyes. We've been lucky enough to get interdisciplinary funding between the social and hard sciences to get environmental samples to see if there are notable similarities."

There was something very different about speaking with Dr. Parks, something that made Jasper want to go off-book. Given his normal shyness, he knew he had to gather his courage and speak clearly. He looked up at Eddie and held up a finger.

"What—" Glenn started.

"*Shh*," Eddie hissed at him. Glenn's jolly mask slipped to reveal a sullen scowl.

Jasper waited another moment to put his thoughts in order, then said, "Dr. Parks, many of our other subjects relate the cryptids they study to the spiritual realm, which connects to the unified theory of the paranormal. Have you spent time viewing your research through that lens? And if so, could you share your thoughts in that vein?"

Out of the corner of his eye, he caught Nico leaning toward them both, hand cupping their chin as if riveted. For his part, Dr. Parks's gaze hung on the microphone in front of him. In the time it would take for lightning to strike, he glanced over at Glenn, then back again. Finally, he leaned forward to speak.

"That is outside my area of expertise," he said, slowly and diplomatically. "I'll let Richard expound on the more metaphysical aspects of the Mothman."

Glenn did exactly that, adding his bluster to an otherwise fantastic interview.

Fantastic interview or not, the tiny room was stuffy as ever when they finished. Dr. Parks was already halfway to the door after Eddie stopped recording. Sweat spots bled through the back of his purple-and-white checkered dress shirt.

"Well, we have almost an entire beautiful Saturday afternoon, so let's enjoy it," Glenn said, gloating as if he'd caused the good weather himself. "Al, will you be joining us for the evening?"

"I'm afraid I have some business back in Seattle tonight," Al said, voice dropping a few degrees in temperature from when he'd been speaking with Jasper. He seemed to like being called Al about as much as Nico enjoyed being called Nicky.

"Well, that's a real shame," Glenn said. The words sounded especially insincere, and Jasper wondered if he was jealous that Dr. Parks actually knew what he was talking about.

"In that case, I suppose you get your room back tonight, Jasper," Glenn said on his way out the door.

An embarrassing blush crept onto Jasper's already overheated face. It was probably for the best after all the awkwardness of the previous night, but part of Jasper still wished he'd get the chance for a do-over. As it was, he doubted he'd ever get a chance to share a bed with Nico again, even when they got back to Portland.

Fortunately, nobody looked at him as he had these thoughts. Parks was gone in the blink of an eye, Nico rushing after him and leaving Jasper and Eddie to clean up the equipment.

"Dr. Parks," Nico croaked, half thinking that there was no way the man would hear them. Thankfully, he turned around at the bottom of the stairs. "Could I have a word?"

The man nodded, face impassive, as if he wasn't surprised that Nico had wanted to speak with him. "Let's go outside," he said. Nico followed as he continued his path out the door. Parks's dress shoes crunched through the gravel as they walked toward a black SUV.

Nico barely knew where to begin. None of this added up. Not only had Dr. Parks's interview been full of well-researched academic material, but he was the only one of their subjects who wasn't already a Unified Theory author. This unknown man with an actual pedigree had flown all the way across the country to spend two hours at Richard Glenn's cabin. And it was clear he held quite a bit of animosity for him.

"Why are you here?" was where Nico finally landed. "You seem to actually know what you're talking about, and you haven't added any unnecessary spiritual spin to it."

Parks took his eyes off Nico's face and scanned the eaves of the cabin behind Nico.

"If you're still recording, you have to tell me," he finally said.

"No! Of course no—" They fell into another fit of painful coughing. "Sorry...laryngitis."

"Alright." Parks politely waited for Nico to stop coughing, eyes still flicking back between them and the front door of the house. "The truth is, this is the only way I could get my research out under my own name."

"What do you mean?"

"I mean someone leaked my research to Glenn, and he told me he'd publish it in his book whether I liked it or not. This is the only way I can lay any claim—if I associate with all these...hm"—Parks screwed up his face—"kooks seems like the right word."

It really did. Nico nodded, a knot of anger forming at the base of their windpipe in addition to the scratchy pain in their throat. It was one thing to disrespect everyone else's time and be a generally off-putting, self-centered person. Stealing a scholar's life's work, however, was a bridge too far for Nico.

Their mind began to race, trying to think of ways that they might help undermine Glenn, no matter what it might do to their standing at the company. And why not? There soon might not even be a company at all.

They dug in their pocket and drew out a pen.

"Do you have a piece of paper?"

Parks dug through the bag slung over his shoulder, then stopped and smirked. He pulled out a copy of *The Unified Theory* and ripped out one of the endpapers, handing it to Nico. The coughing fit that came when Nico laughed was worth it. They scribbled their name and phone number onto the paper and handed it back to the doctor.

"I'm Nico Juárez," they said, then cleared their throat again. "They/them."

"Good to meet you, Nico," Doctor Parks said cautiously.

"The only way this episode will air is with the help of myself and Jasper," they said. "I may not have the same pull as Richard Glenn, but I do have a network who can help you get this published on your own terms, even if it's not in a peer-reviewed form just yet."

Their blood was cold in their veins, with adrenaline rather than dread, as Dr. Parks looked at them quizzically.

"Forgive my bluntness, but why should I believe you?"

Alright, they were at the edge of the diving board. It was time to jump. "Full transparency, for reasons I won't get into, I am not confident this project will see publication. I am also a significant barrier to its completion, and so is Jasper, who is...loyal to me."

(They'd never thought to voice it that way, but it was the truth. They realized they were taking that very much for granted right now.)

"Anyway, there are measures you can take—social media, newsletters, etc.—and I'm happy to help you find them," Nico finished.

Dr. Parks took his eyes off the house to carefully examine Nico's face. Then he slowly nodded and held out his hand. "I will very likely take you up on that, Mx. Juárez," he said, and a mixture of professional satisfaction and gender euphoria fluttered inside Nico. "Now I'd like to be back in the city before it gets dark. Good luck with your situation here. I'll be in touch."

Nico watched him get into his car and disappear down the driveway and out the gate, as they trembled with nervous excitement. Ideas swirled in their head; instead of facing down a dead end, they felt like there was an alternate path coming into focus. As if on cue, they heard footsteps in the gravel behind them and Jasper appeared at their side.

"Jasper," they said, turning toward him before he could even greet them. Their hand closed around his upper arm like a cuff, and Jasper gave a quiet gasp. "Jasper, we need to talk. About...well, about a lot."

They coughed, this time only once, and then the words came faster.

"First, I am sorry I was short with you. You did wonderfully today. And you do make me happy. You make me *very happy*. And I—well, we should still talk more about that. Also, I have some really important things to tell you about Unified Theory, and then the conversation I just had. But we can't do it here or someone might hear us—is that alright?"

Jasper's mouth fell open, and that adorable blush burned in his cheeks. "Ah...okay. Yeah. Fuck. Okay, um. Sorry." He laughed nervously, and Nico's cheeks hurt with how much they were smiling. They were about to lead him away toward the nearby field, when his flustered expression transformed to concern. "Except, maybe we should see who this is first?"

There was a familiar white sedan pulling up in front of the house, and it was Nico's turn to be shocked. A woman with a blunt ice-white bob stepped out and slammed the driver's door behind her. She nodded at both of them in turn. Nico felt adrenaline on top of adrenaline pooling in their system.

"Hello, Nico," Janet said.

CHAPTER TWENTY-SEVEN

RIGHT OF FIRST REFUSAL

They felt like they should have been excited to see Janet again, but none of the feelings swirling inside them were happiness. Questions fueled by spite and betrayal struggled for dominance in their head, but no single thought was well formed enough to come out on top. The pained smile on Janet's thin lips implied to them that she knew exactly what they were feeling. They almost resented her for it.

"Janet, Janet, Janet, looking more beautiful every day!" Richard's voice shocked Nico out of their rumination. He passed by Jasper and Nico as if they weren't there, even as Janet held Nico's eye contact. "We'll get you settled, then you can join us on the patio for a drink. Len!"

Leonard scampered outside to retrieve Janet's suitcase as she followed Glenn inside.

For a moment, Jasper and Nico stood in silence, staring at the front door.

"What the fuck is going on?" Nico rasped, and Jasper let out a spasm of laughter that ended as soon as it began.

"It has to be some sort of conspiracy, right? We've been surrounded by them all week—one of them was bound to be real," Jasper said, earning an eye roll. He laughed again, and there was that warm feeling inside Nico all over again. For a moment, they allowed their eyes to linger on his smile, and they hoped that it would still be there when they talked later. With any luck, they'd be allowed to touch those lips again.

The moment must have lasted longer than Nico thought, because Leonard called out to them from the doorway.

"Nico, Janet and Richard would like you to join them out on the patio," he said, then quickly disappeared. In spite of themself, they thrilled at the sound of their actual name being used for once.

They turned to Jasper and jerked their head toward the house. "Come on," they said.

"But she just asked for—"

"Whatever she wants to say concerns you as well," they said. Without another word of argument, Jasper followed them through the house to the back patio.

The firepit was filled with the ashes of the night before—it was still too early and too bright for that. Janet was reclining in an Adirondack chair, shoes discarded, a clear drink with a lime and a glass straw in her hand. It was the most relaxed Nico had ever seen her, and it was also unnerving. Glenn lounged in the seat next to her, also startlingly barefoot. The two of them seemed to be holding court, unconcerned what the plebs (Nico and Jasper) thought of the sight.

What had happened to her?

They sat on a chair that didn't recline. That was the last thing they wanted to do right now. Even though they had so many questions, it didn't feel right to speak first, so they waited, stock-still, for someone to start explaining.

Surprisingly, it was Jasper who broke the silence.

"It's good to see you again, Janet," he said graciously. "I never really got to thank you for giving me the job."

"From what I hear, you've been a godsend," she replied. "Although that might be arrogant of me to say, given that I'm the god in that scenario." Glenn laughed loudly at that, in a way that could be considered sycophantic. It should have been much more satisfying to see him in that position, but it wasn't.

"So you knew we'd be focusing on audio," Nico said flatly.

Janet grunted in affirmation.

"And you didn't bother to tell me, why?"

This time she sighed, as if she weren't answering this question for the first time. "You're very intelligent, Nico, and I sent you help. I assumed you would be adaptable, even if you had your doubts."

"Wouldn't it have been better to tell me your plans earlier? I could have helped with the planning process. This whole thing could have been much more organized," Nico said.

"Frankly, it wasn't my idea, and I was not interested in leading a project I knew nothing about," she said, an impatient edge to her voice. Janet had always tolerated their anxiety and fielded their concerns. Now they felt that she'd been placating them, like they were nothing but a fussy child to her.

"Then who—"

"Mom?"

As one, everyone turned toward where Brent was framed between the open French doors. Well, that answered the question of where he'd gone. Brent crossed to where Janet and Glenn sat and stood over them, an unseasonably heavy jacket zipped up under his chin. It was puzzling after all the weather-defying tunics he'd been wearing over the past several weeks.

"Take off that ridiculous thing," Janet said.

"But it's cold," he whined.

Janet rolled her eyes. "I'm sure you can guess whose idea the audio project was," she said, head rolling toward where Nico sat.

Over the top of her head, Nico spotted Eddie in the doorway. He had one eyebrow raised, and he made eye contact with Nico as if to ask if it was safe to come out. Nico nodded subtly, and he took a seat on the patio, stuck with the wooden chair that directly faced the sun.

"I'm sorry, and you are?" Janet said to him.

"Eddie—sound production," he said, squinting, a sheen of sweat on his forehead. Nico wondered if they had come off as this imperious when they'd first met Jasper. If so, they had even more work to do on themself than they'd thought. This was not the person they wanted to be.

Janet nodded, her very low-level curiosity satisfied. Her focus returned to her son. "And why are you here, Brent? Finally conceding?"

Conceding?

It hit Nico suddenly that this business may have just been a game to her. The thing they'd built their life around, taken so seriously, was something she'd just handed over to her mess of a son to prove a point. She'd just wanted to see what would happen.

The last drops of their loyalty dried up in the sunlight.

⁓ ele ⁓

"I *hate* it here," Brent said, as if that weren't clear by every action he'd ever taken. "It's cold and boring and...it's so dark and *wet* all the time."

"This was the sunniest spring in years, man." Eddie laughed. He knew exactly who Brent was from Jasper's stories, and Jasper really hoped he didn't go too overboard on the ribbing.

Brent whimpered. Jasper wouldn't have been that surprised if he'd started crying, as he dragged his hands over his face, lips going slack.

"So you're turning down your right of first refusal?" Janet said. Eyes screwed shut, as if he couldn't witness himself admitting failure, Brent nodded. "Then you're handing it back to me."

"Ah, ah, ah"—Glenn interjected—"to *me*."

Nico sucked in a breath, not even bothering to hide their shock. Jasper couldn't blame them; his own heart, which had been in overdrive since Nico's barrage of compliments earlier, pounded against the inside of his rib cage. He held his breath, waiting for an explanation. He couldn't help feeling like he'd been a pawn in this three-person battle of wills. It almost made him feel guilty.

Almost.

"Well, this is what I expected. Sorry, son, but you're just not cut out for this sort of thing," Janet said. She uncrossed her ankles from where they were propped up, standing up and taking her phone out of her pocket. "My lawyer has already drawn up the contract."

"And mine has reviewed it," Glenn added.

"So it's fortunate you're here, Brent. I can have him come out, and we can get this handled tonight," she said. She looked down and tapped at her phone screen.

"Hold on," Nico said, also pushing to their feet. "What about us? What's happening?"

Janet hummed absently, looking toward Glenn. His face was inscrutable to Jasper, eyes obscured by designer sunglasses. Apparently Janet knew exactly what the twist of his mouth communicated. He wondered how long they'd had this planned, how long they'd been prepared to rain this shitshow on the unsuspecting employees of Unified Theory.

"Glenn has plans to pivot from a publishing company and make Unified Theory his personal brand. That may involve audio projects such as this, but..." She gestured to him, as if expecting him to catch her line of thought.

"You're welcome to stay. It would be useful to have all those interviews ready to go," he said. "But we'll have to renegotiate your payments."

"Excuse me?" Eddie said.

"That won't be necessary," Nico said, shoulders thrown back, the wreckage of their voice as stern as it could be. "Consider this my resignation. I'll submit a letter on Monday to that effect."

"I will too," Jasper said before bothering to think it through. Nervous bile welled up in his throat, but he knew he couldn't work for this man—not for another second. He glanced at Eddie, whose expression ping-ponged between amused and horrified.

There was no change in Janet or Glenn's body language, and Brent was obviously too in his own head to notice what was happening. Maybe they had predicted this but had expected Brent to last longer in his position. Jasper was sure even he would have been able to keep things going for longer. (He was an entrepreneur, after all, according to Nico.)

"Your twentieth-anniversary edition likely won't be ready in time," Nico warned, a tinge of sarcasm, of sorry-not-sorry, in their voice.

Glenn shrugged, a cloying grin spreading across his face. "They're doing amazing things in self-publishing these days."

Eddie stood. "So are we getting the hell out of here?"

Nico and Jasper exchanged glances, then Jasper said, "Yup. Time to go home."

He couldn't remember the last time he'd felt such pure relief.

~eee~

"Holy hell, what was that?" Eddie said once they were down the mountain. His voice had climbed an octave, and Nico couldn't blame him. They were still in shock from everything that had just happened. It had been the most bizarre ten minutes after the most bizarre three days of their life, and they didn't think they could have survived another second of it.

"I really don't know." The words came out as a squeak, as not even the nonstop action of the past few hours had healed Nico's laryngitis.

"Um...we're unemployed?" Jasper said.

Perhaps nervousness was filling the vacuum that Jasper's anger and confusion had left behind. That same mood was likely hovering on the horizon, waiting to wash over Nico as well. For now, they were too high on their own display of personal agency and the prospect of being freer than they'd been since they could remember.

Eddie blew out a breath like a deflating balloon, as if he were blowing away Jasper's silly concerns. He turned around and smacked Jasper on the knee.

"You can just walk right into your sexy-voice business. Get that bag, son!" he said. Then his energy and pitch dropped. "Do it soon, too, because I'm going to need some cash—that guy is definitely not going to pay me, and I can't afford to sue him."

"I may be able to arrange back payment with Meera," Nico said. It would be unconscionable of them not to warn her (and Jack too) about what was about to happen. If she found out about it from Richard Glenn himself, she would have every right to hate them forever, as far as Nico was concerned. "Jasper, can you call the office? I think we're back in cell phone range."

The next few hours to Olympia passed in a slow comedown from the high of the afternoon. By the time they dropped off Eddie (whose payment was officially on its way into his bank account), they were as jittery as if they'd had four espressos at the end of an all-nighter. Back behind the wheel, they checked their maps app and groaned.

"You okay?" Jasper said softly.

It was already 9 p.m., and it was only two more hours back to Jasper's house, but by now it seemed like too much.

"I'm just...," they said. "I'm so done. I'm hungry and exhausted and...well, you can hear how my voice sounds still."

"Hm," Jasper said thoughtfully, and there was another thing Nico loved about him. "I'm not suggesting anything...you know, creepy, but, do you think we could expense a hotel to the company? Just for the night?"

Too worn down to feel self-conscious, Nico's laugh stuck in their throat. They wanted nothing more than to get something to eat, take a shower, and get a good night's sleep. Having Jasper there for all of it would make it twice as wonderful.

"We can try," they said, rerouting them to a new destination.

CHAPTER TWENTY-EIGHT

ON MY SIDE

This was it. They were free. Both of them were free.

If you had told Nico two months ago that they would quit their job so abruptly, they would have panicked. They would have looked at the situation as if it were a doomsday clock, counting down to when their career went nuclear. Instead, they had never been so excited about the future. Scared, sure, but so looking forward to whatever came next.

And it was starting to seem much more possible that whatever came next would somehow involve Jasper. They could still hardly believe it, but denying it seemed like an even greater act of self-sabotage than, say, quitting their job with no backup plan.

At the moment, the two of them were perched on a king-sized bed in a Hampton Inn, finishing up the dregs of Chinese takeout with their last remaining stores of energy.

"Are you going to concentrate on your recordings again, then?" Nico asked, shoving the empty dinner container into a paper bag.

Jasper followed suit. "Probably," he said. He sat back against the head of the bed and looked thoughtfully up at the cottage cheese ceiling. "I've got a bit saved up, so I may stay in low power mode to build up that audio drama. Seems like a good opportunity for that. What about you?"

The childish part of Nico wanted to immediately know how they figured into Jasper's equation. They were afraid to be forgotten, left to the lonely life that they were sure to face without having an office to go to every day. Maybe they shouldn't have been so desperate for Jasper to save them from that, but they were.

"Well, I may or may not get that call from Dr. Parks. There are going to be some orphaned authors who will need some help if Dick shutters the place, too," Nico said.

Jasper stifled a giggle and shook his head. "Dick, huh?"

"I think I have the right to call him that now." Nico smiled, fluffing up at their own transgressiveness like a showboating game bird.

The look Jasper gave Nico was curious, and Nico wondered what he was thinking in the ensuing silence.

"You know," he finally said, "I could use a little help myself."

"You can't be serious. After what the last two days did to my voice?" Their throat still ached, but the high, choked pitch had dropped into something huskier over the last hour or so.

"It sounds kind of sexy now, though!" Jasper said. Heat rushed to Nico's face, which they tried to ignore. "Really, you're a natural. You just need practice, and, you know, not to be surrounded by a bunch of assholes. Other than me, of course."

"You can't possibly think you're an asshole. You're talking to *me*, after all," Nico said.

"I won't argue with you there," Jasper said, chuckling and shifting onto his side so he was facing them.

It was comforting that Jasper didn't try to contradict them. If there was one thing that their relationship had proven so far, it was that Nico had a lot of improvements to make when it came to their temperament.

"And yet, you bafflingly seem to want me involved." Nico hoped their fear wasn't too transparent. Part of them thought Jasper might be putting them on, but there was no irony in Jasper's face, only crushing sincerity. It turned Nico's insides to jelly.

"Of course I do. I know it hasn't been very long, but I..." He stopped talking and took a steadying breath. "I think that we make a really good team, and I don't want to lose that. Even if it's just a professional thing."

Uncertainty dripped from every word, and that just wasn't acceptable. Nico reached across the bedcovers to place their hand on Jasper's.

"I've never been as happy as I am when I know you're on my side," Nico said, "professionally or otherwise."

Jasper's brow wrinkled, and he didn't reply. It was only fair that Nico be the one to bring the elephant in the room into focus. After all, they were the one who had said they should put their relationship on pause.

"To be clear," they said, "I'm still very interested in the 'otherwise' bit. If you want to after all...that."

Forehead softening, Jasper flipped his palm to intertwine their fingers. Nico moved closer, then closer still, until they finally climbed into his lap. They always seemed drawn to him like velcro; it had been that way since the beginning.

"I was hoping you'd say that," Jasper said, with a touch of that sweet giggle that Nico couldn't believe they used to dislike. He laid his cheek against the top of their head. The weight of it made Nico feel deliciously grounded. Their eyes fell shut as they breathed him in and let themself doze off. A half-formed dream of this lasting, really lasting, imprinted itself on the backs of their eyelids.

"You know what's pretty great?" Jasper's voice jerked them out of their reverie. "You're not my boss anymore."

"Thank god for that," they sighed, and the lazy ease was replaced by a tightness in their chest. "I should say something."

"Hm?" Jasper murmured. Fingers tangled in Nico's hair, and they tried not to whimper at the gentle tug against their scalp.

Instead, they pulled back and forced themself to look Jasper in his striking blue eyes. "I want to try to be better for you," they said, "but I'm afraid you'll need to be patient with me...I can't stop being difficult overnight."

It was a hard thing to admit, even to themself. By now, after everything, they knew it to be true. There was no way that there weren't more disagreements waiting for them down the road, especially if both their lives were going to weave together in so many ways. Nico had spent years keeping mostly to themself; walking into a relationship like this was like walking into a dark hallway—it left them groping for a light switch that might or might not be within reach.

"That's alright. You're worth it," Jasper said.

There was no better word for it—Nico swooned, and they registered the fond exhale next to their ear as Jasper pulled them closer. Eyes falling shut, they cupped his face and drew him into a kiss. It was gentle and slow, and Jasper hummed with contentment. The ache in Nico's chest felt like it wasn't just theirs anymore. Now it was like a hearth, warming the two of them together.

⁓ele⁓

The two of them had fallen asleep with Jasper curled around Nico's back like a parenthesis. As light from the cloudy day crept into the room, Jasper blinked awake and forgot for a moment where he was. Except this morning, instead of waking up in an unfamiliar bed alone, he was waking up in an unfamiliar bed with a face full of dark hair. For some reason, even after everything that had happened, it felt like he was in the right place.

He breathed in, letting his eyes fall closed again as he savored Nico's scent. Then, of course, he noticed that there was one extremely familiar thing happening this morning. Whoops.

"Something you want, Jasper?" Nico said, sleepy-voiced.

"Sorry." Shuffling his embarrassing erection away from Nico, Jasper swallowed his shame.

With a chuckle, Nico wiggled one of their arms out from Jasper's hold and brought it up to rake through his curls. They guided his face toward them, turning partway around to receive his kiss while still pressing back against him. They hummed, fingers tightening in his hair until they drew a shaky gasp.

"You know," they said, "if you want to use me to get off, you're welcome to."

"Jesus, Nico." Jasper laughed at the audacity, especially in comparison to the swiftly returning waver in his own voice. "What does that even mean?"

Nico hummed thoughtfully. "I think it's called inter-crural?"

Jasper barely suppressed a squeak. "Are you sure?" He had been wondering how Nico was being so smooth about this, but now he felt them tense in his arms.

"Did I misread? If you aren't interested, then we—"

"Nope! Definitely interested. I'll um...hold on." He re-leased Nico and scrabbled ungracefully out of bed.

He returned from the bathroom with the tiny bottle of complimentary moisturizer and a towel, having checked the latch on the door, and pulled back the top sheet to get back in bed. A burst of nervous laughter devolved into a coughing fit as if he'd opened an attic door that had been locked for years.

"Are you okay?" Nico's fully nude body was cast in the cold light of a foggy day. The sight completely blindsided Jasper. Elegant was the first word that sprang to mind, their body a seamless blend of artful lines and angles.

"Fine"—Jasper coughed again and cleared his throat—"totally fine. So I'll just..."

For some reason, he'd forgotten about this part—the no clothes thing. And sure, there had been some making out, and some groping, and a blowjob, but there had also always been clothes. Now he supposed *he* would have to take his clothes off too. He didn't have a great relationship with his body, and he was struck with the horrifying idea that it would be a deal breaker.

"Did I...is something wrong?" There was insecurity in Nico's voice, and that wasn't okay. Jasper was the only one who was allowed to be insecure.

"I'm, um...I'm just worried you'll be disappointed when you see me," he admitted, because he couldn't stand the idea of Nico feeling as self-conscious as he felt right now. His eyes dropped down to the mattress in front of him.

A rustling sound, and Nico kneeled on the bed in front of him. Their hands eased under the hem of his shirt, moving up his sides.

"I very much doubt that will be an issue." A smile shaped every word as they helped Jasper undress, administering gentle kisses down his sternum and the top of his belly. It was so tender, Jasper thought he might shatter before he could even get his hands on them.

Jasper picked up the lotion, squeezed some into his palm, then looked down and noticed Nico's still-soft penis. "Um...are you not..."

Nico's expression was suddenly much less confident. "Right, well. That may not change for me. It's nothing personal, it's just...I still want this, but..."

Jasper wasn't sure what to think, but he believed Nico. They knew their own body better than he did, and this was their idea. He would just make sure he kept getting permission for everything and try not to be weird about it.

"You don't have to explain," he said. "Just let me know if I do something you don't like."

Soon, they had arranged themselves under the covers, much like they were before, with a few strategic changes in angle. As Jasper pulled them to their chest, they released a long, relieved breath, as if Jasper's skin were a salve.

Heart pounding, Jasper slid his cock between Nico's legs. The way they relaxed even further into his embrace at the contact burned off the anxiety Jasper felt when he saw their lack of arousal. They seemed pretty happy to be there, grasping his forearm as he began to rock against them.

"You doing alright?" Jasper murmured through his haze of pleasure.

Nico made a weak, needy sound. "Would you talk to me? Just a little?"

They hadn't really addressed that whole thing yet. Jasper was trying to be respectful, and he had been very nervous to bring it up when they were in that period of limbo. In this position, with the way he was pressing into them, he was a lot less tentative.

"You said you enjoyed the episode you listened to. Care to elaborate?"

For the first time since they'd woken up this morning, Nico was the one who was flustered. They whimpered, turning their face to bury it in the pillow. A wicked smile tugged at the corners of Jasper's mouth.

"Nico," he said in a singsong. "Did you touch yourself to my voice?"

A mortified groan, then, "More or less."

It was much easier to laugh this time, and Jasper hoped it sounded the way it was intended to be—affectionate and encouraging. "Think you might do it again?"

"M-maybe," Nico said cautiously. "If I don't, would that bother you?"

"No, sweet thing." Jasper bent down to kiss the top of their head. "As long as you're comfortable and getting what you need."

There was a contented sigh from the person in his arms. Jasper wondered what they could have possibly been through to make them react this way, whether they'd simply kept away from dating and sex, or if they'd felt like a disappointment in their past relationships. He didn't really want to think about worse scenarios, especially as he pushed slowly into the tight space between their thighs.

"So," he said, forcing his voice to be steady, the way he was used to speaking when he wasn't *actually* in the middle of sex. "What do you want me to talk to you about?"

Nico squeaked, face still buried in the pillow as if they were too embarrassed to say what they wanted. Maybe in the future Jasper would demand they answer him. Something told him Nico might respond well to that. Right now, he took pity on them.

"Do you want me to tell you all the things I'd like to do to you?" There was a sharp intake of breath, and Jasper hurried to add, "No strings attached to actually follow through."

"God"—they laughed incredulously—"yes, that would be…" The sentence hung in the warm air surrounding them, and instead of completing it, they turned slightly and strained toward his lips.

The kiss wasn't quite sloppy, but it wasn't chaste either. For a moment, Jasper stilled the movement of his hips just to fully indulge in it.

"I can't talk if you keep kissing me, sweet thing," Jasper said against their mouth. The noise Nico made, indignant at having to choose, filled him with a warmth completely separate from the one coiling in his pelvis like a spring. Finally they turned away again, pushing backward against him even though Jasper was sure there was no way that could happen without breaking the laws of physics.

There were so many ideas swirling in Jasper's head, so many half-formed fantasies that he'd never voiced anywhere. Most of them were too personal for him to even think of saying into a microphone, and he was thrilled at the idea that he had something to give to Nico alone.

"There's so many different ways I want to fuck you, sweet thing," he said. The pressure of Nico's thighs around his cock tightened and an almost imperceptible rumble sounded in their throat. "I could do it just like this. And I bet I could feel myself inside you if I put my hand just there."

Jasper shifted to interlace his fingers with Nico's, placing their hand at the base of their stomach. With a groan, Nico tipped their head backwards and nearly whacked Jasper in the chin. He laughed again, his normal nervous giggle dropping low in his chest.

"Or, you could ride my cock. I'd love to watch you like that—seeing me splitting you open, watching the pleasure on your face. You're so beautiful all the time; I can only imagine how stunning you would be like that."

"*Jasper*," Nico said, the scandalized "*stop*" that would otherwise follow dying before they could say it. Part of that was because Jasper had shushed them, one of his hands gently covering their mouth.

His hips rocked with more intensity as Nico squirmed around him. Nico took one of Jasper's hands and placed his palm over their cock, which was gratifyingly hard and leaking. With every thrust of Jasper's hips, they rode the momentum to rut against it. He let himself groan as loud as he liked, and he was rewarded with Nico's full-bodied shiver.

"Fuck, I can't wait to taste you," he whispered, adjusting his head so the words flowed straight into their ear. "I know you'd be such a good girl for me while I had your cock in my mouth."

There were frantic, muffled sounds against his palm, and the increased speed of Nico's movements gave Jasper hope that they might be close. He didn't want to pressure them, but he felt his own climax building, wrapping tendrils around his composure in preparation to tear it down.

"You're going to make me come, Nico," he said in a shaky whisper. "I'm going to come all over your legs and your cock. Do you want that?"

They beat him to it, suddenly and explosively, with a frantic cry. As they twisted and writhed, Jasper followed them over the edge. He had barely caught his breath before Nico had pushed him onto his back and was kissing him senseless.

But despite the warmth of their mouth and the weight of their body, all the insecurities he'd managed to ignore refilled Jasper's empty spaces.

"Was that—"

"Perfect. You're wonderful," Nico said. They nestled their face in the crook of his neck, draped over him like a soft blanket. "Thank you," they murmured, ghosting a kiss against his neck that raised every hair on Jasper's body.

Jasper had never ever been in a place where he felt so much promise. Gratitude blossomed inside of him, leaving no more room for his doubts. Shapes of the coming days were starting to come into focus through the blur of his happiness. There were so many adventures ahead, and now he wouldn't have to walk into them alone.

And he was sure now that he could love this person—this frustrating, enchanting little person glowing against his chest. It was too early to tell them this, of course, but he knew it was only a matter of time.

CHAPTER TWENTY-NINE

EPILOGUE: SIX MONTHS LATER

Jasper plonked the cardboard box full of books on the counter at Blossom & Crow, and still it was Nico who released a held breath. They were both sweaty, dressed in clothes that were keeping them far too warm despite it being an especially nippy winter. They had been going non-stop for two days, dragging box after box from Nico's apartment and holding tense discussions about what should be donated and which should be kept as they merged their belongings.

(Where on earth did all that stuff come from? They had always thought themself rather spartan, but apparently they were mistaken.)

The inside of the bookshop looked like it always did, a cheerier take on a mad scientist's basement. Dead-eyed baby-doll heads stared down from inside bell jars. Decorative skulls made of different-colored glass sat atop stacks of worn leather-bound books that were almost sure to leave the reader cursed. The lower shelves around them were lined with taxidermy animals, while the higher ones stretched all the way to the ceiling.

There was only one thing missing.

"Andie?" Nico's call echoed through the seemingly empty shop, dampened only slightly by the packed shelves. It seemed irresponsible to Nico to leave the front unattended like this; any strolling ne'er-do-well could just walk in and take whatever books they'd like.

Before they could worry any longer, there was a shuffling noise and murmuring like actors ducked in the wings. Then Andie approached from the back of the shop. Nico caught the light glint of sweat at the roots of their hairline, white blonde struggling to be seen beneath the black dye.

"Hello, lovebirds! How goes the move?" They slipped behind the counter and manically drummed on it before making a grab for the cardboard box flaps.

"Oh, fine. Just, you know...consolidating," Nico said. Jasper's eyes rested on the counter full of the casualties of their bookshelf massacre. His shoulders were slumped, and Nico assumed he was just as tired as they were. It was probably worse, in fact, since Jasper had carried far more heavy boxes and wrestled more furniture than Nico had the strength to.

Andie pulled out a soppy romance paperback covered in pastel flowers, a painted hetero couple gazing wistfully into each other's flushed faces. It looked like it had been living in the wicker basket beside someone's toilet for the past decade. If they could extrapolate from what they knew of Jasper's life, it probably had.

Andie arched an eyebrow.

"Didn't realize you liked tits so much, Jasper," they said as they scrutinized the front cover. "You're just full of surprises."

"Oh, that one was Mom's," Jasper said, clearing his throat.

Andie set the book aside without another word. They were brash, sure, but Nico knew they were kind enough to wait until the two of them had left to toss it in the recycling. There was undoubtedly plenty of romantic material in this bookshop. It just usually involved vampires, and not the sparkly kind.

Thudding footsteps sounded behind them. Nico whirled around to see Evan hurrying toward them. He looked like he'd overslept before a job interview, top two buttons on his flannel shirt undone, hair rumpled as he ran fingers through it.

"Hey, friends." A wide smile spread across his face. They hadn't seen one another since he'd left Unified Theory in a huff, and Nico knew Andie had taken their suggestion to hire him to help (in some capacity at least). That was, honestly, all they wanted to know about the situation.

"Hold on!" Evan said, glancing back and forth between Nico and Jasper. "What are you two doing here together? Did you—"

"U-um, yeah. We're together now," Jasper rambled. "We got together right after you left—well, a couple of days if you want to be technical about it, and I imagine Nico does at least."

Over the past two days, Jasper had been acting with the sort of nervous, people-pleasing energy Nico hadn't seen since he'd begun working at Unified Theory. It was concerning. Nico had always been a private person themself, and Jasper had spent many years living alone with his mother. The chance that he was regretting his decision lingered in the back of Nico's head like a vengeful wraith.

"And you're moving in together?" Evan's mouth hung open, as delighted as if someone were handing him a puppy. Before Nico could answer, he threw his arms around their shoulders and pulled them into a crushing hug. "I knew it! I knew he'd get to you eventually! One more win for the hopeless romantics. Right, Jasper?"

Nico gazed helplessly at Andie, but they were pointedly not looking at them. Their eyes were glued on the books that they were withdrawing one by one from their box, at a glacial pace. Certainly not at the kind of pace a person who had run a bookstore for ten years would have.

"Y-yeah, we should have you two over to visit when everything's all set up. A little double date night," Jasper said.

Evan's grip loosened around Nico's shoulders, and Andie's hand stopped withdrawing books from the box. The four of them stood for a moment in awkward silence.

"I mean—just a hangout. Nothing...I didn't mean...," Jasper stammered, then sighed with exasperation. "Ignore me, this move has fried my brain."

"No worries, we—" Evan started.

"Should I put this on the same account?" Andie interrupted.

Nico felt their face warm. For some reason, this felt like the most symbolic moment of their coming together so far. One would think it would be their receiving the key to Jasper's front door, but that had already happened months ago, when Nico had started spending most of their time at Jasper's house. It had felt like they'd lived there for a while now, but this? This meant something more permanent. Not just a place they were living together, this was a home. This was a life.

They only realized they hadn't answered yet when Jasper gave them a questioning look.

"Of course," Nico rushed to say. "I'm sure we'll be back for more."

The worry on Jasper's face was replaced with a smile. His hand quietly came up around their shoulder. The unexpected touch wasn't a problem. It was more than welcome, in fact.

"You'd better be." Andie grinned. They tapped the keys on their computer as Nico's chest tightened, as if it were too small to contain their heart.

⁓₰₰₰⁓

The two of them had been hoping that they'd have everything buttoned up by that night. It really shouldn't have been this difficult. Nico had been slowly bringing things over to Jasper's for months now. Even so, there seemed to be an unending supply of *things* in Nico's apartment, and there had also been quite a lot of purging of his mother's old things—which Jasper had never really gotten around to. It had been much more emotionally draining than he had expected, but Nico, who had lost their parents long ago, had been patient in a way that Jasper never could have anticipated.

It was pitch dark by late afternoon this time of year. By the time they were sprawled on either side of the living room couch, grimy and exhausted, it felt like midnight. When Jasper checked his watch, it was only 8 p.m.

They'd been spending most of their time at Jasper's for months now, both continuing down their respective professional paths. Nico had agreed to help Jasper with his new audio drama, with Eddie on board and then some. It had taken off like a racehorse out of the gate and had already had gotten them into talks with a couple networks. Turned out queer horror audio drama was a booming market.

When Nico wasn't helping Jasper, they were helping Dr. Alasdair Parks shore up his platform and publish his work for a wider, less academic audience. Other Unified Theory authors had taken their rights back and were enlisting Nico's help to create new books of their own. There still hadn't been a whisper of any anniversary editions of *The Unified Theory* out there. Jasper doubted there would be. Dick (which was the only way that Nico was willing to refer to him anymore) seemed much more interested in talking about the work than actually doing it.

Conversely, working side by side with Nico had been the thing that Jasper liked the most about his time at Unified

Theory. Getting to keep that part of it without having Brent around to throw wrenches in their system was a win-win as far as Jasper was concerned. The best part was that Nico seemed to agree, showing up morning after morning and somehow still wanting to be with Jasper when they'd packed everything up at the end of the day.

Tonight, though, the opposite end of the couch was awfully quiet, and Jasper didn't have the assurance of contact. The next day, Nico would be cleaning their apartment and handing over the key. It would all be real, permanent. There would be no going back, unless their relationship went sideways, which was an intolerable thought. Even more intolerable was the idea that this was a step too far for Nico and they were keeping their fear to themself.

"You're not regretting this, are you?" Jasper blurted.

Nice. Very nice. Not at all a high-pressure question, Jasper.

Nico jolted a little at his words, forehead wrinkling. "Not at all," they said. They hauled themself up and reached across the couch to squeeze Jasper's hand. "Are you?"

"Nope," Jasper said. *Screw it*, he thought. He leaned closer and planted a decisive kiss on Nico's lips, chapped and worried from the stress of moving. Then he drew back, tucking a clump of dark hair behind their ear. "I love you, and I'm glad you're here."

"Good. I'm glad to be here," Nico said. They looked relieved, as if they'd briefly worried Jasper would turn them out on their ass.

Jasper pulled them to his side. It was always so easy to do; Nico never resisted, going soft as a stuffed toy. For a few moments, the two of them rested in contented silence, staring lazily at the boxes stacked neatly against the opposite wall.

"So what do we do tomorrow when we're done with all of this?" Nico held back a yawn. Jasper didn't bother to hold back his. He luxuriated in a yawn and a stretch before turning to place a kiss on Nico's head. They smelled extra like themself right now, less collected than usual after so much activity. And with them there, there to stay, the house no longer felt like a museum to the loneliest time in Jasper's life. It felt like something altogether new, something that belonged to both of them in equal measure.

"Anything we want," he said.

F or bonus materials, first looks, and the latest news, sign up for M.L. Nolan's newsletter.

Keep an eye out for Andie and Evan's story, *You're the Most*, coming in early 2024.

Acknowledgements

Thank you to my partner for making the space for me to do what makes me happy and for giving me enough faith in love to spend so much time writing about it. Shout out to my beta bestie, Jess, who is my first reader and pulls me out of all my writing slumps with her friendship and positivity. Thanks to Bri, who has been patiently encouraging me to write romantic comedy for years and sharing her insights and experience with self publishing. Gratitude to my other buddy Jess, who unleashes devastatingly good compliments on demand whenever I need an emotional pick-me-up, and who enthusiastically read this book in its earliest form. Lastly, thanks to all my friends from The Magnus Archives fandom, Jay in particular, for cheering me on as I've grown as a writer.